THE MISCHIEF MAKER

*To Kathie,
I am so happy
I met you ♡ Enjoy ♡
Frances Oakes*

THE MISCHIEF MAKER

A LAINEY BUG MYSTERY

FRANCES OAKES

The Mischief Maker
Copyright © 2022 E. Frances Oakes

All rights reserved. No part of this publication may be reproduced, distributed, or transmitted in any form or by any means, including photocopying, recording, or other electronic or mechanical methods, without the prior written permission of the publisher, except in the case of brief quotations embodied in critical reviews and certain other noncommercial uses permitted by copyright law. For permission requests, write to Frances at: francesoakesauthor@gmail.com.

This is a work of fiction. Names, characters, places, incidents or medical situations are either the product of the author's imagination or are use fictitiously. Any resemblance to actual persons, living or dead, events, or locales is entirely coincidental.

Cover & Interior Design by Crystal Heidel, Byzantium Sky Press
Copyediting by Jennifer Westervelt

Print ISBN: 979-8-9852236-0-6
eBook ISBN: 979-8-9852236-1-3

Library of Congress Control Number: 2022902370

Printed in United States of America
Ocean View, Delaware
First Edition

To my Beloved Richard

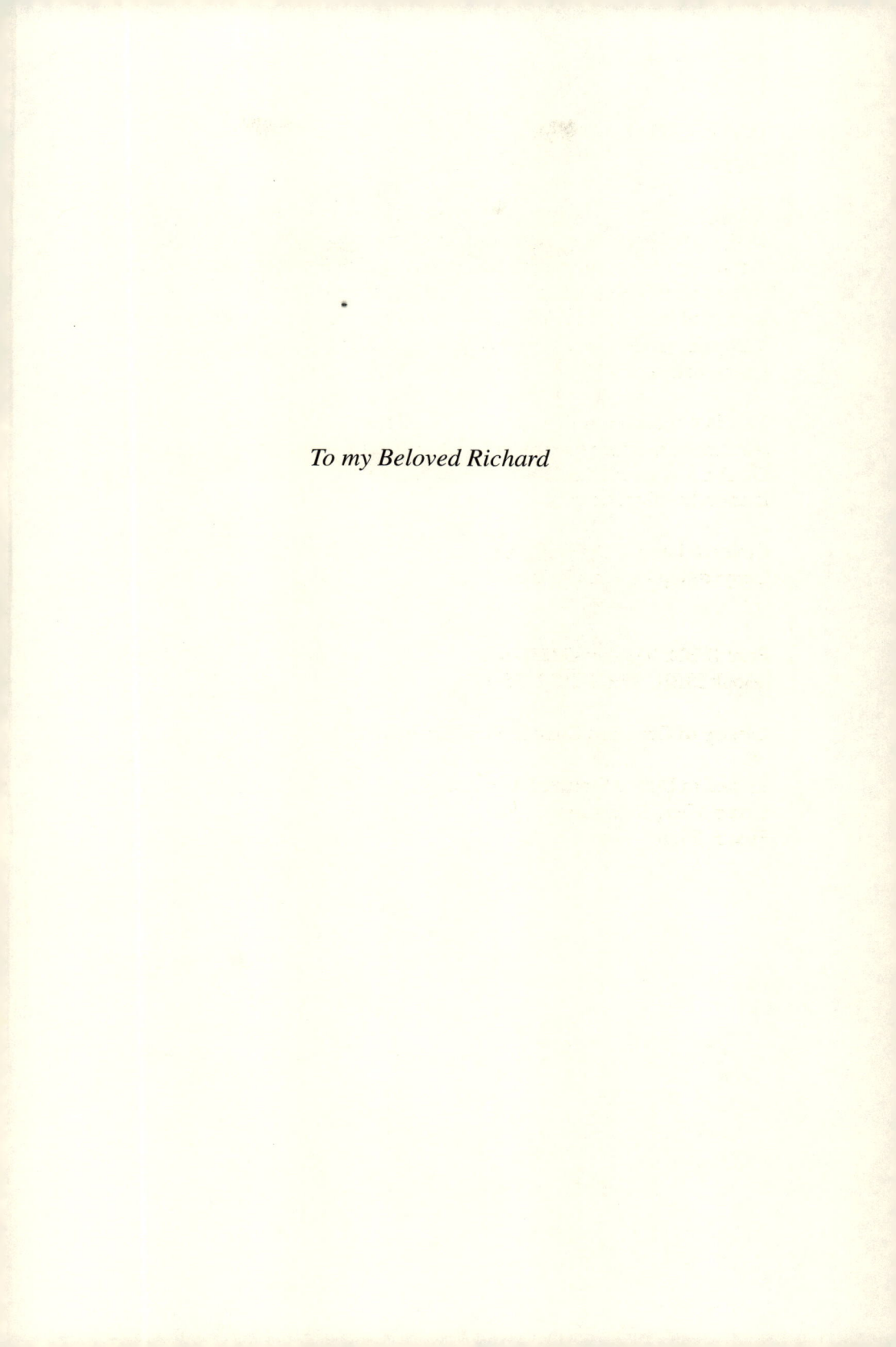

CHAPTER 7

THE INTRUDER

The dark apartment bedroom smelled of beer, buffalo wings, and death. The large digital clock on the stained bedside table illuminated 12:43 A.M. and radiated a ghostly glow over the naked chest and red-stained boxer shorts of Randy Watkins. *Goodbye Mr. Popular.*

Loud, slurred voices erupted in the apartment hallway. *Drunk Idiots.* A door shut and the voices dissipated. *Lucky for them.* Without a thought, the gun was shoved back into its holster.

The killer scribbled two letters on the back of a small, holographic card before placing it next to the worn black Bible resting on the bedside stand. The small calling card glistened as it lay beside God's holy word. *Perfect.*

The killer's heart pumped a triumphant beat at the handiwork of the night. *One obstacle laid to rest.* A chuckle within was held back. *No time to savor this moment.* The face tightened. *One by one they would be taken down. So intricate, so perfect a plan. Nothing would stop what had already been put into play.* And as if wanting to participate in the eeriness of the evening, the night light in the corner of the room flickered off its last breath of light.

CHAPTER 2

A FRIENDLY ENCOUNTER

Blissfully happy. The thought floated into Lainey Pinewood's mind like a gentle breeze of fairy dust while her second graders whispered and waited on the black and white linoleum floor for their turn in the bathroom.

Last night, her husband, Max, surprised her for their thirty-third anniversary with an amazing prime rib dinner. It thrilled her when her daughter, Kate, the detective in the family, had attended as well. Kate often missed family gatherings to deal with unexpected police business. Lainey laughed to herself as she thought about her three grown sons playfully giving their sister a hard time for finally showing up to a family event. Unfortunately, Kate had left early after a call from her station.

Lainey leaned against the blue cement wall surrounding the school's hallway. An odd pins-and-needles sensation crept into her feet and legs again. She shifted her weight to dislodge the uncomfortable feeling, but the tingling remained. What was happening to her? She should call a doctor, but with only seven weeks until summer vacation, things were just too hectic. Besides, what if this is bad? Really bad? Would she really want to know? No, she wouldn't.

She spied Rachel Honeycutt coming down the second-grade hallway without her students, so they were probably in a 'specials' class. Being Friday, it must be music. She observed Rachel's long, golden-brown hair. Although damp from the lack of air conditioning and unexpected eighty-five-degree heat, it showcased her beautiful hazel eyes. *The humidity never made me look that good*, Lainey thought.

Her tension released itself as Rachel approached, and she noticed her students' rising voice levels alerting her that they were done using the bathroom. Both made her smile; the children, because she adored them, and Rachel, quite frankly, because she was her best friend.

"Your class is a little bit frisky this morning. Friendly reminder?" Rachel asked.

"Let's do it." Lainey placed a finger to her lips as Rachel

did the same. The children silenced almost immediately, except for Bobby, who always had one more thing to say. He smiled sheepishly. Lainey made a heart sign by connecting her two index fingers and two thumbs to make a heart. The children smiled and responded with their own heart signs. Bobby's face glowed, as he had been the one that taught the class last week how to make finger hearts. Lainey gave him a wink before giving the whole class a thumbs up. She smiled at Rachel. "I've got the best class." The children beamed with pride. Her heart swelled for her class, and in that moment, nothing else mattered.

CHAPTER 3

PINKY SWEAR

Lainey and Rachel searched for a seat in the crowded teachers' lunchroom. The three round tables were fully occupied by teachers and staff but not the one rectangular table in the corner. Seated at that table were Sara Browner, Isaac Taylor, and someone Lainey didn't recognize. It was the only table with two available chairs. Lainey hesitated before she sat next to Sara, then placed her lunch tray, consisting of a cheeseburger and carrots with dip, down on the table.

"If it isn't the dynamic duo," Isaac said.

"Where did you hear that?" Sara retrieved a napkin from the dispenser on the table and placed it on her tray. "Of course, you heard it in the teachers' lounge."

"Nope. I heard it from the second graders when I subbed." He smiled. "Mrs. Pinewood and Mrs. Honeycutt are celebrities with their kids."

Lainey grinned at Rachel, but the whole conversation had already become awkward because Rachel had taken Sara's second-grade position last year. The gossip mill, fueled by Sara and her little band of cohort teachers, had insinuated that Principal Lopez removed Sara so Rachel could teach with Lainey. Lainey looked over at Isaac and said, "All teachers are celebrities to their students."

Rachel smiled. "Especially if they see us outside of class."

Sara rose and grabbed her tray of half-eaten Caesar salad. She scrunched her brows. "Excuse me. I have recess duty with my fourth graders."

Isaac's expression darkened. To the others, he asked, "Did I do that?"

"No, she's probably had a tough day in class." Lainey answered, feeling bad for Isaac. She suspected he had no idea of the history between Sara and herself, as he hadn't substituted there for that long.

Isaac glanced up at the wall clock. "I've gotta go too." He grimaced. "Mrs. Wyatt's class was lively this morning, so I've got to get the upper hand."

"Anything I can do to help?" Lainey asked.

Rachel set her cheeseburger back on her plate. "Do you need copies made?"

"Thank you both. The morning plans were confusing, but the afternoon is basic math. I'll be fine." Isaac balanced his tray and picked up a black whistle. "Ms. Browner forgot her whistle. I'll drop it off to her on my way back to class."

"She'll appreciate that," Rachel said.

The man Lainey didn't recognize at the table stood up. He looked to be about thirty and was well dressed in a blue suit. She was embarrassed she hadn't introduced herself. "I'm so sorry. I'm Lainey Pinewood and I teach second grade."

"I'm sorry Lainey. I didn't realize you hadn't met Mel yet," Rachel said.

"No problem." Mel smiled. "I'm subbing for Mr. Sanchez for six weeks due to his heart surgery."

"It's very nice to meet you. I'm sure I'll see you next week when I bring my students to your class for physical education."

He nodded and picked up his tray. "See you then."

After Isaac and Mel left, Lainey sat quietly for a moment. She dipped a carrot into her ranch dressing dip. "Isaac is such a pleasant sub, but he seems to have ruffled Sara's feathers with his friendly comment towards us."

"I guess Sara still has hard feelings about being switched to fourth grade," Rachel said.

"According to Lucinda, she's having discipline problems, so that doesn't help."

Rachel pulled a long strand of hair away from her face. "I'm sorry that Sara is unhappy, but I love teaching second grade together."

"I don't know how you and I became friends," Lainey said. They were so different. Rachel was ten years younger and stylish in her colorful dresses and pants, while Lainey's outfits almost always consisted of black slacks and light-colored blouses.

"Perhaps it was divine intervention," Rachel said, choosing a potato chip to eat next.

Lainey poked out her smallest finger. "Friends forever. Pinky swear."

Rachel grabbed a napkin and wiped her hands. She stretched out her pinky finger to attach it to Lainey's. "And all that it means."

Lainey's heart warmed at her words. Rachel had been there for her when her father died from cancer and when her sister abandoned her. Their friendship meant everything to her and always would. She had no doubt of that.

They finished their lunch lost in their own thoughts. Lainey decided she'd call the doctor after school because the tingling in her legs had finally worn her down. She thought about the rest of her school day until her mind shifted. "Are you going to yoga class tomorrow?"

"Sure. Kassidy's going to teach us the Scorpion headstand."

"She's phenomenal but I'm nervous. That headstand is so advanced."

Rachel laughed. "Don't worry. We'll all fumble through it until we get it right."

The bell rang for the children to come in from recess, so Lainey headed for her classroom. She spied Rachel's students outside their classroom door waiting patiently to go in, so she stopped in front of them. "What a nice, quiet line! If your parents could see you, they'd be so proud of you." She surveyed the smiles coming from the youngsters. "I know Mrs. Honeycutt is." Then she crossed the hall to her own line of chatting students.

CHAPTER 4

IT TAKES TWO

Kate Pinewood stood in the doorway of the small conference room and observed Detective Will Burnett as he pulled at the long, black, wavy nose hair. With a quick yank, the nasty hair released itself and fell slowly to the gray linoleum floor. She said nothing as she watched, thinking to the past and figuring that what had happened between them was her fault. In high school, she'd had one date with Will to the senior prom. She had been pleased that a senior would ask her, a sophomore, to the senior prom. It had been a special night until he moved in for a kiss. She had panicked and told him he had a booger in his nose. That hadn't gone well; they never spoke again. *Regrets of the young*, she thought.

Now, fifteen years later, she had been assigned to work with him. Despite his nose obsession, Will was good-looking in a boyish way. The only sign of age was a few wisps of gray in his dark brown hair. The funny thing was that he was humble about his looks. Since she began working at the police station, it was obvious he had captivated a few hearts, but the word was that he rarely dated. None of that mattered to her, though. She just wanted the chance to work with one of the best detectives in Lorianne Falls, Maryland. She had hoped he'd forget their short past and welcome her with open arms, but, so far, he had treated her like she was invisible. Some of the other detectives said it was just the way he was, but this felt personal.

Apparently, Will hadn't noticed her walk into the conference room so she faked a small cough. Their eyes met as he abruptly rubbed his nose and picked up the file resting on the small, metal conference table. Kate slipped off her blue windbreaker and laid it across the back of her chair. She sat down and flipped a blond wisp of hair out of her face while Will buried his head behind an open folder.

Will peered over the file. "Good afternoon, Detective Pinewood." He shook his head. "I took one night off and missed out on the action off of Main Street." He lifted the folder off the conference table and held it up. "I see you had a busy night."

"This doesn't have to be so awkward."

"Awkward?" Will asked.

"You know exactly what I mean."

Will cleared his throat. "If this is awkward, you're the one making it awkward."

"You can't get over one moment in high school." She regretted saying it as soon as it was out of her mouth. She felt her body freeze in place and her eyes shifted downward.

"This is about *that*? Get real."

She felt herself exhale. "You never talked to me . . . after that."

"I graduated." Will opened the folder. "Could we please get back to this investigation?" His face tightened as he rubbed the back of his neck.

"If you want me to get back to this investigation, I need you to do one thing."

"What's that?"

"Stop calling me Detective Pinewood when no one is around."

Will cocked his head and looked her in the eyes.

Kate pinched her lips together and stared into Will's brown eyes. "Use my name. Is that too hard?"

Will tapped his pencil along the edge of the conference table. "No. But you need to get rid of that attitude. Are we in agreement?"

"Yes," she said, even though she wasn't totally in agreement. To her, Will was the one with the attitude. But she liked that he would call her Kate.

"Okay, what did you find out last night?"

"I didn't hear my name in that request."

Will rolled his eyes. "Are you kidding me?" She didn't answer and, after a hesitant moment, he bit his lip. "Kate, what did you find out last night at the crime scene?"

Kate felt the warmth in her heart when she heard Will say her name. Mentally, she felt herself putting a slash in the 'winning' column in her mind. Maybe she did have an attitude, but wasn't she just being assertive by asking for what she wanted? The scowl on Will's face told her she was close to crossing a professional line with her partner. "It's barely preliminary at this point, but you can see the photographs in that file. I'm waiting on lab results on the evidence collected at the scene."

"From the photograph of the crime scene, it looks like a lot of blood, but that's not the case. I assume a bottle of ketchup was not the murder weapon." Will smirked.

Kate prodded on, ignoring him. "It appears our victim was eating wings and fries when he was interrupted by the assailant. The victim may have been intoxicated based on the number of beer cans found at the scene."

"What do you think; foul play or accident?"

"I can't rule out an overdose, but there was mild trauma on the victim's forehead and back of the head."

"Trauma could have been caused by a fall after the overdose or by a hit to the victim's head by an assailant," Will said.

"Exactly, I'm expecting to get the autopsy report in a few days," Kate said.

"Great. What else?"

"Besides the scattered fries on the floor and ketchup all over the body, the victim's wallet was found on the scene, money inside. Rules out theft as a motive. We did find trace evidence of critter tracks on the dead man's chest and down his leg. It seems there was more than one rat involved in this crime," Kate said.

"Those little rodents do have a way of contaminating our crime scenes," Will said.

"Interestingly, I found a hologram card with the initials 'MM' written on the back. It was left next to a Bible. The initials don't match our victim's name. The lab is checking for prints now."

"Victim's name?"

Kate checked her notebook. "Randy Watkins, thirty-five-year-old white male. We did get the phone number for the last person he called: Kassidy Roper."

"Where can we find her?"

"At Yoga Heaven on C Street right here in town. It's the same studio my mom uses, and I used to do yoga there a few years back."

"Whoa, Kate. Please don't mention your mom's name. You know her reputation with this police station is less than desirable."

"She's just under-appreciated." Kate wished her mom would stay out of police business, but she wouldn't defame her own mother.

"Rumor has it that she led this department on a wild goose chase last year. She should stick to teaching."

Kate turned away for a moment. Her mom was always well-intentioned when she interfered in police business, but Kate often had to deal with the fallout of her actions. She agreed her mom should stick to teaching, but she was always so genuine in her desire to help the community. Her mom was a hit in the neighborhood when she found lost children or a pet or two. Besides, her mom was ex-FBI and once in a great while, her mom's intuition had proved valuable. Kate shook her head as her eyes tightened. "Could we stop talking about my mom?"

"Sure. Kate, I'm sorry I made those comments about your mother."

Kate was taken aback by the unexpected sincerity in Will's voice. She felt the tension in her body diminish.

"No problem." She focused back on the investigation. "Yoga Heaven?"

"Let's wait until we've gathered more evidence before we take on Ms. Roper."

Kate stayed silent. He was right. It was too early to start questioning possible suspects. She had let her mixed feelings about Will affect her professional decision-making. After all, she was here to learn from him, not alienate him. Why did she have to bring up the prom? She felt foolish for her insistence that he use her name, but at the same time proud she was a strong woman. Nonetheless, from this point on she would be all detective . . . minus the attitude.

CHAPTER 5

THE HAND

The early morning light cast a curious glow on the hand positioned over an open journal that rested on an oak desk. A chewed pencil twirled around in its flimsy grip. As thoughts began to filtrate down to the fingers, the grip tightened. The hand wrote what the mind thought, so the hand wrote:

Mischief Maker
Mischief Maker
Hide in plain sight

Mischief Maker
Mischief Maker
No time for flight

Mischief Maker
Mischief Maker
Fill them with fright

Mischief Maker
Mischief Maker
What's right is right

    The hand paused. The grip loosened. The grip tightened. The mind thought, so the hand wrote: *One annoyance laid to rest. The prime target in fool's paradise. Let the others fall where they may.* The hand stopped.

CHAPTER 6

LAINEY'S MOM

Doris turned off her bedroom light and pulled back the window curtain to get a better view. The dark figure leaning against her neighbor's car intrigued her. She could only see the back of the head, since the figure faced the new neighbors' house, but the full moon's glow revealed flamboyant white hair that spread out in all directions. What was going on? She felt around for her glasses, grabbed them, and squinted down below. She stepped back and froze when a heavily painted clown face stared back at her. It was the flashlight under the clown's chin and that devilish wide grin that told her this was no ordinary clown. She shuddered. Dare she look again? The clown was gone.

Doris wanted to tell her daughter, but she was afraid

she'd be the one to look like a clown. She'd tell the neighbors, but she had never met them and didn't want them thinking they'd moved next door to a crazy lady. Probably, it was just a teenager who had entertained some kids for a birthday party and thought it was funny to scare her. After all, she was the one snooping out the window. Either way, she'd probably just keep her mouth shut. She'd go downstairs, get her medications, and talk to her daughter about the new health aide.

Her gray hair semi-twirled into a haphazard bun, she sauntered into the living room with her bottled water and retrieved the pill box she'd left earlier in the day. The pill box, which Max had diligently filled the day before, slipped from her hand, sending it across the carpeted floor. Luckily, she had a firm grasp on her water and the only pills that had scattered were her vitamins, which had come free when the lid on their small compartment popped open. She gathered the vitamins and shoved them in her pocket, then stood there for a moment gathering her thoughts.

The new aide had turned out to be a pushover but there was something strange about her. She'd give her another week before she ushered her out the door. She didn't understand why Lainey thought she needed a babysitter. She had always been her own boss, but the rules had changed for her since she moved in over a year ago. She pressed out the wrinkles in her favorite housedress — pink bunnies covering black cloth — which she had worn for the last two days, and headed over to talk to her daughter.

Doris observed Lainey and Max lounging on their comfy green couch, adorned with soft yellow pillows, Max's face hidden behind the comics in the Washington Post. Agatha, their small, sandy brown Welsh corgi, snuggled in Lainey's arms while she stroked the fur between the dog's ears. Where can I sit? Even that dog of theirs has a great spot.

Life was different now that her beloved Ralph was gone. She missed her husband and the love they shared. She talked out loud to Ralph sometimes, but only her own voice answered back and added to her loneliness.

She made her way towards the couch and tapped Lainey's arm. "I need some cards. A birthday card for Sam and another for Bridget's baby shower. And it wouldn't hurt if we had some prune juice in this house and some sugar-free candy." She ignored Max's stare. He had talked to her about demanding so much from Lainey and that she needed to show more gratitude. She hadn't liked his attitude, but she was glad he stood up for her daughter. "Oh, and there's something strange about my new aide."

"Mom, she's fine."

"I'm eighty-seven. I'm helpless to my aide's nefarious ways." Doris expected more of a reaction from her daughter. "What if she starts eating my lunch and tells me I already ate it?"

"Mom, if you know what nefarious means, you can remember if you ate or not."

"Today maybe, but I can go through a whole list of my friends who knew me one day, and then swish - I'm less to them than a bag of potatoes." Even as Doris said it, her heart ached. She prayed God would give her warning before her mind went dark so she could say her goodbyes and express the words of her heart. She mourned the friends that never said goodbye and no longer cared if they did. She tried to believe what her friend, Belle, had said: *You can take the memory out of the person, but you can't take the heart out of the soul.* She guessed that was why she visited Belle at the nursing home every Wednesday and held her hands. Belle's heart knew she was there.

"Where did you go?" Lainey asked. "You seemed lost in the cosmos." She shook her head. "Mom, maybe you're right. Let's do a memory check. Who's the president?"

"I'm not going to say, it will produce a ruckus." Doris thought she knew who the president was, but she wasn't opening up that canister of invertebrates. If she was wrong, she'd be on the way to a nursing home, and if she was right, a heated discussion about politics would erupt. "And I don't appreciate being questioned on the state of my brain."

"You're the one that brought up your mental capabilities."

"I did?"

"You did."

Doris feared the little gremlins within her brain were preparing to overtake the few good minion cells she had left. She'd fight back the best way she knew how. "Could you add crossword puzzles to my store list?" She didn't wait for an answer. "And please do something about that aide."

"Okay, if you start losing weight, I'll talk to your aide."

Doris mumbled. "No one listens to old people like me."

"Mom, I'm listening. I can't terminate someone without just cause."

"You'd rather wait until she starves me, then I'll be all wrinkly skin and brittle bones, and then my veins will bulge out, and you let it happen to your own mother." Doris heard Max cough and saw his narrowed eyes directed at her. Her daughter's reaction was harder to read, and she felt a flutter of guilt. "I guess I'll go to bed." She pouted her face, but the dog had jumped on her daughter's lap and now Lainey's attention was on that mutt. "Don't forget those things I need from the store."

"I won't." Lainey lifted her dog from her lap. "Goodnight, Mom. I love you."

The clown's face flashed across Doris' mind. She trembled. She wanted to believe the clown was a teenager, but she remembered those menacing eyes. She knew she should tell her daughter, but after the senility test Lainey tried to give her, there was no way she'd be believed, and then Max would put in his two cents. She'd just have to leave her bedroom light on.

"Are you alright, Mom?"

Doris nodded. "Night, night, I love you." She hugged Lainey.

"Good night, Doris," Max said.

Doris kept her eyes away from Max and grumbled her goodnight.

CHAPTER 7

POINT OF VIEW

Max grabbed Lainey in a soft embrace. "How come your mom gets more hugs than I do?"

Lainey felt his eyes search hers. Was that amusement or concern that she detected? She pulled him closer and planted an affectionate kiss on his waiting lips. "Technically, you get better hugs and longer kisses, but I know what you mean."

"Do you?"

"I work too long at school, and you have more responsibility now that my mom lives with us. You never complain but you wish we had more time together."

Max lowered his brows. His face tightened. "You forgot the part about your uninvited meddling in the workings of our local police department which takes time away from us."

"That was last year. Nothing much happens around here." She hesitated. "I graduated from the FBI academy, and five years later, it was over. We got married, and that was that."

"Sorry I said meddling. You earned your creds."

She took his hand, but the comment hurt. "I love teaching now, but a part of me yearns . . ."

Max interrupted. "It's more about your mom. When you're home, she demands your attention, even with the aide's assistance. It's not right that your sister offers no help. I'm glad to do my part, but don't let me fall too far into the shadows."

Lainey jumped when Agatha suddenly barked, perhaps perceiving doggie dangers, like the sounds of leaves rustling, metal trash cans banging, or the neighbor's cat prowling, which were her dog's usual triggers. It was the howling wind filtering through the screen door that caught Lainey's ear. No, not a howling wind, more like a chilling high-pitched whistle. Lainey locked the screen door.

"Let's go to bed," Max said. He slid his arms down to Lainey's hands and held them.

Lainey gave him a soft kiss. "Where's our cat?"

"I'll let her in and let Agatha out for a minute."

Lainey felt tiredness overcome her and plopped down on the end of the couch. She watched Max open the back door as Agatha scurried out. Bailey, their little black and white fur ball of a kitten, stinking like an old fireplace, sauntered in through the opened door. Her cell phone pinged and a message appeared. *Randy is dead.*

CHAPTER 8

THE HAND

The bright morning sun shone through the window onto the gloved hand that gripped the pencil above the open journal. The hand wrote what the mind thought, so the hand wrote:

Mischief Maker
Mischief Maker
Stop with the talk

Mischief Maker
Mischief Maker
Time to go stalk

Mischief Maker
Mischief Maker
Head to Main Street

Mischief Maker
Mischief Maker
Time to go greet

The hand twitched. *So many disguises; what shall I choose?* The hand's fingers twirled the pencil and then held on tight. *Of course. Senior Delight.* The hand stopped.

CHAPTER 9

MAIN STREET FESTIVAL

Main Street came alive on the second Saturday of May every year and today was no exception. The familiar sound of the Lorianne Falls Ragtag Band penetrated through the breezy air. Lainey delighted in the view at the top of the hill next to the Lorianne Falls Steakhouse. Hundreds of people had already filled the street. She had missed the parade, but the delightful smells of Thai chicken, sausages, and yummy funnel cakes filled her senses. The brightly colored tents that surrounded both sides of the street raised her imagination as to the crafts and treats that were waiting for her undivided attention. This was exactly what she needed to forget that awful text last night.

Lainey felt Max grab her hand and, before she knew

it, they were swinging their arms as they headed to the center of the Festival. In the center were the funnel cakes, sausages, and corn dogs. She hustled Max over to the grilled sausages as the tantalizing aromas seemed to alert her very hungry stomach.

After about two hours, Lainey's abdomen had found its saturation point for food. Max had headed over to their son's sports bar, Sam's Brewpub and Grub, to watch the Orioles game. She eyed the crowd but saw no sign of Rachel. She expected her to arrive at the Festival around three and it was already half past. Lainey strolled past the Louie's Meat Market towards the railroad station but still no Rachel. It was unlike Rachel not to text or call her if she'd be late. Where was she? The sight of a park bench drew her attention, and she plopped her tired, tingling legs down for a rest.

Fifteen minutes later she received a text from Rachel. She'd meet her at the Mexican restaurant at five. The change of plans disheartened Lainey, but her mind was disturbed by a new thought. What if the murderer was someone in this crowd?

The drop in temperature chilled her. She wrapped her

blue hanging scarf around her neck. Someone pushed harshly against her shoulder. She felt the painful sting of an object pelting her side and her body tensed. Lainey turned around to see an old lady in a blue dress with a bright yellow sweater carelessly swinging her huge purse in the air as she whistled. *I know you're old, but can you at least say you're sorry?* Lainey thought, but didn't actually expect to hear such an apology as the woman had disappeared into the crowd. She scolded herself. That old woman looked to be about ninety and surely meant no harm. *My goodness, she was whistling.* More likely, she didn't realize she hit someone. Her side ached. What was in that purse?

Although Lainey assumed it was an accident, it tainted her mood and put her mind back on Randy's killer. It's funny how she could have two opposite thoughts at one time. The ex-FBI agent in her wanted to find the perpetrator and deliver justice, but the mother and grandmother in her wanted to hide. It was all moot. Randy's killer was probably across state lines by now. Besides, the Main Street Festival was no place for a killer.

CHAPTER 10

FRIENDLY DISTRACTION

With Rachel delayed, Lainey bought her favorite blue cotton candy. Another park bench across the way seemed to beckon her to take a break. It felt so good to just sit there. Before long, students and their parents stopped by as they made their way through Main Street. All the kids wanted to know where she had purchased the cotton candy, and then off they went with their parents following behind.

It was a great distraction, but as soon as they left, her mind drifted back to Randy. Who would want to murder him; a beloved substitute that everyone at her school admired? She frowned. Clearly, someone didn't admire him.

Lainey's thoughts turned to a recent conversation she'd had with Randy in the teachers' lounge about his plans for the summer. His thirty-something, freckled face had glowed with youthful excitement as he showered her with details. *She doesn't know it yet, but I'm taking my girl to Bermuda. Wow! Me and her in Bermuda! Sorry, I'm buzzin' like a bee.* Lainey sighed sadly, thinking, *A vacation never meant to be.*

Lainey opened the glass door leading into Enrique's Mexican Restaurant. The enticing smells of spicy tacos and stuffed burritos intertwined with the sounds of sizzling steak and softly playing Mariachi music offered her the promise of a relaxing evening. She caught sight of two student teachers from her school waiting for a table.

Within moments she engaged with them in a lively discussion about discipline problems they faced in their first experience with front-line teaching. She sensed their apprehension but their enthusiasm for their students lifted her spirits. She was disappointed her discussion with them was cut short when the hostess arrived to show the two of them to their table.

The hostess came back and directed Lainey to a corner

booth. The patched red cushion seat was worn but clean, so she sat down. She smiled at the toddler poking his head over the adjacent booth. He started to climb over, but his mother quickly pulled him back. Lainey missed those days when her children were babies. Now her youngest was twenty-six; the same age she was when she married Max. If she could go back thirty-three years, she'd slow down and treasure every moment she spent with each of her kids. Why didn't anyone tell her how much she'd miss those days?

By the time Rachel showed up, the young toddler and his mother were making their way out of the restaurant. Lainey noticed Rachel had pulled back her long hair in a ponytail and wore her purple-and-pink-striped Zumba attire, which highlighted her great figure. She admired Rachel's dedication to fitness and nutritional eating. Lainey wished she had that same resolve to stay fit, like when she was in the FBI.

Rachel slipped into the seat opposite hers. "Did you order yet?"

"Just got here." She understood why Rachel was late and didn't want her apologizing.

"Sorry, I didn't make the Festival. I ran into Jamal and his mom at the lemonade stand, and next thing I knew, we were in the library choosing suitable reading books.

I'm glad I did. It felt so good seeing Jamal be enthusiastic about picking out books. It was worth the time getting him to tell me about his interests. He'll benefit from the extra reading, particularly when they are on his reading and interest level."

"That is so you." Lainey smiled.

The waitress approached them with a warm smile and Lainey smiled back at her former student. She could still picture her as she was in second grade. She wore a different color hairband on her head every day and was the kindest student.

"Hi, Mrs. Pinewood and Mrs. Honeycutt." She pulled out a pencil from the side of her hair. "May I take your order?"

Lainey ordered beef tacos with extra cheese and a diet coke with lots of cherries before Rachel ordered her usual chicken fajitas and a glass of ice water with lemons.

"I'm so happy I started ordering cherries in my diet soda. You always got free water and free lemon while I paid two dollars for a diet soda and no fruit. It just didn't seem fair."

Rachel laughed. "Life is so tough for you." She leaned back in her booth. "How was the Festival?"

"It was fun until I got hit in the side by a careless woman swinging her purse."

"Getting pushed around happens sometimes with the large crowds. I accidentally stepped on someone's foot last year at the Festival."

"I guess you're right." Lainey frowned. "I'm shocked about Randy."

"The whole school is." Rachel said nothing as the waitress came by with their drinks and set a bowl of chips and salsa in the middle of their table. "Thankfully, the kids seem oblivious."

Lainey pulled one of her red cherries from her drink and bit it off its stem. "Who would want to kill Randy?"

"I have no idea." Rachel spooned some salsa on her plate and scooped some onto a chip. She then squeezed a lemon into her glass of water. "Randy is — was one of us. It has me rattled."

Fifteen minutes later, the waitress arrived and placed their food before them with a warning that the plates were hot. It looked delicious. Lainey couldn't wait to bite into her tacos. She looked up to see Rachel waiting to begin grace. She hated to admit it, but she sometimes felt shy and uncomfortable saying grace publicly.

"Let's pray. Thank you, Lord, for bringing Lainey and I together to share in your bounty. Bless our friendship, bless our husbands, bless our families, and bless our students." She paused. "And please keep our community safe from the evil that killed Randy. Let your love be our armor. Amen."

"Thank you." Lainey bit into her beef taco, cracking the hard shell into pieces.

Rachel meticulously layered her fajita before she took her first bite. Then she sipped on her lemon water. "I interacted with Randy whenever he was your substitute, and he attended my Bible study. He didn't seem like the kind of guy who would attract enemies."

"Apparently, he was that kind of guy." Lainey felt bad for demeaning Randy. He had always been friendly and one of her most reliable substitute teachers. She was in FBI mode even though she no longer worked for the agency. Some things she couldn't forget.

Rachel shrugged. "Unless it's random."

Lainey took a long sip of her drink as she deliberated on Rachel's comment. "You have a point, but let's assume it's not random. Did Randy get along with everyone in your Bible study?"

"We talk about God and his love for us. Not a topic that causes conflict."

"That doesn't answer my question. Surely, different interpretations can cause friction."

"We're civilized. We avoid friction."

Lainey tilted her head and pressed her lips together

before she spoke. "Let's approach this differently." She paused as the waitress tried to drop off their check, but Rachel ordered a fried ice cream for them to share. Lainey continued, "Who are the members in your Bible study?"

"I think you know everyone. Kassidy, Lily, Marilyn, Juan, Randy, and of course, me." Rachel jerked her head back in realization. "You're treating my group like we're suspects."

Lainey didn't know if Rachel was really miffed or faking the indignation, but she was on a roll. If the murderer was someone Randy knew, then the Bible study group had to be checked out. She knew Rachel wouldn't like her next question. "Since you mentioned suspects, where were you two nights ago?"

Rachel stared straight back into her eyes. "Where were *you* two nights ago?"

She didn't know if it was the intense look on her friend's face or the absurdity of it all, but Lainey couldn't stop herself from laughing. Before she knew it, Rachel was overcome with laughter too. "Okay, okay. I guess we're both off the suspects' list."

"If you weren't my best friend, I wouldn't tolerate this abuse. Do you really think that I, or a member of my Bible study, am capable of murder?"

"No. But I didn't expect someone to kill Randy either." Lainey's eyes widened. "That's the woman who hit me."

Rachel turned around to observe the woman sitting alone at a table at the far end of the restaurant. "Lainey, she's like, ninety and, with all those wrinkles, I suspect she's had a tough life."

"Wrinkles or no wrinkles, she hits hard." Lainey grimaced. "And she was whistling after she did it."

Rachel laughed. "The whistling granny. Bless her heart for coming to the Festival to give herself some joy. You should want that for her too. You'll be old someday." Rachel glanced back at the old woman. "I like her long gray hair. I plan to keep my hair long when I'm in my nineties too."

"Well, I hope I'm as strong as she is when I'm that old." Lainey stared over at the woman and thought she may be staring back, but the woman wore large sunglasses, and she couldn't tell. As if the woman read her mind, she placed some cash on the table and left. "I bet I'll have a bruise on my side."

"Could we talk about something else?" Rachel said.

"Sure."

"How's your mom?"

"She's doing well right now and I do need to spend more

time with her. Max wants me to spend more time with him. It's a balancing act that I'm not winning."

"Have you heard from your sister?" Rachel said.

"No." Tears threatened at the corners of her eyes. Her sister's words still stung. *I'm done with my role. Don't ever expect to see me again.* And she hadn't. Those words echoed in Lainey's mind each day ever since her sister had said them.

"It's been over a year since your father died. You can't let your sister continue to have this power over you."

She hated that Rachel was right. "I thought I was helping my sister by asking my mom to live with me. Now I'm in my sister's doghouse."

"Earth to Lainey. It's not about you. Families can become very dysfunctional when a parent dies. Sadly, you're the scapegoat for all her irrational feelings."

"Well, her goat kicked me right in my microvalve prolapsed heart. I bet you didn't know about that condition. If I don't take an antibiotic before I go for dental work, I could die from bacteria leaking into my bloodstream."

"You're so neurotic about your health. It's hard to believe you're a Quantico girl."

"I'm not neurotic." She wanted to say one more thing in her defense, but the waitress showed up with the fried ice cream and two spoons.

"Lainey, you've forgotten something," Rachel went on.

Lainey smiled. It's funny how well she knew her friend. She had kept the conversation too long about herself. Four years ago, they started a tradition of alternating each year and making one of them the star. "It's the year of Rachel."

"And what was last year?"

"The year of Lainey."

Rachel tilted her head back and tossed her hair. "And did I do right by you?"

"Yes."

"So, I wonder, what we should be talking about now?"

Lainey waited for Rachel to take the last bite of their shared ice cream. "How's *your* sister?"

CHAPTER 11

A CASE FOR MEDDLING

Where are those car keys? To Lainey's disappointment, they weren't on the kitchen hook. She wiped the sweat from her forehead. Was it the humidity or her frustration? She was about to give up when she recalled wearing her denim jacket last night and remembered hanging it up in her bedroom closet.

She opened her closet and felt inside the jacket's pocket but found no keys. She was about to search downstairs again when she spied her special jewelry box on the top shelf of the closet. Without thinking, she pulled down the box. It was ridiculous to think the keys were there, but she felt drawn to the contents within. She shuffled through her high school ring, her passport, a picture of her grandmother, but still found no keys. She checked under her birth certificate and then her eyes froze.

Before her lay her old FBI badge. She stared at its gold beauty and the magnificent eagle resting on top. Underneath stood Lady Justice in her splendor. With the impartiality blindfold covering her eyes, Lady Justice held the scale of justice and the torch of truth. Lainey's heart swelled. The embossed letters — on the top, *Federal Bureau of Investigation*, and on the bottom, *Department of Justice* — still held her in their power. She had been so proud of those words and so glad they hadn't been diminished by acronyms like FBI. She could still remember the overwhelming pride she felt when she received her badge and credentials at her graduation.

She had been on top of the world the day of her graduation. She had excelled in all aspects of FBI training despite competition from other brilliant and physically trained men and women. Despite that, she had remained humble, utterly shocked, and so proud when she was presented with the Director's Leadership Award. The thrills just kept coming that day. When she was presented with her pistol and carbine, she felt the tremendous weight of responsibility. She remembered that her hand trembled a little when she was handed the shotgun. It was a day she would never forget.

She gazed down at the badge again. That was over thirty years ago. How could that be? Where had the time gone? She knew where the time had gone. She met Max and they had four wonderful children. It was all great, but sometimes she really missed her life as an FBI agent.

Her eyes swelled slightly with tears as she remembered the other night. It still hurt. After how they had met, and what Max knew about her earlier career with the FBI, how could he say she was *meddling* in police business? Meddling was what people did when they didn't know the situation and put in their two cents. She knew police business and she had earned a measure of respect that *meddling* didn't connotate.

She leaned back and thought about the years after graduation. She spent four years investigating human trafficking. She investigated crimes and followed leads about suspicious activities involving children or young adults. Her willingness to risk her life, her insights into the criminal mind, and her flair for deception proved valuable traits. She took a breath as she remembered how she tricked a trafficker into trusting her so that she became one of his Bottoms. As a Bottom, she booked hotels and oversaw other activities that kept the young victims in line. Trusting her was a mistake that their leader and the rest of the members never recovered from.

It was during that investigation that she met Max. As a CIA officer, he was involved in the international components of the case. Lainey and two other agents met with Max and created a plan to disrupt this elite group.

The meeting was held at a satellite FBI site in Brooklyn. She could still remember her first impression of Max. At six feet, three inches, his height had captivated her, but it was his presence — his confidence — that fascinated her. When he spoke, his ideas seemed to roll off his lips like butter, melting into her thoughts and making them her own. His eyes mesmerized hers and brought power to his views on how to proceed. He was so different from the other CIA agents she had come across; not so egotistical and he actually wanted to know what she and the other agents thought. When they were done, it wasn't just an FBI plan or a CIA plan, it was *their* plan.

She felt a slight chill down her back. The implementation of the plan proved to be a bit more dangerous than expected. While in the final stages of their infiltration, one of the gang members, Four, asked her to meet in a dilapidated section of the old warehouse. Once inside the room, Four questioned her about one of the undercover agents, whom he thought was a buyer. She tried to convince him that the agent could be trusted but it only made him more suspicious. He drew his gun on her and warned she'd better follow him to see One, the boss. Just as they were about to walk out, his cell phone rang. The timing was so perfect; as he pulled the phone out of his jeans pocket, she kicked the gun out of his hand and pulled out her own. It was the first time she had to shoot her gun. It was hard to admit, but she had frozen at first. Four was a dad. How many times had she watched his five-year-old twins playing soccer with their friends in the parking lot next to where the women were housed? She often wondered how Four could have his children so close to the despicable trafficking business. She remembered her hands sweating and the look in Four's eyes when he realized that she may not be able to pull the trigger.

Even now, her heart skipped a beat when she remembered Max blasting through the warehouse door. He had not seen the hidden weapon in Four's hand. Her instincts and professionalism took over when she saw the point of the long-bladed knife close in on Max's chest. Within seconds, she fired two shots and watched the knife drop from Four's hand as the first shot hit his thumb. The second shot landed above Four's right knee, sending him to the floor. She hadn't killed him, but she still recalled how she trembled. Max was okay and that was all that had mattered.

At the safe house in Queens, she had felt so much relief. She was so glad to be away from the strong perfume and cigarette odors that fouled the air in the warehouse; relieved in that moment not to see another young, frightened girl or boy walk into the warehouse and become part of the human trafficking network.

Once they had settled Four in the safe house and Max had taken the time to talk to Lainey, it was his gentleness that had her hooked. For over an hour, they talked about what had happened at the warehouse. Max admitted he had seen her through the broken glass window and saw her hesitancy to fire. She realized it was willingness to risk her life, but not someone else's life that was a problem for her. And then Max had stared into her eyes and taken her hands into his and her heart had fluttered in her chest at his touch.

The capture of Four escalated their plan and within days they had taken out both the leader called One and the entire gang. Over a hundred teens were released from bondage following the arrests.

Lainey was reassigned to an FBI facility in Fairfax, Virginia when she reconnected with Max months later. During a lunch with a friend at Artie's restaurant, she was surprised when he walked in. She remembered him looking so handsome in a dark blue suit and blue-striped tie. He proposed six months later in New York City at the famous Carmine's restaurant.

When they were first married, Max raved about her abilities as an FBI agent. He had even told her not to give up her career. She tried to listen to that, but Sam was born ten months after they were married. She quit her FBI job and tried to live vicariously through Max's CIA job, but he would never talk about his work. She missed the thrill she got from being an FBI agent. When Pete, Steve, and Kate were born, her passion turned to raising their four children. She substituted at her children's school and realized it was her second calling. After four years, she got her teaching degree and began her new career. Her passion to live the agent's life subsided but never died.

She pressed her fingers across Lady Justice. How could Max forget who she had been or underestimate her contributions to the police force? She hadn't forgotten all she had learned through the academy. What about her experience — their experience — together? She didn't understand this Max. Her Max would understand, even encourage her. Where had he gone?

She felt her anger rising as she placed her FBI badge prominently in the center of her jeweled box. If Max thought she was *meddling*, she would show him some *meddling*. She placed the box back on the top shelf of the closet before she collapsed on their bed. *Where in the world were those keys?* She laid her head on her lavender pillow and looked up at the very still fan. Where are those darn keys? And then it happened: her brilliant mind came back in full force. She remembered thinking it was not a good place to leave her keys, but she was hungry and tired, and it was so handy to just place them there. Let the *meddling* begin, she thought as she headed downstairs to grab the keys off the top of the refrigerator. First stop: the doctor, and then off to see Kate. Perfect time to find out if the police had any leads on who killed Randy. She smiled to herself as the thrill of the chase crept into her soul.

CHAPTER 12

THE FIRST DIAGNOSIS

Where were the other patients? The large, empty waiting room and the mostly vacant parking lot surprised Lainey, but she rationalized its meaning as she waited for the neurologist. It was the reason she was able to get a quick appointment.

She wiped her wet palms across her pant legs and waited. Eventually, an elderly nurse escorted her to an examination room. Moments later, Dr. Healey stepped in, bringing with him the potent smell of nutmeg and musk. Her chest ached as she recognized the familiar scent of Old Spice, her dad's favorite. Her throat tickled. As much as her dad liked it, though, he'd never doused himself in it.

Dr. Healey's appearance astonished her, and not in a good way. That photo on his website must have been taken twenty years earlier. The man standing before her was a short man of about seventy, with dyed red hair that draped over his balding head. His eyes were tiny behind thick black glasses.

"Mrs. Pinewood, it's nice to meet you." He shook her hand. "Now, what's going on?"

"I have no problem walking around, but it's been difficult lately walking up stairs and getting up from a chair." She watched him intently to see if he was dismayed by this news. "And my legs have a prickly sensation." So far, so good. Obviously, he didn't think this was a major problem.

"Have you had any recent injuries?"

"A few months ago, I hurt my back."

"I see." Dr. Healey tapped on a small device.

"What's that in your hand?"

"It's my PalmPilot. Data in, data out." He smiled.

His use of an outdated PalmPilot was a bit disarming. What else was he outdated on? Lainey bit her lip. "What does it tell you that I might have?"

"Not much yet."

"Would your PalmPilot be able to tell me if I have Lyme disease?" She cleared her throat. "My computer said

I might have Lyme disease." She rubbed her arms as the room seemed to have gotten chilly.

"You apparently have your diagnosis. Why are you here?"

She felt her face flush. "A second opinion."

"At least you're honest." He rolled his neck and projected his beady eyes straight into hers. "I'm not going to waste your time or mine." He put down his PalmPilot and crossed his arms. "You obviously prefer a computer over a real doctor."

She cringed as the realization hit her that she had offended him. Why didn't she think before she spoke? Kate was always warning her of being so blunt, but she had done it again. Leaving here without his diagnosis was not an option. "Sorry, Dr. Healey. I do believe in doctors. My anxiety got the best of me."

His smile was weak but appeared genuine. "We'll try again Mrs. Pinewood. I'd like you to answer a few questions."

His list of questions turned out to be lengthy, but she didn't want to get on his wrong side again. If these questions helped him cure her, she'd answer a hundred of them.

He stopped tapping her responses into his PalmPilot and instead tapped her knees and ankles with a small hammer. She thought her knees were supposed to jerk but they hardly moved. She had no idea what her ankles were supposed to do.

Dr. Healey scratched his head. "Please sit on the floor and let me see how you get up."

She felt foolish and feared she couldn't get up. "Do you make all your fifty-nine-year-old patients drop to the floor?"

"Just the ones who say they can't do it."

Smart-aleck, she thought. She was five feet, eight inches tall, but the distance to the floor seemed like ten feet. She hesitated and slowly toppled to the floor.

"Now, please get up. You may use the chair if you need it."

She took a deep breath and grabbed the cushioned arm of the chair and forced her body back to the vertical position.

Dr. Healey removed his glasses and nibbled at a side hinge. "This is puzzling. There is some weakness in both your arms and legs."

She'd never heard a doctor use the word *puzzling* before. Her tongue went dry while wetness touched her eyes. "Am I going to die?"

"At this point, we should stay positive."

Lainey hated the words *at this point* because they turned

her anxiety into fear. It was just as likely that bad news was waiting at the end of that point. "So, what's next?"

Three hours later, Dr. Healey called her into his office.

"Mrs. Pinewood, your x-ray implicates a pinched nerve. And based on my exam, you have diminished reflexes in your ankles and knees. Your nerve conduction test was a bit inconclusive, but I still feel a pinched nerve may be the culprit of your current condition. I recommend physical therapy and an antidepressant."

Lainey should have felt calm — felt relief — that it was just a pinched nerve, but he had to toss in the word *antidepressant*. She wasn't depressed, and she worried that taking a pill that altered her mood was not a good idea when she had her students to think about. Her mom's mood had gotten worse since she started taking pills and she didn't want that to happen to her too. "I don't understand why you want me to take an antidepressant. I'm not depressed."

"We've found that antidepressants help conditions like yours. The dose is less than what we would give a depressed patient."

"And none of the side effects will kill me?"

"Assuming you've told me every medical condition that you have, you shouldn't worry about such deadly consequences."

"Dr. Healey, it's just that when I see those commercials on different medications, the side effects seem worse than the original condition."

Dr. Healey put his PalmPilot into his shirt pocket. "Make an appointment for six weeks."

On her way out, Lainey walked past the receptionist and the empty waiting room with no intention of ever going back. Relieved that she had escaped a death sentence diagnosis, she figured physical therapy should do the trick and there was no way she'd fill that antidepressant prescription. A glance at her cell phone told her the hour. Perfect. She couldn't wait to find out what the police had learned about Randy's murder, and she knew exactly who to ask.

CHAPTER 13

YOGA HEAVEN

One hour before noon, Kate and Will arrived at the tiny yoga studio just off C Street. The first thing Kate observed upon entering was Kassidy Roper at the front of the class demonstrating an upward-facing bow pose. Five yoga students duplicated the pose with relative ease while an elderly woman struggled. Kate remembered doing the pose a few years ago when Kassidy first opened her yoga studio. The pose required good shoulder flexibility to lift you up, and strength in the arms to keep you up. Being back in the studio reminded her how much she enjoyed the fitness and relaxation of yoga.

It was time to forget about yoga and, instead, to survey the studio with the eyes of a detective and not the eyes of a yoga student. She noted the bright pink cubby area full of cell phones, keys, and bottles of water. She detected that one of the iPhones had a little plastic gadget attached to it. She wondered about it and then refocused her attention on the young yoga instructor. She approached Kassidy just as Will had displayed his badge.

"Ms. Roper, we hope you have time to talk to us," Will said.

"I guess so." She turned back to her class before facing Will again. "Please give me a few minutes. I need to give them a cool down first." With that, she began an Om chant with her waiting class.

After Kassidy had ended class, she turned to the two detectives. "What is this all about?"

Kate had no doubt that Kassidy knew what this was about. Randy's demise was front-page news this morning in the *Lorianne Falls Gazette*.

"Detective Pinewood and I have a few questions for you about Randy Watkins," Will answered.

Before the detectives could start asking questions, one of the yoga students approached Kassidy. "Are you okay?"

"I'm fine, Lily. Just go back and practice your bow pose and the Chaturanga for the next class." She turned back to the detectives. "Sorry about the interruption. My friend can be a bit overprotective."

"We're here because you're the last person Randy Watkins called." Kate pulled out her notepad and pencil. "Why did he call you?"

Kassidy bit her lip before answering, "He wanted to go out. The last I'd seen him before that, except for a few times in Bible study, was two years ago."

"Did you go out with him last Thursday night?" Will asked.

"We went out to dinner at the Red Hot & Blue restaurant on Main Street. We had a few drinks."

"Did you do anything else with Mr. Watkins?" Kate said.

Kassidy's face reddened. "I slept with him in his apartment, if that's what you mean. I left around midnight."

Interesting that Kassidy felt it necessary to mention the time she left, Kate noted mentally, but stayed focused. "So, you were lovers?" She studied the uneasiness in Kassidy's eyes at the question.

"We had sex. He decided we weren't lovers long ago."

Kate said, "Then why did you sleep with him?"

"I don't know. Maybe I hoped he would care again."

"So, what happened? Why did your relationship end two years ago?" Will asked.

"Randy broke it off with me." Kassidy shrugged. "He didn't like my personal maintenance plan. I believe in freedom of mind and body. Let nature be. His ideas just didn't mesh with mine."

Kate wanted to refocus the questioning. "You said you left Randy at midnight. Are you sure?"

"We were just chillin' in bed and I asked Randy for the time. He said midnight. I said I needed to go." She paused. "He asked me to order him some wings and fries from Wing King for delivery."

Will glanced down at his notepad. "Were you there when the food arrived?"

"No, I called and left."

The yoga studio door opened, and two yoga enthusiasts came through the door engaged in active chatter. They must have noticed the solemness in the room and the business attire of the two detectives because they immediately stopped talking and just stood there gawking.

Will closed his notebook and looked over at Kate.

"My last question is, what time did you get back to your place after you left Randy?" Kate asked.

Kassidy pulled a damp brown curl from her face. "Around twelve-thirty A.M."

"Did you stay home?" Will asked.

"Yes."

Kate tilted her head. "Can anyone confirm that?"

"Snuggles, my cat?"

Kate smirked. "You'll have to do better than that." She closed her notebook. "Thank you, Kassidy, for your time. Do you have any questions?" She noted the girl's trembling hands.

"How did he die?"

Will moved in closer to Kassidy, his face inches from hers. "At the hands of a killer." He folded his arms and stepped back. "Randy Watkins was murdered, Ms. Roper."

Kate watched as Kassidy's face froze. Will had a way of making suspects feel very uncomfortable and he had certainly done that. Kate recalled him telling her that everyone is guilty until *he* proves them innocent. Now she would have to soften his words. She turned to Kassidy. "We can't discuss the details of the murder, but we want to thank you for your cooperation. It's very much appreciated."

"Ms. Roper, you're sweating. Perhaps some yoga will calm your spirit." Will moved close to her face. "And don't leave town."

So much for softening his words, thought Kate. Kassidy had fair warning that Will considered her a prime suspect. For now, Kate would give her the benefit of doubt.

CHAPTER 14

MISDIAGNOSIS

Bills and opened envelopes were strewn in a pile across the table, alerting Lainey that Max was tackling the finances. She took a breath and hoped to sneak past him before he complained about the gerbil cages she purchased for her class.

"I heard that sigh." Max set down the bill he'd been reading and met her eyes. "What are you doing home from school so early?"

Lainey took a breath. "I took sick leave so I could talk to the doctor about my sluggishness that I mentioned to you the other day."

"So, what's the news?"

"Dr. Healey thinks it's a pinched nerve." Lainey said.

"He gave me a prescription for physical therapy and an antidepressant."

Doris rushed into the dining room with her lips quivering, but her voice was loud and steady. "Antidepressant! I knew it, Lainey. I'm driving you into a depression."

Lainey scowled. It was obvious her mother had been eavesdropping again. "Mom, it's not about you."

"Of course it's about me. I'll grab some leftovers out of the ice box and be on my way. I never wanted to be a burden." She lifted the cat off the couch. "Any chance I can take Bailey? You two never seem to pay him any attention."

"Mom, you're watching too many soaps. You know we love you." Lainey patted the cat encased in her mother's arms. "And we love little Bailey too." She paused for a moment. "I just need the antidepressant for a pinched nerve in my back."

"In that case, erase everything I just said and consider it a senior moment." Doris took a cupcake from the kitchen and headed upstairs to her room.

Lainey turned back to Max. "Would you like to know what else the doctor said?"

"Yeah."

"He said that the physical therapy should help bring back my strength. With that said, I need to do something."

"What's that?"

Lainey gently lifted Bailey. "I'm going to hug our cat."

Lainey felt the moisture drip down her back and threw her blanket to the bottom of the bed. She fluffed her pillow the way she liked it and then snuggled her head on its softness. Her eyes shot wide open when she heard a whirling, high-pitched sound. *What was that?* She looked around the room and strained to hear the sound again. The room was dark but a soft glow from the streetlight below the bedroom window provided enough light to survey the room. Whatever caused the buzzing, it wasn't in the bedroom. The sound seemed to be coming from outside. She glanced over at the window. Was she dreaming? She closed her eyes and pulled the blanket close to her face. After a moment, she opened her eyes again and her mouth went dry. A black drone hovered close to the window; a blurry whiteness hung from its bottom. The only thing keeping it from crashing into her was the fragile window screen.

Lainey frantically poked at Max's arm, but he didn't move. She poked him harder and called his name.

Max mumbled, "What's wrong?"

"There's a drone at the window."

"Sure, there is. Go back to sleep."

Lainey's voice cracked. "Please."

Max sat up and looked over at the window. "I don't see a drone."

"It was there."

Max put on his pajama bottoms and went over to the window. He groaned. "We've been pranked."

"What?"

"Well, our whole cul-de-sac has been pranked. Come take a look."

Lainey peered out the window. Everywhere she looked was toilet paper. Houses, trees, sheds, and yards were covered in streams and strips of whiteness. If it had been snow, it would have been beautiful, but this whiteness harnessed creepiness. Maybe it was that awful drone that stalked her window that made her feel violated. She understood now what was hanging from the bottom of that flying machine. "What's this about?"

"Probably teenagers."

"Don't teenagers usually go after their friends' homes? And what about the drone flying at our window?" So far, Lainey wasn't comforted by Max's explanation.

"Maybe the mayor upset someone." He put his finger to his chin. "Maybe the drone came by our window because it was open. Drones usually have cameras."

"You might be right about the mayor. A police car just showed up in his driveway."

"The mayor will get to the bottom of this."

"Do you think that drone did all this?"

"No, my guess is there was a ground crew creating this havoc. I think the drone kept an eye out so they wouldn't get caught." Max rubbed the top of his head. "I'm going back to bed. I'll need to get up early to clean up this mess in our yard."

"Why not take care of it tonight?" Lainey didn't like the idea of going back to sleep with strips of toilet paper hanging outside her window like an ominous omen.

Max grunted. "Because if the teenagers responsible for this are still hanging around, I don't want them to have the pleasure of seeing me clean up their chaos."

Somehow, Lainey didn't think this was the act of teenagers, and she didn't like that the drone's camera had been pointed directly at her.

CHAPTER 15

TWO STRIKES

After a quick meal at the Lorianne Falls Diner, Kate and Will arrived at the police station to discuss their interview with Kassidy. Even though it was past eight in the evening, Kate had decided to meet while it was still fresh in their minds.

Will rubbed the back of his neck. "What are your instincts telling you about Ms. Roper?"

"My instincts tell me that the words flowed too easily out of her mouth," Kate answered. "No real sign of sadness for someone she once loved. But I do believe they slept together and that she ordered the food."

"The real question is, did she actually leave at midnight and, if she did, does she have an alibi to prove when she left and that she never came back?" Will asked contemplatively.

"The wings and fries were delivered after she left. I'll check with the delivery person at Wing King whether the order was called in and if she was there at delivery," Kate said.

"Great."

Kate was informed earlier that some of the reports were in from the evidence collected at the Watkins crime scene. She saw the orange file sitting on the table in front of Will. Orange was the color for toxicology reports. She looked down at the folder. "I assume the toxicology report is in?"

"Joe handed it to me when I walked in." Will handed Kate a copy and they both read in silence.

"According to the toxicology report, Watkins had a high dose of zinc phosphide in his blood, along with a point-zero-five blood alcohol level. Basically, our victim died of rat poisoning," Will said.

Kate raised her brow. "If we can link Kassidy to the poisoning, perhaps through analysis of the ketchup and fries, we may find our killer."

"It would still be circumstantial since the fries were delivered." Will pointed out.

Kate nodded. "It's also possible he was poisoned by

what he ate at dinner." She noticed a strange, worried expression on Will's face. "What's up?"

"I have information I haven't shared with you yet. Joe did an analysis of the hologram card left at the scene of the Watkins murder and actually, the killer left us a clue. The hologram showed all kinds of items found under a kitchen sink. All the items are in miniature form except for one item: a bottle where the label is magnified in glistening 3D."

Within seconds she made the leap. "Rat poisoning."

"Exactly, the killer is playing with us." Will drummed his fingers against the metal conference table. "What about those initials 'MM' that were scribbled on the back of the card? Another clue?"

"Or a red herring?" Kate thought about that for a moment. No, not a red herring. This perpetrator was too brazen and had already displayed a willingness to tease the police. The bottle of rat poison in the hologram was a clue, not a red herring. She had to assume the initials were a clue, at least until proven otherwise. "This changes everything."

"It definitely makes this a premeditated murder." Will furrowed his brow and slid his finger down the file. "What really bothers me is that whoever murdered Randy wants to play games with the police. The hologram was meant for our eyes. Killers that want to play games with police aren't happy with a one-game move."

Kate didn't like the creepiness of this case. Murder was bad enough, but to be a pawn in the murderer's game was unsettling. Kate knew exactly what the next game move would be. "There's gonna be another murder."

CHAPTER 16

YOGA MISCHIEF

The next day, Kate met with Will at the police station after checking out Kassidy's alibi. She had been able to verify that Kassidy had eaten at the restaurant with Randy, but her alibi fell apart after that with no one to corroborate her whereabouts. At the police station, Kate debated back and forth with Will the logic of arresting Ms. Kassidy Roper. The circumstantial evidence was condemning, but, most likely, any good lawyer would have her out on bail in no time.

Her real disagreement with Will was over whether Kassidy was capable of the devious way the killer carried out Watkins' murder and the taunting of the police. Kate had taken a few yoga classes from Kassidy and didn't see a devious bone in her, let alone the ability to kill someone and taunt the police. Will had thought Kassidy was a bit strange from the start and had no problem believing in her guilt. His most persuasive point was the number of grandmothers in jail across the country; if a grandma can commit murder, anyone can.

In the end, Kate decided to err on the side of caution. Two hours after their discussion, they interrupted Kassidy's yoga class and read her her Miranda rights before she was escorted out in handcuffs in front of six yoga clients, including her wide-eyed mother and a closed-mouthed Rachel.

CHAPTER 17

FOOD FOR THOUGHT

Lainey turned right, towards the mall, but her mind obsessed about Randy's murder, even as the golden, cloudless morning sky suggested that more pleasant thoughts were in order. Rumors were rampant in her West Lorianne Falls community; some believed Randy was caught in the middle of a drug war, or he messed with the wrong man's woman, or that he was involved in some other nefarious activity. Her school community was much kinder and gentler in their assessment of Randy's unfortunate demise as they conjectured that he must have been a random victim, or a case of mistaken identity, or he picked the wrong friends. Either way, he was dead and that was disturbing. And if that wasn't bad enough, her daughter had arrested Kassidy Roper.

She made a left into the crowded parking lot and drove towards the front of the Food and Things Supermarket. At least two cars were circling the area in their own desperate attempt to beat out the next driver to a newly opened parking space. The odds were against her as an aggressive driver showed up and overtook a spot that she had eyed for herself.

"Yes!" she shrieked, seeing a green Honda pulling out of a parking space, allowing her to pull right in. The recollection of the long red light on Fourth Street, which had frustrated her at the time, now seemed the reason she had arrived at the grocery store at the most opportune moment.

She sat for a few minutes in her car and stared at the sticky note above her car's dashboard that reminded her to get a second opinion. Despite the advice of her family doctor and her talk with the physical therapist, she had let two weeks go by without any attempt to schedule an appointment with a neurologist at the Baltimore Research Hospital. How could she focus on her health problems with Randy's death and Kassidy's arrest? She couldn't. Rachel had asked her to go visit Kassidy and clear her name. She'd seek the truth and no less. She really liked Kassidy, but in her experience with the FBI, the most dangerous criminals sometimes masqueraded as demure young ladies.

It wasn't just the murder of Randy that kept her

distracted from her health, but the end of the school year had its own list of demands. The added responsibility of being a co-chair with Rachel on the Second Grade Talent Show only added to that list.

Lainey had to admit it was getting harder to dismiss her symptoms as a temporary inconvenience. It wasn't until this morning that she realized she was using her hand to lift her right leg into the car to get into the driver's seat. How long had she been doing that? Now she wondered about last week when she walked up the steps to the stage during the talent show rehearsals and she hadn't felt the light-footed steps she was so used to. It all seemed unexplainable and alarming. How could she be normal two months ago and now this? Her heart sank, but she wouldn't let this bother her. Besides, Agatha and Bailey were home waiting for their pet food. With their hungry faces in her mind, she hoisted herself out the car door, dragged herself past cars that crowded the entrance, and opened the door for an elderly lady before she grabbed a grocery cart.

Even for a Saturday, the place was busier than usual. Lainey eyed the carts that passed next to her and noticed the big buys were burgers, sodas, and watermelons, with steaks coming in a close second. How she wished she had time for a cook-out.

It didn't take Lainey long before she was waiting in the cashier's line behind a mother, whose cart was filled to the brim and whose toddler's feet were kicking through the open leg space as he threw a tantrum for a candy snack. Lainey smiled at the child and practiced patience waiting, but the longer she stood there, the more enticing the candy rack became to her as well. She checked to make sure the toddler's eyes were elsewhere, but the renewed screaming told her he had seen her grab an Almond Joy. His kick to her cart forced her to step back and she accidentally bumped into the cart behind her, sending it into its shopper's side.

Ready to give a quick apology, Lainey turned and met the unforgiving stare of Sara Browner. Oh no, not Sara. Why did she have to act this way? Teachers are switched around to different grades by principals all the time. Lainey stammered her apology for the cart bump and hoped for the best.

The stare and silence that followed gave no clue that Sara was about to back out of the cashier's line and march herself right over to self-checkout. In a tantrum of her own, Lainey turned around, unwrapped the Almond Joy and took a huge bite. It wasn't until the toddler cried again that she realized she had let Sara get under her skin. There was only one thing to do now: buy that snickerdoodle of a child a candy bar.

CHAPTER 18

MEET AND GREET

An hour later, Lainey pulled into her driveway and parked her car. Roadwork had added fifteen minutes to her drive home. Usually, she enjoyed seeing other teachers from school out and about in the neighborhood, but she hadn't felt joy in her encounter with Sara.

What did bring her joy were the red azalea bushes that lined the right side of the driveway, which seemed to melt her worries away. She was pleased they still had quite a few blooms left, despite the windy night.

Her legs felt sluggish under the weight of two shopping bags, but she attributed it to the exhausting morning. She turned the key in the door while using her right knee to keep the bags from falling. As she opened the door, she threw the lighter bag into the house, and cans of cat food slid, banged, and littered their way across the wooden hallway floor. Without warning, the five-pound bag of dog food fell as her knees buckled under her and propelled her backward into the rosebushes that encased the front porch entrance. Her backside hit the cement walkway while her head landed among prickly thorns. She quickly moved her head away but not before a barb pierced her neck. At the same time, Agatha came flying through the opened door, tail wagging, apparently wanting to be part of the action.

"Agatha, how embarrassing." Lainey tried to pull herself up and lift her body farther away from the rosebush. One prickly thorn stuck to the back of her pink cotton shirt. She pulled it out with a careful yank and glanced back to her dog. "I can't just lie here." She tried to stand up, but her body strength seemed nonexistent. Now alarm overtook embarrassment and she felt nausea on top of everything. What was going on? Her body felt like a dead weight matted to the cold cement porch floor.

She looked at Agatha, the dog's sympathetic eyes upon her. "I can't believe this!" She couldn't see past the bushes but the usual sounds of neighbors being out and about were absent. Through the open front door, she heard her mom's television blaring *Justice Judy*. Her mom wouldn't be any help. She bit her lip as she remembered that her cell phone was still connected to her car charger and Max was out shooting pool. "Agatha, I'm going to have to crawl into the house." Agatha set a paw upon Lainey's chest and licked her face.

Lainey tried to crawl, but her arm strength was too weak. She regretted that she hadn't taken Zumba along with Rachel. But it was more than that; something was terribly wrong. Agatha rested her head on Lainey's chest. She stroked her fur. "Why me?"

Agatha licked her face before she jumped up and started barking.

"Are you okay?"

Lainey heard the nearby voice behind her and scooted her body so she could face the man. She recognized her new neighbor as the one she saw bringing cartons into the house next door around midnight. She had been alerted to this late-night activity by Agatha's insistent barking. His tall physique and long dark hair were the clues that it was the same man. His deep brown eyes seemed to be assessing the situation and she couldn't tell if he thought she was a lady in distress or a buffoon. It was embarrassing to meet her new neighbor as she was flat on her back, but she was also relieved that he might help her. "I don't know what happened. My legs just gave out," she stammered, then added a weak smile. "Oh . . . and I'm Lainey Pinewood. Welcome to the neighborhood."

"I'm Rob." He bent down towards her. "Are you hurt?"

She shook her head. "Just rattled."

Rob extended his hand out, but Lainey kept her hand to herself.

"I'm afraid you'd break your own back trying to lift me. I have no strength to help you." Lainey sighed. It wasn't her weight that concerned her. At around 150 pounds, she might be a bit heavy but not unmanageably so. She couldn't trust her limbs to do their part.

"It's okay." Rob stepped off the porch. "I'll go get my secret weapon."

Lainey thought, *Secret weapon? Was he planning to put me on the hand dolly I saw in his yard this morning?* She chuckled to herself. If it got her up, who was she to quarrel?

The sun was not so bright, as clouds partially covered and dulled its bright face. *What a way to meet our new neighbor*, she thought. Oddly, thoughts of her home crept into her mind. *Oh my God, my house is a mess!* How she wished she had cleaned before going to the grocery store. It didn't help that she'd thrown her groceries all over the hallway.

It wasn't but a few minutes when Lainey thought she

was seeing double. It was Rob, but with short hair and a mustache. "Oh! There's two of you."

"This is my twin brother, Al. I'm sure we'll be able to help you into your house." Rob took Lainey under her right arm while Al helped support the left side of her body. She was unsteady, so Rob and Al very carefully held her and kicked the groceries to the side that had scattered across the front hallway. Lainey limped towards the couch, then Rob and Al gently set her down.

"Are you sure you'll be okay?" Rob asked.

"Yes, I'll be fine. Thank you both so much for your help. I'm so thankful for your kindness."

"You're welcome." Rob stared at Lainey. He pulled out from his shirt pocket what looked like a yellow envelope but just as quickly returned it. "I've got a letter to mail." Without another word, he motioned to Al and they left.

Lainey wanted to remind Rob to put a stamp on his envelope, but she held back. Her grown children would moan when she reminded them to bring a sweatshirt on a breezy summer night as if she was still treating them as young children.

She tried to stand and felt relief to find that her strength seemed to be back, so she cautiously headed into the kitchen and got herself a diet soda.

Before long, Max walked in the front door. He looked

concerned and a bit off-kilter. She knew that to be the look of agitation. And that an 'I told you so' was coming her way.

"I just met our new neighbors and they told me about your fall." Max sat on the end of the green sofa next to her. He gave Agatha a pat on her head and a quizzical look at Lainey. "What happened here?"

"I lost my balance and then I couldn't get up. Rob and his brother were kind enough to rescue me. It was so scary."

Max raised his eyebrows. "You could've been seriously hurt. Call the Baltimore Research Hospital to get that specialist. I think there's more to this than a pinched nerve."

"I know." Lainey stared down at her fingers. "I should have already called."

"Your procrastination is ridiculous. Call tomorrow."

Lainey stared at him. "Don't micromanage me."

"Sorry, my micromanagement saved lives in the CIA. It's hard to change." Max slid across the couch and leaned close to Lainey before he kissed her forehead. "My love, please call."

CHAPTER 19

THE TALK

Lainey approached the front desk officer at the Lorianne Falls police station with great anticipation. After her fall into the rosebush on Saturday, she had worried her health would keep her from visiting Kassidy, but the weekend moved on without another incident. Her confidence grew that whatever was wrong would reverse itself. Max disagreed with her and purchased a pink cane which she now dutifully dragged around with her. Unexpectedly, the cane created quite a buzz with her students today, so much that she felt like a celebrity.

The instant she walked through the door, she felt like Sherlock Holmes and Watson, who she remembered had both walked with a cane during certain periods in their lives. She tapped her cane gently on the floor and then twirled it until she nearly hit an incoming officer bringing in a woman in handcuffs. His harsh stare told her he was more than annoyed. She gripped her cane and muttered, "I'm sorry," before she turned her attention back to the desk officer.

Within minutes, another officer came and directed her to a small room, which was surrounded by concrete walls and contained a gray, rectangular table in the center. An unpleasant pine disinfectant odor scratched her throat. Lainey's mood darkened at the sight of Kassidy, still dressed in her colorful yoga leggings and matching stretchy top. Her normally neat hair frizzed out in all directions, but it was her drooped face that tugged at Lainey's heart.

Kassidy glanced up but stayed bent over at the metal table as she tapped the tabletop with the ends of her long fingernails. The frantic *tap-tap-tap* on the metal was in deep contrast to the rigidity of the rest of her body. It was difficult to see her looking so forlorn.

Lainey placed her cane on the back of a chair and slid into the seat across from Kassidy. She gently touched her arm. "I'm so sorry you're in this predicament."

Kassidy pulled at a strand of her brown hair as if trying to straighten out the frizz. "Please get me out of this place!"

The officer stepped forward and warned Kassidy not to yell.

Lainey scooted her chair closer. "Try to simmer down so we can talk."

Kassidy yanked her wrist, rattling the cuff attached to the table. "I can't stand it here!"

Lainey checked the clock on the wall to see that she had only eleven minutes left of the fifteen minutes the officer had given her for this visit. She needed to get Kassidy to relax a bit so they could talk. "I'm not seeing any evidence of the peacefulness that you perpetuate in your yoga class." Lainey noted the weak smile she received back, so she pressed on. "I might as well quit your class if yoga doesn't work when the going gets tough."

Kassidy moaned in apparent realization. "Okay, you've made your point."

"Maybe you should try the Corpse Pose."

Kassidy chuckled. "In here, I'd rather you call it by its traditional name of Savasana."

"The pose of *complete* relaxation," Lainey added.

"I'm starting to feel better just thinking about doing that pose." She glanced over at the officer. "I'll do it when I get back to my cell."

Kassidy's warm eyes and smile seemed to express gratitude and a calmer spirit, so Lainey was hopeful. "I'm glad."

"I created this mess." Kassidy pulled her fingers through her hair and flicked off a loose hair. "I should have never gone out with him."

Lainey motioned to Kassidy to lower her voice. She didn't think the officer was in hearing distance, but she didn't want to take any chances. "Why did you?"

"We were a thing a few years ago, so after he joined my Bible study a few months ago, we became friends again."

Lainey picked up her pink cane, which had fallen on the floor, and rested it on her chair again. "So, you rekindled your relationship?"

"When he joined my Bible study, we became a bit friendlier, but we only had that one night together."

"Unfortunately, the same night he was murdered." Lainey thought about how timing was everything. If Randy hadn't been murdered, Kassidy might have been with him right now, kissing on some park bench.

"Yeah."

Lainey noticed that the clock showed that five more minutes had passed. "So, what happened that night?"

"We went dining and dancing, then . . ."

"Skip that for now," Lainey interrupted. "How was Randy when you left him?"

"Happy. He and I have uh . . . had great chemistry."

She stopped speaking for a moment as if she was reliving that night. "He always wanted fries after sex, so I ordered him some and went home."

"What time did you leave?"

"I left around midnight."

Lainey frowned. "Not good. Randy was killed sometime between midnight and 2 A.M. It still supports opportunity. I wonder what the police suspect your motive is." The voice of a man yelling about his neighbor's dog penetrated itself through the walls of the small room and brought a halt to the conversation before Lainey spoke again. "Were you ever so mad at Randy that you wanted him dead?"

"Of course not! How could you even suggest that? I thought you were my friend."

Lainey questioned the use of the word *friend* as it sat in her mind. Does having someone instruct you in yoga for a period of time make them your friend? She remembered the pleasant way Kassidy had encouraged her when she struggled with poses or welcomed her back when she had dropped out. "Yes, you are a friend." Lainey gently reached across the table and held Kassidy's hand. "I'm sorry, I had to ask. I wanted to observe your body language and consider how the police might interpret it. It's not raising any alarms for me."

Kassidy considered this for a moment before responding, "That's good, I guess." She shifted her weight in an apparent attempt to get comfortable in the hard metal chair.

"Yes, but the cops followed some kind of trail to put you here." Lainey rubbed the back of her neck. "Do you use social media?"

"I like to tweet a lot and I use Facebook."

"No Instagram?"

"Nope."

Lainey rubbed her earlobe. "Maybe your social media accounts implicated you."

Kassidy didn't respond to her comment but instead glanced up at the officer before she focused again on Lainey. "He'd be alive if I had just stayed home."

Lainey gasped. "What?"

Kassidy hunched her shoulders and stared down at the table. "Um, I just meant we did so much drinking he probably couldn't defend himself."

"I've never thought of yoga people as being heavy drinkers."

"I limited myself to two glasses of wine, but Randy had more than a few drinks."

Lainey raised her eyebrows. "Okay, new question on an earlier theme. Did you kill him?"

Kassidy looked down at the floor and back up at her. "You know I didn't."

"Do I?"

Silence, except for the wall clock that ticked loudly as if suddenly connected to a speaker, and the clank of a metal door sliding to a stop. Lainey had no doubt a prisoner on the other side of the wall had just been put in lockup. She wasn't sure if the anxiety she saw in Kassidy's face was because she heard the clanging of jail cell bars, or if it was the unanswered question left hanging between them. She could at least do something about the latter.

"No, I don't think you killed Randy," Lainey conceded.

Kassidy held her hand to her heart as her voice trembled. "Thank you."

"You don't need to thank me." She leaned forward. "I'm not the one you need to convince." She raised her finger just high enough for Kassidy to see it and then pointed it towards the police officer. "Make them believe."

"How do I do that?"

"Tell the truth. The fastest way for them to find you guilty is catching you in a lie."

The officer reminded Lainey she had three minutes left. The hands on the wall clock verified he was correct to the minute. A few more questions and that would be it. "If you didn't do it, who did?"

"How should I know?"

"Are you protecting someone?"

"No. The police asked me the same thing and I gave them the same answer."

"I don't think the cops believed you." Quite frankly, Lainey wasn't sure she believed her. The beads of sweat across Kassidy's forehead gave Lainey a clue that her questions were making her yoga teacher feel very uncomfortable.

"You don't?"

"You're still in here," Lainey said.

"Don't you have some leverage with your daughter to get me out?"

Lainey had little leverage with her daughter when it came to Kate's investigations, and she couldn't force herself into this one either. "Kate is the one investigating your case, but I'll help in any way I can."

"That's fair."

Lainey looked thoughtfully at her friend. On some level she believed Kassidy couldn't possibly have done it, but, so far, she didn't have anything to go on. A kernel of a thought popped into her head and exploded its way to the forefront of her mind. It was something Rachel had mentioned at lunch. "Did you know Randy had a girlfriend when you slept with him?"

"No."

"Did you know Randy planned to take his girlfriend on a cruise next week?"

Kassidy winced. "No." She slumped in the chair.

Kassidy's body vibe didn't match on either question, which left Lainey weary. It didn't necessarily mean she was lying, but it struck a nerve. It was time to go. Lainey gave Kassidy an encouraging smile. "I'll do what I can." She patted her hand. "Hang in there."

Kassidy said nothing, but a small smile crept from her lips.

Lainey motioned to the officer that she was ready to go. With a tap of her cane, she ambled out the door.

CHAPTER 20

FRIEND SUPPORT

Lainey had intended to catch Rachel up about her visit with Kassidy, but it soon became evident that Rachel had another conversation in mind as Lainey ordered Chicken Chow Mein and Rachel ordered Moo Goo Gai Pan at Tangy's Chinese Restaurant.

"I spoke with Max today when he brought in the Popsicles for your class. Why didn't you tell me you fell Saturday?" Rachel asked, concerned.

"I didn't want to worry you." Lainey was annoyed that Max had shared about her fall. She knew if Rachel heard about it, she'd make a big deal out of it.

"What concerns you, concerns me," Rachel said. "I'll let you know if you go overboard."

"You're younger, but sometimes you're the wisest."

"Correction. I'm *always* the wisest."

Lainey laughed. "I don't understand why I fell."

"You're reckless for someone who just had an unexplained fall." Rachel rolled her eyes. "I saw the way you used your cane as a marching baton when you walked your class down the hall today."

As the waitress placed their hot food on the table, Lainey inhaled the savory smells of garlic, ginger, and green onions that teased her empty stomach. After the waitress left, Rachel led them in a short grace before Lainey devoured her first bite.

Rachel took a sip of her lemon water. "As your friend who knows you and all the nuances of your body language, it didn't take much for me to notice that you were having difficulty walking up the stage steps at rehearsal last week. Too bad you didn't have your cane then."

Lainey was surprised Rachel had observed her sluggishness ascending those steps. "I thought it was all in my head."

"It's not. Call the doctor."

"You'll be happy to know I called the Baltimore Research Hospital yesterday."

"Fantastic. When's your appointment?"

Lainey sighed, taking a sip of her drink. "In two months."

Rachel's jaw dropped. "You've got to be kidding."

"I asked the booking nurse if she was comfortable with me waiting two months. I told her I could be worse or even dying by then."

Rachel wrinkled her nose. "And what did she say to that?"

"I think she melted a bit because she said she'd call if there was a cancellation. Otherwise, I should call nine-one-one." Lainey caught the eye of one of her second graders and they both waved.

Rachel sat back. "You're so funny sometimes. You either think you're dying or you're completely dismissive of your health." She moved her soiled plate out of the way. "I can't keep up with you."

Lainey stared down at her crumpled napkin before she lifted her head. "I don't really like to talk about this event in my life, but it may explain why I am so phobic about my health. You'd think a former FBI girl would be fearless. I was, until the car crash that changed my perspective on life and death."

"How did I not know you were in a car crash?" Rachel placed her hand over Lainey's. "I'm so sorry. When did this happen?"

"You couldn't have known. It happened over twenty years ago, before I met you, when my boys were toddlers."

She understood the alarm in Rachel's face and smiled reassuringly. "The boys weren't with me, and no one else was hurt, but I remained in a coma for two weeks from a head injury."

"A coma?"

"When I came out of the coma, intellectually, I felt the same, but emotionally, I had lost my feeling of being invincible. I had come too close to death. Staying alive for my children became a tremendous responsibility and an unwanted burden." Lainey took a sip of her drink to relieve her dry mouth. "As if things weren't bad enough, when I was in the coma, little Steve came down with a high fever and ended up in the hospital." Lainey stared across at Rachel. "I should have been there for him."

"You would have. It's not your fault."

"Anyway, I became a hypochondriac. I was convinced indigestion was a heart attack and a cough was throat cancer. I worried something would take me away from my children when they needed me most. I kept this behavior going through my thirties and eventually a short bout of therapy helped. I guess when I'm trying to pretend nothing is wrong, that's when I come across as dismissive."

Rachel grinned. "That explains one of your many idiosyncrasies."

Lainey couldn't help but smile back.

The waitress approached with the check and then placed a small black tray with two fortune cookies in the middle of the table. Rachel excused herself to go to the restroom.

Lainey seized the moment to enjoy the vintage red and yellow silk lanterns that hung from the ceiling of the restaurant. She caught her breath at the beautiful mural on the adjacent wall of a majestic Ginkgo tree. Its abundant yellow leaves were showcased by the glow of a sunset and the scattered shadows of regal mountains.

"Fortune cookie time!" Rachel said, returning from the restroom. She passed a cookie to Lainey and took the other one for herself.

Lainey opened hers. "Mine says, *Seek your guide first, before you take the treacherous path to the truth.*" She pretended to cringe. "What does yours say?"

"Mine says, *Curiosity killed the cat and satisfaction brought him back.*"

"I know something you should be curious about."

"What's that?"

"I met with Kassidy earlier today," Lainey said before crunching down on the rest of her fortune cookie, then sipping the last drop of her diet soda. She frowned when she noticed Sara Browner being escorted to a booth directly across from theirs.

Rachel grabbed Lainey's hand. "Oh my gosh, that's great!"

Lainey grimaced. "Yes, but mentally, Kassidy's not in a good place." She paused before continuing. "But I was able to calm her down so we could talk."

"How did you do that?"

Lainey smiled. "Yoga for a yoga teacher."

"Glad it worked." Rachel pierced her fork through a water chestnut and bamboo shoot and took a bite. "Can you get her out?"

"It won't be easy. She definitely had opportunity."

"Because she was with him that night?"

"Exactly."

Rachel tilted her head and sighed. "That doesn't make her guilty."

Lainey was concerned that Rachel wanted a quick fix for Kassidy's predicament. "It doesn't make her innocent."

"What reason would she have to kill him?"

Lainey leaned back against the booth cushion. "Ah, motive. It's the piece of the puzzle that could set her free or put her behind bars for a very long time."

"Cut the extra yap. Do you think she has motive or not?"

"She admitted she had a prior relationship with Randy, and we know she slept with him."

Rachel raised her eyebrows. "That doesn't give her a motive."

"If she knew about the girlfriend, I'm just saying."

"I don't get it."

"She may have lied to me today about her knowledge of the girlfriend." Lainey wrinkled her nose. "Do you know if she knew about Randy's girlfriend?"

"I just know Randy never mentioned a girlfriend at Bible study."

"Kassidy said she didn't know about the girlfriend, but in my experience, her body language suggested she lied."

"You could be wrong."

"I could, but the question obviously unsettled her."

"Go see her again." Rachel leaned forward. "Do I need to remind you it's the year of Rachel?"

"Alright, you win." She didn't really want Kassidy left in jail and even without Rachel's insistence she would have gone again anyway. Kassidy was hiding something. Why was Kassidy so uneasy with just the mention of a girlfriend?

CHAPTER 21

THE CALL

It seemed like only yesterday that Max had told Lainey about his billiards tournament this weekend. She observed her cat chase after a small chipmunk that had just appeared from underneath the red azalea bushes. Agatha wagged her tail when Max walked outside. Lainey's thoughts turned to her appearance. She knew Max loved her no matter how she looked, but she wished that she had put on makeup so Max would remember her looking pretty and miss her on his trip. Instead, here she stood, in her baggy blue sweatshirt and sweatpants.

Max tossed his large, black duffle bag into the back seat of his red Ford Taurus. He ran his hands through his hair before he leaned against the car.

Lainey walked over to him and planted a big kiss upon his lips. "Have a great trip. Knock those pool balls in."

"Thanks, honey. Are you sure you'll be okay?"

"I'll be fine. I have my trusty cane; or is it my crusty cane? My kids at school have had their hands all over this thing. Somehow, it has become a status symbol."

"You're adorable. You know, you're a bit quirky but so very lovable," Max said.

"I'll take that as a compliment." She glanced down at her watch. "You better get going."

"You're right. I'll try not to worry about you. What could happen in a week?" Max pulled her close and gave her a quick kiss. Max stroked Agatha on her furry head before he hopped into his car. With a wave out the driver's side of the window, he accelerated and headed on his way.

Lainey looked down at Agatha and realized it was time for her precious pets to get some food. "You must be hungry! Let's go inside and I'll fix you and Bailey some yummy food. Only the best for you two." She opened the side door to the kitchen to let herself and Agatha inside.

Lainey noticed that the phone's message light was on. She pushed down on the message button and listened. *'Lainey Pinewood, this is Agnes from Dr. Barnes' office in Baltimore. We have a cancellation for Tuesday, at 9:30 A.M. If you want this appointment, you must call by 7:15 A.M. on Monday, or it will be given to someone else. The office opens promptly at 7:00 A.M. Thank you.*' Lainey pushed the button again and listened to the message once more. Joyful news! She wouldn't have to wait two months, after all. She would only have to wait a couple of days.

    A thought crept into her mind and there was no taking it back. Did they give her the early appointment because they saw her records? Was there really a cancellation, or did they need to see her right away? Lainey no longer felt good; she felt scared. She felt nauseated. If it wasn't for Agatha, with her cute brown eyes looking at her, she would have cried. Instead, she put on her big-girl pants, as Rachel would say, and opened a can of gourmet dog food for Agatha and Kitty Supreme for Bailey. They didn't usually get high-priced food, but she had saved it for a special occasion. This wasn't a special occasion, but she felt like giving them comfort food. She opened the freezer and grabbed a pint of double-loaded cherry ice cream. Agatha and Bailey would have their comfort food, and she would have hers.

    Lainey sat on the couch and devoured her pint of ice cream. It wasn't long before Agatha and Bailey joined her and found their spots on the couch. It was going to be a long weekend until she could call the doctor. It was after six on a Friday night, so she would have to call from school first thing on Monday morning.

The ice cream would have to be her dinner tonight. While she wanted to wallow in her worry, she had to take care of her mother. She would need dinner, an insulin shot, and mother-daughter time. Lainey finished the last spoonful of ice cream. She had wanted to lose a few pounds before Max came home, but now, she probably just added a few. *Well, if I'm dying,* she thought, *it doesn't really matter about my weight.*

CHAPTER 22

THE HAND

The nightly breeze flowed into the dark, one-bedroom apartment, gently whipping the top pages of an open blue journal that rested upon an old oak desk. With the switch of a Tiffany lamp, a small light cast itself on the lined journal paper. A small pencil nestled within its inner fold. The dim light hid the figure sitting on the cushioned desk chair, except for the manicured fingertips that grabbed the nibbled pencil. The hand wrote what the mind thought, so the hand wrote:

Mischief Maker
Mischief Maker
Be the director

Mischief Maker
Mischief Maker
Get the projector

Mischief Maker
Mischief Maker
I've got an itch

Mischief Maker
Mischief Maker
To kill a snitch

The hand loosened its grip on the pencil and tightened again. *One more night for the next target. One more night before my victim will have life's last breath. Death to bring the fools' chase anew. Muddy the waters, stray their minds.* The hand twitched. *There's no going back to the time when good was prized and evil despised. I turned the corner. I embraced the change.* The hand stopped.

CHAPTER 23

THE SHOW

The predawn rain pounded against the car's windshield as Kate maneuvered her way through the torrential downpour. Between the windshield wipers failing to keep up with the rain, and the fog clouding her windshield, she felt her anxiety rising. She clenched her teeth and continued the battle with the elements that obstructed her view. She rolled her window down, but that did nothing to clear the fog; it simply resulted in rain plastering her shirt to her skin. With the window rolled back up, she put the heater on and then the A/C. Sometimes that worked and sometimes it didn't. She was relieved that this time it worked. With clearer vision, she picked up the speed. She had feared a second murder and it had happened.

Within fifteen minutes, Kate arrived inside the condo on C Street. She presented her badge to the officer in the doorway and entered the yellow-taped area leading to the bedroom. A cold tremor went through her. The air conditioning must have been set on full blast, but it was not the temperature that sent a chill through her bones.

The bedroom was buried in artificial snow that extended over all the bedroom furnishings except for one, and a bizarre robot. In a blue-cushioned chair, she beheld a man's lifeless body slumped back with an apparent trauma to the head. His hands were tied to the arms of the chair with white zip ties in keeping with the wintery theme. There was no doubt he was dead. She had seen dead bodies before, so none of this was new to her. It was the eerie, creepy, and disgusting holographic projection of the victim's last moments as he was being killed by a huge robotic snow person. The large robot had a carrot-colored nose that twinkled on and off, and a black hat that spun around on top of a round metal head. A sinister smile was painted on its face in bright red. The absence of eyes only made it appear more wicked. The buzzing of the running projector sickened her. Her stomach churned and nausea closed in. The murderer had recorded the dead man's last words in this dastardly projection. Over and over, the man's weak voice repeated, "I . . . Help me! Help me!" as he struggled under the attack of the snow-bot pounding his head with a heavy metal shovel. The heartbreaking sound of the man's voice crying for help dug deep into her soul; the look in the victim's eyes before he took his last breath captured in 3D. Kate shuddered, but then suddenly exhaled. She caught something in the projection that brought peace to her heart. Mercifully, the victim was only hit one time before his death as she realized the same fifteen seconds were being replayed over and over. This maniac was so vile, so cruel, that her desire to find this killer filled her blood with fire.

Will motioned to her to come over to where he was talking with a member of the forensic team. He looked tired, but in control. His brown eyes intensified as he showed her the clear evidence bag and pulled out a small holographic card with his gloved hand. "See the small robot with the shovel glistening in the killer's hologram? It's all part of his distasteful game."

"I recognize this robot from an article I read. It was designed to shovel snow for the elderly to prevent heart attacks after a major snowstorm. The killer found a way to weaponize a robot meant for saving lives to taking lives."

"This is more than a killing; it's a performance." Will

shook his head. "We're the audience for this one-night show." He stared down at the floor. "Come on. The turning black hat and that insidious smile on that robot; all this, just to kill someone? The whole scene disgusts me."

Kate flinched. "It's an ego thing and the thrill of the chase."

"Yeah, and our killer is feeling invincible. Who knows what will happen next?"

Kate had noted that the initials 'MM' were not on the back of this holographic card. Was it an oversight, or an intentional omission, or had the details of the first murder been leaked and a copycat was at work? She doubted the copycat theory, as she had total trust in her department to hold the details of the crime close to their hip. Perhaps there were two of them: one an egomaniac that needed to identify his handiwork and another just out for the kill. "It's urgent that we find a connection between our two victims."

"Or find out there's not one." Will paused. "Kate, please find out all you can on this victim. According to the driver's license we recovered in his wallet, his name is Jesse Sparks."

"Will do." Kate couldn't wait to stop this killer.

"Great. I'll focus on our first victim, Randy Watkins." He glanced down at his phone. "We'll meet this afternoon.

That will give me time to check out Watkins' employment and interview his best friend, Matt Adler."

Kate wanted to spend more time observing the crime scene before she researched background information on Jesse Sparks. After Will left, she put on her gloves and got to work. She didn't expect to find any prints in this snow mess and wanted to focus on any physical clues she could find. When she inspected the robot, she found the word 'Holotech' etched in the bottom corner of it. A good start. The projector had been powered by a battery. Most likely, the killer had done the actual killing by remote controlling the robot. She was about to leave when she discovered a clear, plastic gadget on the floor. Hmm, hadn't she seen this somewhere else? But where?

CHAPTER 24

DETECTIVE BUSINESS

Sixteen hours later, Kate and Will collapsed into their conference room seats. Kate noticed that Will chose the chair farthest from her, or had she chosen the chair farthest from him? It didn't really matter. As she eyed Sergeant Rodriguez rubbing the back of his neck, his eyes seemed to pierce through her. Were they late? She looked at Will, but his eyes were clearly aimed at Sergeant Rodriguez. Kate didn't recognize the young, blond-haired man, wearing a blue sweater-vest and pink cotton shirt, seated across the large, brown conference table.

"Kate, this is Joe Morgan. He's our technology and research expert," Sergeant Rodriguez said.

Kate gave Joe a firm handshake and a brief smile.

"Will, I know you have experienced, firsthand, the tremendous insight and knowledge that Joe brings to our table," Sergeant Rodriquez said.

"Wouldn't have been able to solve the Reagan or Mortelli cases without him." He clasped Joe's hand.

"What questions do you have for him that will aid you in this investigation?" Sergeant Rodriguez asked.

Will cleared his throat and directed his attention towards Joe. "We think there may be a connection between the two cases: the use of the hologram card in the first murder and now the 3D holographic projection of our most recent victim. With the use of the projection and the crazy robot used to kill our second victim, I guess our question to you is, who would have this kind of technological expertise?"

"Short answer. The applications for this kind of technology is growing. The field of experts capable of creating and using holographics is expanding every day. For example, the military uses it for intricate battle management. A construction company may use holograms to create test models of planned projects to determine if safety measures are effective. Basically, it's being used everywhere. Just recently, there was a holographic fashion show in New York City. If you look in your wallet, you probably have a hologram on your credit card for security purposes."

Joe took a deep breath. "As for robots, tech companies have put them on the fast track."

Will grimaced. "Thanks Joe. You just increased our suspect pool."

After Joe left, Sergeant Rodriguez signaled for Will and Kate to stay seated. "What the hell is going on with you two? I've heard the rumors, then you both walk in here and take seats at the opposite ends of this large table. Will, I have never seen you like this before. Three weeks with a new partner, and you've got problems. Work it out."

As Kate listened, she felt the room close in on her.

Will said, "We are doing better, but I will work on it."

"I would expect no less." Sergeant Rodriguez turned to Kate. "Your opinion on this?"

Kate shifted in her chair. "We had an adjustment period, but I am appreciative of my opportunity to work with Will. My choice of seats when I walked in was random."

"I'm glad to hear this," Sergeant Rodriquez said.

Kate gave Will a sidelong glance, then drew back in her seat. For the moment, Sergeant Rodriguez seemed to fade into the background. She felt the nearness of Will, a fluttering in her stomach, and the sense of a heatwave. She might have broken out into a full-fledged sweat if her eyes hadn't caught the quizzical look in Sergeant Rodriguez's eyes.

CHAPTER 25

THE SECOND FALL

It was 6:30 A.M. on Monday morning as Lainey sat in front of Lorianne Falls Elementary School anxiously waiting for Principal Martin Lopez to open the doors. She hoped the wait in her car wouldn't be long, as she needed to call the hospital by seven and she wanted to be calmly sitting at her desk when she did that. She took a moment to admire the beautiful flowers surrounding the school; not because they were beautiful but because the children had planted the different flowers depending on their grade level. Her second graders planted beautiful pink and purple impatiens. She was proud they had been so dedicated to the project and took ownership of beautifying their school.

Principal Lopez finally pulled into the school parking lot. Lainey grabbed her cane and the moment he unlocked the door she entered the school. She gave a smile and 'hello' to Martin, then went into the teachers' lounge. Each day she purchased two diet sodas out of the vending machine, and today was no exception. One was for herself, and one was for Danielle, who also taught second grade. Lainey held the two drinks in one hand as she made her way to Danielle's classroom, then placed one beverage on the corner of Danielle's neat desk.

Lainey's legs trembled and she steadied herself with her cane before entering her own classroom. With one step inside, both knees gave out. Her diet soda, purse, and cane went flying into the air as she plummeted down onto the hard, linoleum floor. She tried to pull herself up but collapsed back down as she realized she didn't really have the strength to get herself up. She yelled into the hallway. "Help me, please! Somebody help me!" She tried again to move, but to no avail. Principal Lopez and another teacher hurried to her.

"What happened, Lainey? Are you okay?" Martin asked.

"Both my knees just gave out," said Lainey, now beginning to feel embarrassed about the fall, and then even more embarrassed as she realized they would have a hard time getting her up. Max was right: she should have taken her weight issue more seriously.

Martin motioned to the other teacher. "Thelma, please go get the wheelchair from the nurse's office and then go find the custodian. I'll need some help."

Lainey felt bad that Thelma had to get the wheelchair and custodian for her. Teachers value every minute before school to get ready for their students. She made a mental note to do something nice for her.

Martin rubbed the back of his neck. "We'll have you up in a few minutes. I'm worried you may have injured yourself."

"I'll be okay once I get up," Lainey replied.

"I'll get a substitute for your class."

"I won't need a sub. Just give me a few minutes," Lainey said. Her mind raced. There was no way she wanted a sub. That would be a nightmare. She hadn't made copies yet for her students, and her lesson plan only contained brief notes. It would be easier to hobble around than try to get her sub plans together.

Within minutes, the custodian arrived, pushing the wheelchair close to Lainey.

"Cal, if you take one side, I'll take the other," Martin said. He and Cal struggled a bit, but before long placed Lainey gently into the wheelchair.

Lainey couldn't help but notice that one of her ankles appeared swollen. "Thank you both for helping me."

"No problem. I'll take you to my office. I don't want to upset the children by their seeing you in a wheelchair. I'll send Maggie to cover your class until we decide if we need a sub or not." Martin pushed Lainey across the hall and into his office.

While Martin had wanted to keep news of the incident quiet, Lainey saw her student, Bobby, waiting outside the principal's door, having arrived early for school. His wide eyes told her that he wouldn't wait to spread the news to his classmates.

Bobby frowned. "Are you alright, Mrs. Pinewood?"

"Yes, Bobby, I'll be fine."

"I'll make you a special card to make you feel better," he said, his small hands reaching for a sheet of paper from his Spider-man book bag. "I'll get everyone to sign it."

She smiled back at him. "Thank you, Bobby."

Lainey was pleasantly surprised when Bobby rose from his seat and gave her a hug. She gently hugged him back, grateful for this sign that maybe it wouldn't be such a bad day.

CHAPTER 26

STILL A BAD DAY

The wall clock in Martin's office displayed five minutes past seven. Lainey's heart raced. "Martin, may I use your phone? I really need to confirm my appointment at the Baltimore Research Hospital."

"Of course," he replied, gesturing toward the phone.

Lainey scooted her wheelchair over to the phone on his desk and searched frantically through her purse for the doctor's phone number. The clock was ticking away her opportunity to make her appointment. She dumped her purse out into her lap searching for the small yellow sheet of paper with the number she needed. It wasn't in her purse. *Where could it be?* Then, she remembered. She slipped her hand into her front pants pocket and pulled out the crumpled yellow paper before she dialed the number. It seemed like minutes before a voice answered. With relief, she recognized the voice belonging to the woman who had called her on Friday. The appointment was still available, so she hung up the phone and smiled at Martin as she gathered up all the stuff from her lap and put it back into her purse. She looked again at her swollen ankle and hoped this would only be a minor complication in getting to Baltimore tomorrow. At least it wasn't her driving foot.

"Thanks for letting me use your phone."

Martin nodded to Lainey, then said, "Ellie, take a look at her ankle," as the school nurse appeared in the doorway.

"Mrs. Pinewood, so sorry to hear about your fall," Ellie said, lifting Lainey's legs gently. "Your left ankle is very swollen. You could have sprained or broken it when you fell. This needs to be looked at by a specialist, today."

"Your wonderful second-grade team will keep an eye on your class until we decide if you're staying or going home. Please use the phone again to call your doctor," Martin said, handing the phone to Lainey.

She dialed the number to her physician and reached the office receptionist. "Hi, this is Lainey Pinewood. I just fell and I need to see Dr. Holmes right away." Silence. "Is that the earliest? You're not worried that my leg will swell out of control?" She heard the usual response from the receptionist. "You're asking me to overwork the nine-one-one system, so I'll just take the appointment for tomorrow. Thanks."

Ellie asked, "Did you get the appointment for today?"

"I couldn't get in today, but he'll see me first thing tomorrow."

"I'll call for an ambulance. There is no way you can leave that untreated until tomorrow."

"I agree with Ellie. I lifted you up off the floor. You're in no condition to drive anywhere." Martin clasped his hands together. "I'm sorry, but I'm going to call nine-one-one."

Lainey's mind went back and forth between thinking about going into the ambulance to wishing she had taken the time to clean off her desk after class last Friday. She shuddered to think what the other teachers would think about her messy desk. She was usually well-planned for her class, but today, her desk belied that fact. A sad thought occurred to her: if Randy hadn't been murdered, she would have called him. She pressed her fingers through her hair and leaned back.

Vice-Principal Wanda Jackson marched into the office with her car keys dangling from her fingers. "Lainey, I'll follow the ambulance to the hospital to make sure you're okay."

"Wanda, it's kind of you, but I'll be fine," Lainey said.

"Don't be silly. I'm worried about you." She smiled. "Martin gave me the go-ahead."

Lainey felt humbled by her support. "Thank you so much."

"Rachel stopped me in the hallway and wanted to come with you, but I told her she's to stay with her class. I'll give her an update later," Wanda said.

Lainey fretted about worrying her friend. "I'll call Rachel at lunchtime."

Wanda abruptly commandeered the handles of Lainey's wheelchair and pushed her through the office door. Lainey saw what Wanda apparently had seen: the ambulance had just stopped in front of the school.

Lainey wanted to cry. She wanted to call Kate but held back. The arrival of the ambulance signaled the seriousness of the situation. It wasn't going to be a good day.

CHAPTER 27

CONNECTING THE DOTS

Kate and Will were prepared to narrow down their suspects. Late spring rain drizzled upon their heads as they approached the police station. White, yellow, and green leaves, torn and withered, glistened from the wet air as they littered the narrow, cobbled sidewalk in front of the police building. As they entered the station's long hallway, Kate heard Will's black leather shoes squeak on the speckled linoleum floor, even though they had both wiped their shoes against the brown woven floor mat situated near the entrance. Will motioned her into one of the small conference rooms to the left of the doorway.

Kate settled into one of the black vinyl chairs while Will hung his jacket on a nearby coat rack. She noticed the worn, grease-stained Orioles cap hanging on a chair at the end of the brown, water-stained conference table. Obviously, it was Don Parson's cap, as he was the Orioles fan extraordinaire of the police department. Through the thin walls of the conference room, she could hear Frank, one of the old-timer detectives, coughing and hacking in the adjoining room. It worried her that he may have lung cancer from years of smoking. Would he check it out? No. Frank didn't believe in doctors or giving up cigarettes.

Kate glanced over at Will. He had taken a moment to wipe off a sticky area on the conference table. She felt Will's annoyance as he complained about the inconsiderate nature of some of his fellow cops. Kate smelled coffee in the air and then noticed the small amount of coffee left in the glass carafe. Kate agreed with Will: cleanliness among the ranks was not always evident. What was evident, she thought, was that cops worked long, hard hours trying to keep people safe, so if cleanliness took a backseat, so be it.

Will pulled out a chair and sat across from Kate. He reached into his shirt pocket and pulled out a small, yellow-lined notebook and a blue pen before he looked across at her. "Here's what I got. Watkins had been employed by the county school system for the last six months. Based on Human Resources comments and a few teachers from Lorianne Falls Elementary School, Watkins had been a model substitute. Before that job, he worked for a construction company for ten years. So, I talked to Watkins' supervisor at Hammer and Nails Construction Company. He was fired last year for sharing design plans for a new technology the company planned to patent. The company didn't press charges because they believed he innocently shared it with his girlfriend. I also talked with Watkins' best friend, Matt Adler, who's a small-time film director. He hadn't seen his friend in weeks. Watkins slept with Adler's wife and that pretty much ended their friendship."

Kate wrinkled her brow. "So, Adler has a motive for killing Randy Watkins but is there a holographic connection?"

"It's a possibility. We can't ignore Adler as a suspect. Betrayal is a powerful motivator." Will leaned forward in his chair. His brown eyes focused on Kate. "If you get a chance, go check out Adler. There's something about him I didn't like. Maybe you will detect something I missed." He folded his arms and leaned back against his chair. "Now, what have you got on Jesse Sparks?"

Kate shifted in her chair, aware of the closeness of his body, but met his gaze — man to woman, professional to professional. "I discovered that the robot was manufactured at Holotech, where Jesse worked. I also found a small, clear plastic piece that may be relevant. I saw it somewhere; I can't remember where. Interestingly enough, when I checked Jesse's desk, I found a brochure about the Holographic Trade Show that was held in Montreal last year. I also found a yoga mat at his apartment, which could connect him to our own Kassidy Roper. We're checking for prints on the yoga mat that might clarify the owner and connection."

Will massaged the back of his neck. "Check out Kassidy's friend Lily too. She may be a missing link we haven't investigated thoroughly."

"I agree. I have looked into her background, but I'm not done." She felt a soft flutter in her chest and a hint of an adrenaline rush. She was at her best now. She felt her confidence rising that they would catch their killer soon.

Kate smiled at Will. His body was stretched out on the conference room couch. His unshaven face meant he hadn't intended to be disrupted this morning, but she was so excited to share the results of her investigation into Lily's background that she couldn't wait until they were on duty.

Will sat up. "You called this meeting. What's up?"

"I found some interesting facts on Lily when I investigated her previous employment. Lily had worked at Holotech and was there at the same time as Jesse Sparks." She paused. "And I remembered where I saw that plastic piece. When we were at Yoga Heaven, I noticed that one of the cell phones in the storage cubbies had a clear plastic gadget attached to it, and during my research on holographic technology, I learned that gadget was a mini hologram projector for smartphones. It's minor, but a link to a knowledge of holograms. Whoever owns that cell phone may blow this case wide open." She flipped through her notepad. "And that's not all. After quite a bit of digging into her college records, I discovered a few things like she has an IQ of 168."

"A closet genius," Will said, surprised.

"So, her intelligence and her connection to Holotech make her more of a suspect than even Kassidy." Kate pushed her chair closer to Will. "When I looked into her academic history, a pattern evolved. I discovered Lily grew up in eight different foster homes starting at age two. Going from school to school, I assumed she couldn't keep friends. It's evident that Kassidy and Lily are close friends. Randy and Jesse threatened that relationship. If Kassidy fell in love with either man, Lily would be pushed into the background. Jealousy plus dysfunction plus genius is the perfect collaboration for murder."

"Kassidy did say Lily was overprotective, which supports that theory." Will smiled. "Great job on the research."

"Thank you; that means a lot." Kate leaned back in her chair. She had presented her findings and her hard work was validated by Will. For the first time, she felt like he valued their partnership. Now all they had to do was figure out who the real killer was.

CHAPTER 28

EMERGENCY ROOM

Lainey and Wanda waited in emergency room number seven for the doctor to arrive. A nurse had taken Lainey's vital signs and informed her that the doctor would see her when he could. Based on what she had already seen and heard, she expected a long wait. When her gurney was wheeled past rooms one through six, they were all filled with patients. How she wished the hospital staff had kept the curtains drawn on these unfortunate occupants. For eight o'clock in the morning, there was a packed house of injuries and illnesses. She was still having trouble blocking out the red-stained bandage around the man's eye laying in the bed in the room next to her and the young boy in number three screaming frantically for his mom while a nurse attempted to give him a shot to make his pain stop. The more she listened to the sounds around her, the more her anxiety grew. In a hospital was nowhere she wanted to be. She was so thankful Wanda had stayed with her.

To her surprise, it hadn't been a long wait when a tall doctor stepped in.

"Hello, I'm Dr. Assad. What brings you here?"

"I was walking to my classroom and my legs just gave out," Lainey explained.

"Let me take a look." He examined both her ankles and asked if any other part of her body was injured. "Hmm. Have you been subjected to any domestic abuse?"

With that question, Wanda started to head out the door. "Maybe I should wait outside," she said.

"Wanda, please don't leave. My husband doesn't hit me." Lainey felt embarrassed by this whole discussion. She felt offended for Max that anyone would ever think that. "Dr. Assad, there's no abuse."

"I need an x-ray of your right and left ankles," Dr. Assad announced, then pulled back the curtain to the room and spoke to the nurse standing next to Lainey's bed. As Dr. Assad left, another nurse walked into Lainey's room.

"Mrs. Pinewood, there is someone who would like to see you," the nurse said.

Wanda looked across at Lainey. "I'll go see who it is. I have a feeling I know." Wanda pulled back the curtain and left.

Five minutes later, Wanda came back with a familiar face. "I told her to stay at school, but here she is." Wanda pursed her lips. "Well, I'm going back to school then, since Rachel's here now. Feel better Lainey, and Rachel, you take care of her." With that, Wanda left.

Lainey embraced Rachel when she came over to the hospital bed. "I can't believe you just left school like that. You could get yourself in trouble!"

"Stop fretting. Martin okayed it. Although, I did do a bit of begging and volunteered to help him with the next fundraiser. Anyway, you're the one in trouble!"

"Me?" Lainey pulled the sheet over her head and then back down.

"Why didn't you send someone to tell me? I had to hear it through the teachers' pipeline."

"I'm sorry, Rachel. Everything happened so fast. I didn't want to disturb you and your class." Lainey saw the nurse coming in through the drawn curtain.

"I'm taking you to x-ray," the nurse announced. "Your visitor can wait here until we get back. It should only take a few minutes." The nurse helped Lainey lower herself into the wheelchair.

"See you when you get back," Rachel said.

Within twenty minutes, Lainey was back in the room with Rachel, waiting for the results of the x-ray. She was feeling overwhelmed when Rachel got up from her chair and hugged her. Rachel was such a comfort. Lainey still couldn't believe she had such a wonderful friend.

"I hope my ankle isn't broken. I must see Dr. Barnes tomorrow. Then I'll need to cancel my appointment with my primary doctor since I ended up in the emergency room," Lainey said.

"Did you really think you could see two doctors in one day? They're not even near each other," Rachel said.

"I got caught up in the moment. It's like when I go to McDonald's drive-thru; I'm planning to order a salad, but I hear myself say, 'Big Mac.'"

"Sometimes your thinking eludes me."

Dr. Assad interrupted their conversation when he came back to discuss the results of the x-ray. "You do have a broken ankle. You'll need to see a specialist." He handed her a business card with the specialist's name and her discharged papers.

Rachel took hold of the handles on Lainey's wheelchair and unlocked the brakes. "Dr. Assad, thank you for your time and expertise. I'll take her to see the specialist. Today, if we can get an appointment."

Five hours later, Lainey sat exhausted from all the running around that came with her injury. They had been able to see the specialist and no surgery would be needed. Six weeks in a cast and she would be good as new. It felt good to just sit and relax with Rachel on the couch. She couldn't walk, but other than that, her life was back on track.

CHAPTER 29

FAMILY SUPPORT

It had only been a few hours since Rachel left, but Lainey felt like evening would never come. Despite it being only seven o'clock, she longed for sleep, but she needed to call one of her sons for a ride to the hospital. Relieved that her mother had already been given dinner by her caregiver, she lowered her head onto a couch pillow. Her thoughts turned to the cumbersome cast that she would have to endure wearing for the next six weeks.

A loud knock on the door and her son's voice woke her. Agatha ran over, tail wagging, and jumped up on Pete. "What's going on? I got a call from your school telling me that you fell. I tried to call you on your cell but got no answer and your voicemail was full. I thought of calling

Nana, but I didn't want to worry her." He eyed the cast. "Are you okay?"

"I have to wear this cast, but I should be fine."

"Where's Dad? Does he know?"

"No. He left for a pool tournament on Friday, but I'll tell him." Lainey gave a weak smile. "Is there any chance you can take me to Baltimore Research Hospital tomorrow?"

"Weren't you taken care of in the emergency room?"

"Yes, but this is something else. Pinched nerve I think." She hoped he wouldn't worry, a pinched nerve sounded pretty common to her. "My appointment is at 9:30."

"I have an important appointment for my security clearance, but I can take you, if you don't mind getting there early." He hesitated. "I can come back for you."

"I'm very grateful, Pete. Could you kindly help me to the bathroom?"

"Sure." Pete took hold of Lainey's arm to give her support.

"Mom, this is more than a broken ankle." Pete continued to support his mom's walking, even as she made her way to the hallway bathroom. Lainey could feel tears building up, but she suppressed her emotions before Pete noticed.

Pete put his arms around her. "Mom, don't worry."

"I think I'm only tired right now." Lainey pushed open the bathroom door and maneuvered her way to the toilet. Pete stepped away once she had entered the bathroom. She closed the door and yelled out to her son. "It may take a while." She hated being helpless and hated that Pete saw her this way, but she had no choice. After about ten minutes she banged gently on the bathroom door.

"Are you done, Mom?"

"Yeah, are you ready to help me out?"

"Mom, Agatha is even ready."

CHAPTER 30

AN ARREST

Kate and Will strolled into Kassidy Roper's yoga studio. Kate called a cell phone using the number found in Jesse Sparks' wallet. Kate nodded to Will and the two detectives walked up to the two yoga friends meditating at the front of the studio.

"You're under arrest for the murders of Randy Watkins and Jesse Sparks," Will said.

Kassidy's face paled. "Oh my God, I just got out of jail!"

Lily stepped in front of Kassidy. "Leave her alone. I'll get her a lawyer."

Kate tried to harness her contempt for Lily. How could Lily betray her friend and then act innocent? "You're the one who needs a lawyer this time. *You're* under arrest for the murders of Randy Watkins and Jesse Sparks."

Two police officers walked in and placed handcuffs on Lily and read her the Miranda rights. Kate ignored the tears in Lily's eyes; her police training had taught her how to do that. Lily was such an itty-bitty girl that no one would've suspected her, but killers came in all sizes. She signaled for the two cops to take Lily down to the station.

Will turned back to Kassidy. "Ms. Roper, we knew it was your friend when she answered the iPhone with the holographic gadget attached to it."

"None of that means anything to me." Kassidy lifted her chin and glared. "You're making a big mistake. Just like you did with me."

"I'd keep quiet if I were you. I'm not convinced you're not involved in this," Will said. "Both of the male victims were once your boyfriends."

Kate noted Kassidy's facial change when Will told her he knew Randy and Jesse were once her boyfriends. It was obvious she was shaken by Will's comment. Was it possible they had let Kassidy out too soon? Kate glanced down and noticed the white envelope protruding out of her jacket. Time to put this little piece of information to rest.

Kate handed Kassidy the white envelope with the

outline of a purple heart drawn in the middle. Inside the heart, were two letters and a word: *R loves K.*

"What's this?"

"It's two plane tickets to Bermuda." Kate tapped at the envelope in Kassidy's hand. "You were the one Randy planned to surprise, but then he was murdered."

Tears welled up in Kassidy's eyes, but she stayed silent.

"I remembered you wanted that second chance with Randy. You almost had that." Kate needed to say more, her heart told her that. "I'm sorry for your loss."

Will motioned to Kate to wrap it up. With nothing else to say, they both walked out the door.

CHAPTER 31

DOCTOR BARNES

Lainey sat in the waiting room at the Baltimore Research Hospital contemplating all the possible outcomes for her visit today. The room seemed to spin. The worst possible outcomes skyrocketed her anxiety through the roof. The loads of other worried patients in the large waiting room did nothing to calm her fears. She watched the patients coming through the doors after their consultations and they didn't look happy either.

The double doors swung open repeatedly in that hour, which soon became two hours. Finally, the door sprung open to reveal a woman in a white lab coat with curly, ruffled hair and black glasses. "Lainey Pinewood?"

"That's me." Lainey smiled and tried to maneuver her

wheelchair towards the doctor. *It might have helped if I had shifted the brake handle so it could move.* Lainey pulled on the brake handle and moved her wheelchair towards the doctor.

"Hello. I'm Dr. Sheila Barnes." She reached out and shook Lainey's hand gently. "I'll wheel you down to my office." Dr. Barnes pushed her down a long hallway filled with many closed patient doors. It seemed to Lainey that they would never get to the doctor's office.

"Mrs. Pinewood, what's been going on?" Dr. Barnes asked once they were settled.

"As you can see, I broke my ankle. It just happened yesterday. I've been trying for months to find out what's happening to me. When I fell yesterday at school, both of my knees gave out at the same time."

"That's unfortunate. What other symptoms do you have that brought you to see a neurologist?"

"My feet tingle and feel kind of numb," Lainey explained. "Sometimes, it feels like it is tingling all the way up to my knees. I also have trouble getting up from a chair."

"Anything else?"

"The other day, I couldn't even lift my foot up onto a curb. A school bus driver had to help me." Lainey hoped her list didn't sound so long that she thought she was a hypochondriac. A knock on the examination door sent Dr. Barnes across the room.

Before the door had fully opened, Lainey yelled out, "You're incredible! What are you doing here?" She couldn't stop gawking at her dear friend.

"The field trip was to the park for leaf identification. We got back early, and I took a half-day," Rachel said.

"Dr. Barnes, this is my best friend, Rachel. Is it okay with you that she stays?"

Dr. Barnes nodded. "Nice to meet you," she greeted Rachel, then turned back to Lainey. "Please continue with your symptoms."

"Two months ago, I saw a different neurologist. He thought my symptoms were the result of a pinched nerve in my back. I didn't get better, so my husband suggested I see a specialist at this hospital."

"So, would you say you are getting progressively worse?"

"I fell yesterday. Before that, it seemed to be about the same."

"It hasn't stayed the same." Rachel piped up. "She's a lot worse than even two weeks ago. Her walking is slower and she's a bit more unstable."

"Thanks. Sometimes friends are better observers of what is happening than the patient," Dr. Barnes said.

"Do you know what is wrong with me?"

"I have an idea. I'll have to do some tests first before I can confirm my diagnosis." Dr. Barnes squatted down with a small metal hammer in her hand and tapped Lainey on her knees, then her right ankle, and then her elbows. Dr. Barnes took out a small pin and gently touched her feet, legs, and hands. Still, Lainey felt nothing. "You seem to have minimal or no reflexes in your ankles and knees, and you exhibited little response when I touched you with the pin. Let's try something else. Please close your eyes and touch your nose."

Lainey closed her eyes and was thrilled that she could touch her nose. That had to be a good thing.

"Good. Do you have time to stay for some more tests?"

It felt like Groundhog Day. Hadn't she been through all this with Dr. Healey? "Yes," she answered. She just hoped she'd get a different diagnosis this time.

Dr. Barnes made a call to make the arrangements and then folded her hands together. "I made the plans for your test. Someone will be by in a moment to wheel you down to the lab. By the way, Mrs. Pinewood, your son is in the waiting room. He can come to the testing lab if you want."

"Lainey, I'll get Pete and meet you in the testing area," Rachel offered.

"Thanks, Rachel. See you in a few minutes."

CHAPTER 32

THE DIAGNOSIS

After the conduction test, Lainey was wheeled back to the waiting room by the lab technician with Pete by her side. Rachel went home to avoid traffic in Baltimore during the rush hour and wished Lainey good news. It was good to have Pete by her side, but she missed Max. Lainey closed her eyes. She wished she had heard from him. He usually never let more than two days go by without calling. Her thoughts broke when she felt Pete nudge her right arm.

"Mom, Dr. Barnes just called us over." Pete pushed her wheelchair through the double doors as he followed Dr. Barnes to her office.

"Mrs. Pinewood, I have the results of your conduction

test. I can't be completely sure until you take the lumbar test, but I believe you have the symptoms of CIDP."

"What's that?"

"It stands for Chronic Inflammatory Demyelinating Polyneuropathy. It's caused when your body's immune system attacks the myelin sheath on your nerves. Some consider it the chronic form of Guillain-Barre disease." She scratched her head. "It's a rare disease."

Lainey trembled. "Am I going to die? Is it curable?"

"It's not curable, but it's treatable."

"What caused this?" Pete asked.

"We're not sure. There are various theories, but none have been proven conclusive."

Lainey grimaced. "Is it my weight? Is it because I color my hair? Once, a beautician colored my hair and it smelled like formaldehyde. Is it because I drink too much diet soda? Is it because I used to live near power lines?"

Dr. Barnes interrupted her before she could say another word. "Like I said, we don't know. If the things you mentioned were the causes, we would have loads of cases. CIDP is relatively rare. If untreated, it's possible you might not be able to walk, and it can affect movement in your arms."

Pete glanced over at Lainey and back to Dr. Barnes. "What's the treatment?"

"Some options are intravenous therapies, or we could use a combination of steroids and immunosuppressant drugs. You'll need to schedule a lumbar test before we make decisions about the treatment," Dr. Barnes answered, then put out her hand. "It was nice meeting both of you. Try not to worry, Mrs. Pinewood."

"Thanks. Is there anything I need to do before I see you again?"

"Schedule the lumbar test."

CHAPTER 33

INSIDE INFORMATION

It was six-fifteen A.M. on a sunny morning when Lainey held tight to her crutches and knocked twice on Kate's condo door. Her daughter would be surprised to see her out of the wheelchair since it had only been a few weeks since her visit to Baltimore.

No response. Thinking Kate might be upstairs, she pounded against the hardwood door. She waited. She readjusted her black shoulder bag. She bit her bottom lip and pounded again. *Calm down*, she told herself. Kate's blue Ford Fusion was sitting in the driveway. She was home.

Kate finally opened the door. Her eyes grew wide. "Mom?"

Lainey eyed Kate's pink ruffled blouse and gray slacks

and was pleased that her daughter wore the blouse she had given her for her birthday. It looked great with the gray slacks. However, she had more important things to discuss. "I just couldn't wait. I heard you've made another arrest."

Kate waved her mom in, and they each sat down on a kitchen stool, albeit Lainey did it less gracefully. A leftover aroma of bacon and maple syrup nestled over them. "Yes, we did. We took Lily Proctor into custody last week. How did you know we made an arrest?"

"Rachel called me." Lainey paused. Her daughter didn't like to be questioned about how she handled her investigations. She knew this from experience, but she had to say something. She gritted her teeth. "You've made a mistake."

Kate groaned. "Mistake?"

Lainey took a slice of bacon from Kate's plate. "Yes, just like when you arrested Kassidy Roper. There's no way Lily killed Randy or anyone else. She's harmless."

"She's not harmless. Her background check said otherwise." Kate also took a piece of bacon off her plate.

Lainey narrowed her eyes and raised a brow. "I don't know what you think you know, but Lily wouldn't do this." She slowly got up from her stool and retrieved a mug from the cupboard.

"Mom, I would've gotten that for you."

"I know," she said, pouring herself a cup of coffee. "Lily was in my class the year I taught fourth grade. She was so smart. The only issue she had was that she socially isolated herself. I assumed it was because she had changed schools so much, but by the end of the year she was blooming. I believe that was the year she met Kassidy. It was a shame she moved the next year."

"She's changed from the young girl you taught."

Lainey sat back down on the stool and took a sip of her coffee. "She hasn't changed."

"She's not the same person from *fifteen years ago*," said Kate. "I can't disclose the details, but we believe she's capable of murder."

The answer to Lainey's next question might give her an answer that she didn't want to hear, but she was confident that her impression of Lily was right on. She looked directly into Kate's eyes. "Has she killed someone before?"

Kate paused. "We're not sure, but when Lily was in college a friend of hers disappeared. It makes us wonder if she was involved." Attempting to curb her irritation, she jabbed her fork into the last fluff of buttermilk pancake resting on her plate and poured a small amount of maple syrup as she prepared to take a bite.

Lainey grabbed Kate's fork from her hand. "But you don't know for sure?"

Kate didn't hold back her irritation this time and grabbed the fork back. "No."

Lainey exhaled. *No* was the answer that gave her hope. She took another sip of coffee and was grateful for its soothing effects, but it still didn't calm her frustration at Kate's stubbornness. She had to think of something to change her daughter's mind. "I saw Lily at yoga every week. Nothing about her makes me think 'killer.' "

"Mom, let's just say people have secrets and you don't know hers." Kate lifted herself off her stool and stood up. "Let us do our investigation and stay out of this."

"While you're figuring it out, Lily will be stuck in a jail cell for a crime she didn't do."

"She can post bail." Kate shrugged.

"You have an answer for everything," Lainey sighed. "You can't undo the harm of arresting an innocent person. Social media will be all over this in no time. They'll have her convicted the second the first Tweet goes out."

"Mom, please, you're overreacting."

Lainey felt herself tapping on the end of the kitchen island. She was feeling disheartened by her lack of progress in changing Kate's mind. It really shouldn't have surprised her. She had dealt with the mindset of a detective before. "If you were the one falsely accused, would you think I was overreacting?"

Kate shrugged. "Of course not. That's different."

"You only think it's different because you've already judged her guilty." Lainey drew a breath and bit her lip. "It's obvious you've made your decision."

Kate frowned. "Can we just agree to disagree?"

"Can we agree that I've given you something to think about?" The old-fashioned cuckoo clock on the blue kitchen wall tweeted its message of the passing of time. Lainey placed her mug in the kitchen sink before she tossed her napkin in the metal trash can.

Kate shook her head and paused. "Don't you have school today?"

"Yes. My wheelchair is in the car; I use that in the classroom and going down the hall so I don't have to use the cumbersome crutches." Lainey paused. She bit into her last morsel of bacon and then quickly slid a finger through the maple syrup still clinging to Kate's white plastic plate. She licked the delicious syrup off her finger.

Kate handed her a napkin. "Mom, I've got work. You have school. It's time for both of us to leave."

"You're right, but I feel so unsettled. There seems to be a rush to judgment about Lily."

"If anyone is rushing to a judgment, you are. Your mind is so closed that you won't even consider that Lily could be guilty. Chew on that while you make your way out my front door." Kate grabbed her car keys and jingled them in the air.

Lainey lowered herself off the kitchen stool. She didn't like the weakness she felt in her legs but the steroids Dr. Barnes prescribed helped keep her strength up so she could walk. She lifted her shoulder bag over her head and got her crutches into position while Kate put on her gray blazer. Kate assisted her out the front door and they both stopped at the end of the sidewalk. Lainey gave her daughter a hug. "Love you."

"Love you too. Have a great day," Kate said, then paused. "Are your students behaving better? Last week you said they were doing more talking than listening."

"It's the end of the school year so that is to be expected. But funny you should ask that. They're doing better, but based on this morning, they're not the only ones not listening to me." Lainey smiled. "I hope you have a great day too." She wasn't worried about her students' behavior. It was her daughter's behavior that riled her. Why couldn't Kate see the truth? She would prove to everyone, especially to Kate, that Lily was no killer. She felt the adrenaline rise in her body as she contemplated how she might do just that.

CHAPTER 34

TEACHERS' LOUNGE

Four hours after her talk with Kate, and after a morning filled with reading groups and questioning students, Lainey was ready for lunch. Her students' questions had been exhilarating and she felt wonderfully spent. For whatever reason, her class had been engaged. It was a teacher's dream.

It all started with Bobby's usual comment about reading. He said the book they'd read was boring. She wished she had said the next comment but Latisha, apparently tired of his complaining, asked him what makes this story so boring to him. Bobby looked her straight in the eyes and said the *words* were boring. And then the fun started.

Lainey asked Bobby how they could make this story less boring. He grew silent, but the rest of the class stepped up. Benjamin said maybe the author could add funny words. Lainey asked the class what some funny words were that they could add to this story. Five hands went up. Raoul thought this story was not meant to be funny so then they all came up with serious words. Lainey said maybe the story needed more adjectives to describe the characters. With a brief reminder about what adjectives were, the children came up with ten descriptive words. Michael came up with an adjective for the porch in the story. By the time they ended the session they were discussing setting. Lainey thought her heart would swell with pride when Michael asked if they could write their own stories during writing class.

Lainey found an empty seat at one of the round tables in the teachers' lunchroom and wheeled herself over to it, balancing her food tray carefully in the process. She could hear Jacob from Mrs. Howard's kindergarten class crying in the hallway. He was a new transfer student and, according to Mrs. Howard, was having a hard time adjusting to a new routine.

Her eyes focused on the sun glaring brightly into the room, highlighting the food particles resting on the very used lunch tables. She brushed some leftover crumbs out of her way and placed her tray on the empty table. The other tables were filled with third-grade teachers chatting about their day and a few other staff members sat scattered around the room eating their lunches as well.

A familiar substitute sat alone at a table eating an egg salad sandwich. That sulfuric odor coming from her sandwich was palatable. It was the woman's demeanor, however, that caught Lainey's attention. Her eyes were downcast as she stared at her food but made no attempt to eat. It was the look of a substitute on a bad kid day. If Lainey had noticed her when she came in, she would have sat with her. She made a mental note to sit with her the next time she was at her school. Instead, catching the woman looking up, Lainey just smiled, and was pleased to see the woman smile back.

Lainey looked at her own tray, filled with spaghetti, a small cup of salad, and garlic bread. It was her favorite cafeteria lunch. She swirled some spaghetti and placed the delicious forkful into her mouth. She was about to swirl another when Rachel walked in, grabbed a bottled water from the old refrigerator, and sat across from her. Rachel was the only teacher in the school wearing high heels, but she did it so well. She was a chic dresser, but today she looked a bit frazzled, which was unlike her. Beads of sweat dampened her forehead and brown hair. Lainey put her fork down and gazed at Rachel. She felt she knew the answer, but she still asked. "How's your day going?"

"It was going great until one of my students vomited in class. If that wasn't enough, another student accidentally spilled her bottled water all over another student's desk. At that point, I lost their attention and went into recovery mode. How's your day so far?"

"I had an awesome morning with my class, but my morning visit with Kate didn't go so well." Almost as if mimicking her feelings, the room darkened as the clouds covered the sun's brightness with their graying shadows.

"You went to see Kate before school?" Rachel took a sip of her water before she raised her eyebrows. "What's going on?"

Lainey finished swallowing a forkful of spaghetti. "I still can't believe she arrested Lily."

Rachel nodded. "Unbelievable. Besides yoga class, Lily's in my Bible study. She's such a gentle spirit."

"I know. You mentioned Lily was in your Bible study the other day."

"Thanks for reminding me. I forgot to mention that Mel is in our Bible study too, but he has only attended a few meetings," Rachel said.

Lainey didn't give much thought to Mel being a member of the Bible study. Her mind was laser-sharp on

Lily's arrest. She lowered her voice when another teacher walked in. "Well, I don't believe Lily murdered Randy. First, like you said, she's a gentle spirit. She even works at the animal rescue league. Second, I don't think she knew Randy or the second victim. No real connection there. Third, she's not egotistical. That's a common characteristic of murderers. I tried to convince Kate, but her mind seems made up about Lily's guilt."

Rachel tapped a finger to her chin. "Mmm, I'm going to agree with you on one thing. Lily is a gentle spirit. Hands down. The rest of your argument is a bit sketchy, which is why Kate shut you down. Apparently, you've forgotten this: I already mentioned to you that Randy and Lily were in my Bible study group when you interrogated me about Kassidy. My guess is that Kate, the detective, already knew this too." Rachel tossed her brown hair out of her eyes.

Lainey winced when she remembered what Rachel said was true. "Okay, then what other reasons do you have for not believing in your best friend?" she challenged.

"Calm down Lainey Bug. Put on your big-girl pants. I'm just trying to save you from some wild goose-chasing and get your credibility back with Kate."

Lainey delivered a half-smile. She looked around the almost empty lunchroom, the third-grade teachers now gone, before staring directly into Rachel's hazel eyes. "Thanks, so what's the problem with my third argument?"

"It's in describing murderers as egotistical. You taught me everything I know about detective work. You've told me, or I've learned it, through a kind of osmosis, by being your friend. Serial killers, commonly, are egotistical. We need three or more murders for this case to qualify as a serial killing. We only have two."

"You make two seem inconsequential."

Rachel didn't reply to the comment. "You once told me murderers come with a diversity of motives and personalities." Rachel smiled. "Shall I go on?"

Lainey took a deep breath. "No, you're right. I need to get the facts before I go to Kate again."

"You also need to think before you question Kate. I know she hates when you meddle in her police work."

Lainey moaned. "I'm not a meddler as everyone seems to think. I don't call it meddling when I see an injustice being made. Sometimes I've been right, but she forgets about that."

"I remember when you've been wrong, and Kate listened to you. You made her look foolish in front of the other officers. I'm sure she still remembers that."

Lainey nodded. She knew exactly what Rachel was talking about. Last year, she had talked Kate into convincing Sergeant Payton that a suspect was hiding out down at the Swenson farm. Guns blazing, the police, with Kate and the Sergeant in the lead, had stormed the Swenson's barn. Within minutes, they had the suspect surrounded. Two suspects, to be exact. However, there would be no arrests. Before them was a standoff . . . between a raccoon and a big black cat. The cat stood in a full hiss and the raccoon was ready to pounce. Lainey could still remember the mortification she saw in Kate's eyes. The Sergeant had given her daughter the evil eye while the other officers were laughing and doing "meow" calls. If the Sergeant hadn't put a stop to their unprofessional behavior, Lainey would have. She still couldn't believe she had been wrong. All her leads said the suspect would be there. She had heard human footsteps in that barn, not animal steps. She was convinced they had just missed him, but it didn't matter. Her daughter had taken the fall. It was probably why she had been transferred to work under Sergeant Rodriguez. She shrugged. "I know and I get that. But this time, she just has to listen."

"Tread lightly, my dear friend. She needs to know her mother believes in her ability to do her job."

"I do believe in her, but I also believe in me. I'm just going to have to find the evidence to set Lily free." Lainey was about to say more when Isaac approached them. She knew what he carried in his hands: a diet soda for her and an iced tea for Rachel. Ever since he started last year, he would stop by McDonald's during a long break and get drinks for certain teachers. Isaac said they were chosen because they left good sub plans.

Isaac smiled. "Hello ladies. Anyone care for an ice-cold drink?" He handed them each their beverage while they expressed their thanks. Isaac then said goodbye and headed out the door.

The smell of body odor filled the lunchroom as the door opened. It was the typical smell of fifth-graders at this time of year, especially after recess. Lainey saw a former student, Jason, in the hallway and smiled at him as he passed by the lunchroom door.

She glanced at the large, circular metal clock on the wall. Rachel wanted to talk to her about something she didn't want to discuss: whether Lainey felt better after her appointment in Baltimore. She didn't feel better. The diagnosis seemed to commit her to a long-term problem when she wanted a quick fix. She tried to change the subject, but Rachel stormed on. Finally, Rachel did what she did best: she had them bow their heads in prayer. She prayed that her student who vomited would get better, that the Lord would comfort Lainey, and that He would give the doctors the wisdom to find the right diagnosis and treatment.

The prayers did make Lainey feel a bit better, but for some reason she couldn't get Lily out of her mind. Could Lily be the killer? It didn't seem likely, but the police had something on her. The minute school was over, she'd go to the jail and get Lily to tell the truth. And she could only hope that the truth didn't prove Lily guilty.

CHAPTER 35

LILY'S LOCKUP

The Lorianne Falls police station was unusually crowded when Lainey arrived after school. Apparently, a drug bust had proven fruitful, both in arrestees and drugs. The hallway leading to the jail cells smelled of cigarettes and weed. Finally, after twenty minutes, an officer led her down that hallway to visit Lily.

Lily was sitting in the corner of her cell reading a book when Lainey arrived. *Such a difference from the way Kassidy had handled being locked up*, she thought. She watched Lily place the book on the metal chair before she approached her.

"I'm so glad to see you. Why are you on crutches and wearing that medical boot on your foot?" Lily asked.

"I fell and fractured a bone in my ankle, but I'm fine. Curious about the book you were reading; you seemed so calm."

"It's a book of Biblical meditations," Lily answered, then pressed her hand to her heart. "The meditations ground me to a spiritual place. No matter what happens, I know I'll be okay."

"That's a philosophy that Kassidy could use."

Lily pinched her lips. "It's not a philosophy. It's a truth."

"Speaking of the truth, did you kill Randy Watkins or Jesse Sparks?" Lainey asked. She didn't expect to get an answer, but Lily's body language would provide a clue.

Lily looked down at her red and white sneakers. A suppressed smile crossed her face. "Mrs. Pinewood, when I was in your class those many years ago, I lied numerous times when you asked me if I did Kassidy's homework for her. You never figured it out. You won't know if I'm telling the truth or not."

The use of her teacher's name amused Lainey, and Lily's comments reminded her just how close Lily and Kassidy had been. It reminded her how Lily had cried on her last day of school when she had unexpectantly announced she was moving the next day. She should have been suspicious of Lily at the time, with Kassidy getting all A's on her homework but doing poorly on tests. But Lily was so smart, so good in class, that she went under Lainey's radar. *Is she going under my radar now?* She pressed her hands against the bars. "If I were you, I wouldn't relay this story to the police. They might just think, 'once a liar, always a liar.'"

Lily winced. "I didn't kill anyone. Please believe me."

Lainey wanted to believe her, but her story about knowing how to lie because of having done it so convincingly when she was a student in her class gave her pause. Yet, murder didn't make sense. "It doesn't matter what I think. What connections do you have to Randy and Jesse?"

"Randy was in my Bible study, and I worked with Jesse at Holotech."

"Hmm, I had no idea you knew Jesse Sparks." How many wrong assumptions had she made about Lily? She had to get to the bottom of this. She moved her chair closer to Lily. "What kinds of questions did the police ask you?"

"Most of the questions focused on Jesse and our time at Holotech. They kept asking me how well I understood holographics and artificial intelligence. The rest of their questions were about my relationship with Kassidy," Lily frowned.

Lainey raised her brow. "I hadn't heard about any holographic technologies or robots being involved in this case. I'll ask my daughter about that. What does your relationship with Kassidy have to do with Watkins and Sparks?"

"I once dated Jesse and so had Kassidy."

"Murder Motive 101," said Lainey. This meant the police suspected that jealousy may have fueled these two murders. *Too circumstantial*, she thought. There must be something else. It must be the holographic connection that had Lily in this jail.

"What does Murder Motive 101 mean?" Lily asked.

"It means they think jealousy may be your motive. Did you ever love Randy or Jesse?"

"I liked them both, for a time, but I never loved them."

Lainey had to dig deeper. "Can you think of anyone who may have wanted to harm Randy or Jesse?"

Lily rubbed her forehead. "Matt Adler. I told the police this. Matt and Randy had a falling-out over Matt's wife. That's all I know."

"Do you know how I can find him?"

"He doesn't live near here. He's somewhere by the University of Maryland."

"I'll find him," Lainey said. She saw the tiredness in Lily's eyes and decided she would come back another time.

"Great. I'll come back once I figured out why holographics are so important to the police."

"Thank you so much for coming. Kassidy said you used to be an FBI agent. If anyone can get me out of here, you can."

"That was a while ago, but I'll do my best."

Lainey stopped by Kate's desk on her way out, but she was gone for the day. Why did she have to leave early the one day she needed her? The holographic and AI connection had been unexpected information and she wanted to get to the bottom of it. No matter; she'd catch up with her later and determine the significance of this newest information. She had to get home. The long day had caused her arm to be sore from the crutches, and her cast boot was itching her to death. Well, not quite death.

CHAPTER 36

HOLOGRAPHIC CONNECTION

Lainey massaged her temples and rested her head on her kitchen table. She wanted to trust the experts, but they didn't seem to know how she got this autoimmune disease. Thank goodness the six weeks were finally over, that darn boot was removed, and she no longer needed crutches. Dr. Barnes' steroid prescription for her CIDP seemed to be the miracle drug for her great return to walking, but she took each pill with dread. The Internet was full of stories of people on steroids going over the edge. But so far, she hadn't had any creepy side effects and that suited her just fine.

She wasn't happy that Lily was still in jail and her bail denied. Where were the good lawyers in this town?

What was the evidence that was so damning that it kept Lily as a prime suspect? She had no doubt her daughter was looking at other suspects. Kate knew her stuff, and even Lainey understood that, while the circumstantial evidence supported Lily's guilt, the actual crimes fit the profile of a deeply disturbed individual. The only problem was that her FBI training taught her that the most evil and devious of individuals can go through their lives appearing normal to those around them. It was the reason most of them went undetected for so long, some never coming to justice. She so hoped Lily wasn't one of them.

The sound of the doorbell broke Lainey's thoughts and sent her to the front door. It was a nice surprise to see Kate smiling in the doorway.

"Hi Mom."

"Kate, I'm so happy to see you." She gave her daughter a hug and tossed some scattered newspapers off the couch onto an end table nearby.

"Where's Dad?"

"Golfing." Lainey directed Kate to sit down beside her on the couch. Agatha wagged her tail and Kate hugged her.

Lainey went to the kitchen, opened the refrigerator, and grabbed a small bottle of sweet tea. Bailey meowed below her feet. "Not now." Lainey walked back into the living room and handed Kate the bottle.

Kate accepted the drink, then frowned. "Agatha doesn't seem her normal self."

"She's getting older." Lainey didn't want to alarm Kate about Agatha's deteriorating health and now was not the time. "I've been wanting to talk to you."

"I figured you would. Some of the guys at the station told me you went to see Lily last week."

Lainey caught the annoyance in her daughter's voice. "I really just went to give her moral support."

"Hmm, moral support. So kind of you, Mom."

"Yes, but I do have one question for you," Lainey said carefully, not really wanting to ask the question. Kate already suspected that her mother was interfering in her case and Lainey knew she wouldn't like it, but that was too bad.

"Thought so." Kate waited to hear what it was.

"Why did you ask Lily about holographic technology and what does that have to do with these murders?"

Kate sighed before answering. "Please keep this to yourself, Mom." Kate hesitated, seeming unsure if she should reveal the information, but went on. "The killer left clues using holographic technology."

"What role do robots have in all this?" Lainey pressed.

"That's it. Our conversation is done. Now I need you to back off." Kate groaned and put her hands in the air. "Your *help* will get me in trouble, just like last year."

Lainey felt the distress in her daughter's voice. "I'll stay out of your way and stay behind the scenes. If I come up with anything, I'll let you know. Otherwise, you won't hear a peep from me," she conceded.

"Mom, why don't you work on your own mystery?" Kate suggested.

Lainey's eyes widened in surprise. "My mystery?"

"Yeah, I don't get how you got CIDP. I read it's rare. It's so weird." Kate stood up from the couch. "I read it could be from an environmental toxin, among other things. You need to ask your doctor what caused this."

Lainey didn't know what to say to the question she had asked herself so many times. She had scolded herself for opening her big mouth when Dr. Barnes was about to share the various theories about what caused CIDP. By the time she shared her theories, she had other questions and they never returned to the causes. "I don't know why this happened to me."

"I want you better, so maybe you could work on your health mystery before you try to tackle mine. No kidding Mom. You're more important than any case."

When Kate finally left, Lainey was sure of two things.

She would put more effort into getting answers from her doctors, but not before she found out what holographic evidence the police had.

CHAPTER 37

A TIME FOR AGATHA

It was mid-August and the heatwave had lasted longer than expected. Lainey turned the air conditioner down a few notches. She waited patiently on the couch for Max to get home from the veterinarian's office. When he finally came through the door, Agatha was nowhere to be seen.

Max took Lainey's hands and held them gently. "I did what you asked. Dr. Cur was going to put Agatha to sleep but I told him you weren't ready, so he put her on steroids. It may give her a week; maybe more."

"Where is she?"

"I'll get her. She doesn't look good, but the vet said she will feel better once the steroids kick in. She's resting on the front porch."

Max was only gone a minute when he walked back into the living room carrying Agatha in her old, worn-out, pink blanket. Lainey took her gently from Max. The small furry body seemed to melt into her arms. Tears slid down her cheeks as she looked into Agatha's warm brown eyes, and she pulled her closer to her chest.

Max patted Lainey's back. "I'll handle dinner and check with your mom to see what she wants."

"Max, thanks so much." Lainey repositioned herself and lay across the couch, keeping Agatha close to her heart.

A few hours later, Lainey cleaned up the dishes after attempting to eat the spaghetti with meatballs that Max had served for dinner. Tonight, she just twirled the spaghetti around her fork. When the dishes were done, Lainey sat down on the couch. Max held Agatha and rubbed her under her chin. She knew this was hard on Max too, but he would never be one to talk about his feelings.

"Let's get to bed, Lainey. It's been a long day."

"I'm going to sleep on the couch," Lainey said. She really wanted Agatha to come upstairs and sleep with them, but Max was a 'no dog in the bed' person and she didn't think tonight would be any different. "I want to be here to give her moral support." Lainey hugged Max.

"Sorry I'm staying down here," she apologized, "but I don't want to have any regrets."

"I know." He leaned in and kissed her. "Love you."

"I love you too." Lainey stared down at Agatha and stroked her back. She and Agatha had something in common that she would have never expected. They were both on steroids.

CHAPTER 38

AGATHA'S SECOND WIND

Lainey sat in her green Coleman camp chair enjoying the soft breeze of another August night. It wasn't quite dark yet and the mosquitos had not made their presence known. It was a great night to be outside. Max sat in a blue outdoor lounger chair, beer in hand, and watched Agatha scamper after a yellow tennis ball that he had just thrown. Bailey was curled up in a black and white ball, snoozing happily on a small, wicker table.

"I can't believe how well Agatha is doing. It's only been a week and it's like she's her old self," Lainey said.

"It's not going to last. Steroids are only a temporary fix. I'd hate to see you get your hopes up," Max replied.

"I'm hoping for a miracle," Lainey said, stubbornly. She

zipped up her windbreaker as the soft breeze had turned chilly. "I did want to talk to you about something that happened today." She waited for Max's attention. "I was buying supplies for school . . ."

Max interrupted, "Whoa! Spending money on those kids again and then never turning in your receipts."

"It's not about my spending, so you just wasted that tirade."

"Yeah, but don't make light of your spending issues."

"Anyway, today was Teacher Appreciation Day at Office Depot. When I tried to sign in to get the twenty percent discount, a strange thing happened: I'd forgotten how to use the pen. I kept flipping it around in my hand, wondering why it didn't work. Finally, a teacher behind me grabbed the pen from me and pushed the top of the pen in. I was so embarrassed."

"You were probably just distracted."

"You're making light of this. It was scary," Lainey insisted.

"I'll make you a frozen daiquiri. That should make you feel better," Max said.

"Thank you, but I'm fine. The whole experience was just unsettling." A thought came to her that maybe Max was offering a drink because he really wanted one. "Would you like another Bud Light?"

"I can get my own."

"I'll do it. I need to check Mom's blood sugar anyway," Lainey said as she opened up the back door. When she passed by the wall mirror in the hallway, she grimaced at the puffiness in her face. It hit her like a bat to a home run ball that this puffiness was a side effect of the steroids. Steroids. School was starting in a few weeks, and she would still be on steroids. Her inner voice told her to put on her big-girl pants. The image in the mirror was disheartening, but there was one good side effect of a puffy face: her wrinkles were less noticeable. In a few months, she would be back to her normal self. *Just one day at a time.*

CHAPTER 39

THE COOKOUT

The pleasant sundown glow spread over the small cul-de-sac gathering hosted by Lainey and Max to celebrate the end of summer. The cheerful voices came from the remaining neighbors who shared their wonderful, and sometimes disastrous, summer vacations. Lainey and Max's annual end-of-summer cookout was a smash hit this year with a record number of people attending. The lingering smells of barbecued beef and Chesapeake Bay crabs highlighted the delicious foods enjoyed by all. Max sat in the green Coleman lawn chair debating local politics with Rachel's husband, Jake. At this point having enjoyed a few beers, their discussion was boisterous but remained friendly. Lainey and Rachel were busy chattering and cleaning up with the last few neighbors. But truth be told, Lainey had done more gabbing than helping as her body had taken a sluggish turn.

One dim streetlight illuminated the gentle quietness of her neighborhood as Lainey sat in silence. Her eyes focused on the scattered stars sprinkled between clouds in the night sky. She stretched out on her lawn chair and embraced the night's beauty. Max had gone in to watch Washington play the Baltimore Ravens, so here she sat by herself reveling in the success of her cookout when she had the sudden feeling of being watched.

The wind blew against her skin, giving a brief chill. She felt goosebumps forming on her arms, so she put on the blue sweatshirt that she had draped over her chair. She looked across her cul-de-sac to see a full-grown red fox partially hidden from sight by a neighbor's bush, his eyes glowing in the darkness. There was no way she planned to stay seated in this chair. The comfort she had felt was now gone and replaced with a paralyzing fear, her mind on overdrive with a killer fox nearby. The intense desire to escape from this perceived imminent danger was more powerful than her common sense. Common sense told her it was just a fox; go inside. But her fear kept her glued to her seat. Only it wasn't just her fear: she couldn't get up.

Her weak arms struggled to lift her weight while her legs seemed leaden. Why weren't the steroids working? Her mind raced. She felt trapped. Had the fox moved? She could sense his red piercing eyes focused on her. Her mind was in overload now. She sensed a new danger, an unknown danger; new eyes, unseen. She trembled. Sweat dripped down her chest and off her forehead. Her sweatshirt felt tight. She wanted to rip it off. She felt claustrophobic. She looked behind her at the front door of her house. She needed Max. She could hear the television booming, accompanied by an animated Max hollering his disagreement with the coach's calls. Her frustration and desperation mounted. She had to get out of this chair and do something. She would crawl her way back into the house. Using her body, she dumped herself and the chair over, just missing a prickly rosebush. *Déjà vu*. Slowly she dragged herself across the lawn. She heard rustling in the leaves behind her and she let out an alarming scream.

A deep voice penetrated through her fears. "Are you alright?"

Lainey lifted her head to see her neighbor, Rob, hovering over her. His presence should have calmed her, but for some strange reason, it didn't. "I saw a fox over there by the bushes."

Rob looked over at the bushes. "There's no fox now. Can I help you get up?"

She remembered how he was there after her last fall. The fox was forgotten now. She was just embarrassed and wasn't sure she could get up. "If you could get my husband, he can help me up."

Rob went immediately to the house and returned shortly with Max.

Lainey saw the concern in Max's face as he and Rob lifted her up. Knowing that he didn't like anything that messed with football, she apologized, "I'm sorry this happened in the middle of your game."

Max said, "I paused it. What in the world happened here?"

Rob answered, "I heard your wife scream and found her lying on the ground."

"I don't think the steroids are working. I tried to get out of my chair, and I could barely move, but I feel better now."

Max thanked Rob and he left to return to his house.

Lainey tried to relax while Max finished watching the game. It unnerved her that she had panicked over a fox. That wasn't like her. It scared her even more that she had the unsettling feeling that she had been watched. She wondered if there was really someone watching her or if that was paranoia from taking high doses of steroids?

She had told Max that the steroids weren't working, but she knew it was her fault. She had never liked taking medications because of their side effects, and the steroids were no different. She didn't like having a moon face and she didn't like the mental changes. She was a schoolteacher. There was no way she'd put her students at risk. She had heard of people on high amounts of steroids harming people. If she ever hurt her school children, well she couldn't bear to think about that. Who knew what she would do under the influence of this odious drug?

When she had started walking better, she decided to take her steroids every other day, instead of every day, hoping it would decrease the swelling in her face and diminish the unwelcome changes in her mental state. She realized now that it was a stupid decision. It was probably why she struggled to get out of that chair and why she was so scared that the fox would attack her. She would never let Max know she had played around with her meds.

Lainey's thoughts were interrupted by a loud cheer

from Max as his team beat the Ravens by two points. He was ecstatic and gave her a big embrace. She couldn't help but give him a huge hug back. It was a nice reprieve from her unsettling thoughts about steroids.

"Are we ready to try and get up from that chair?" Max asked, placing his hands near her elbows as if ready to pull her up. "You were up and about at the cookout. Let's give this a try."

Lainey wasn't ready, but she also knew she couldn't sit on the couch all night. She hoped the fact that she took her steroid medication about a half-hour ago would boost her chances of getting up. She stared at her legs and then back to Max. His eyes were hopeful and pleading. She stared back at her legs, then pushed down on her arms to determine their strength. She felt some strength and felt hopeful. "I think I'm ready now." She felt nauseous but determined. "I have to do it all in one motion or I can't do it at all," she said. Taking a deep breath, she continued, "and I have to do it fast."

Max raised his eyebrows, but simply said, "Okay." He stepped back to give her room to stand.

Lainey hesitated before lurching herself out of the chair and into Max's arms. She felt relief that she was now standing, even if being supported by her husband. She felt him back away and she slowly took a few steps. She felt some weakness but was able to walk on her own. It felt good to start feeling a bit normal again. She sat on the arm of the couch to maintain some height for when she wanted to get up later. Bailey purred softly, curling around her legs before he jumped into her lap.

"Well, I'm glad you're walking again. You scared me," Max said.

Lainey moaned. "What about me? I thought I'd get eaten by a fox."

"Yeah, like you ever really believed that."

"Crazy as it seems, I did. Luckily, Rob was there."

"Luckily, Rob's always there when you fall," Max commented.

"I'm very grateful for his help."

Max shrugged. "There's something bothering me about him."

"He's fine. He's just being neighborly," she said, smiling. "Besides, he's actually kind of hunky."

"I call that overweight bulge," Max countered.

"Wow. You're awfully hard on him. You almost sound jealous," Lainey teased.

Max rubbed the back of his neck. "I'm not jealous."

Lainey felt like saying more but fatigue was beginning to settle in. She wanted to get to bed before her legs tired again. "Alright then, let's just go to bed."

Without a word, Max assisted Lainey upstairs to their bedroom. He helped her out of her sweatshirt and pants, and into her favorite nightgown with the pink clouds. It felt so good when he helped her get under the blue comforter onto the luxurious soft mattress. Their cookout had been a success and, although the fox incident had been scary, she survived it all. She closed her eyes, but her thoughts crept to Max's comments about Rob. *He was always there.*

CHAPTER 40

READY FOR SCHOOL

There were no other cars in the school parking lot except for the custodian's black Ford truck. A late afternoon breeze spread across Lainey's body, momentarily cooling her from the humid ninety-degree day. She stood at the front entrance of Lorianne Falls Elementary and rang the school's doorbell.

It wasn't a great day to come to school, especially with the air conditioner turned off for the summer, but she really wanted to just sit at her desk and plan how she would decorate her classroom for the new school year. She knew that Cal, the school's custodian, wouldn't be surprised to see her. She did this every year, showing up weeks before teachers were expected to return.

Cal opened the door and grinned. "You have nowhere else to be?"

Lainey laughed. "I'm just excited for school to start."

"Yep. Every year. Right, Mrs. Pinewood?" He didn't wait for an answer before continuing, "Sorry your room hasn't been cleaned yet. It's slated for next week." He pushed his back against the door to help her walk past him.

"That's okay. How long do I have?"

"About two hours."

The hallway leading to her classroom was dark, as it was in a part of the school with few windows. Her room was part of a pod and had a small window near the chalkboard. A musty odor invaded the air as she opened the door to her classroom. The children's desks were piled up in a corner, the chairs stacked nearby. She felt a small leap in her chest as she saw her desk and cushioned chair. She couldn't wait to sit down and begin imagining all the ways she could surprise her students with a wonderful room; a room that would excite her students on their first day of school.

She grabbed a notebook out of her purse to jot down her thoughts. She felt around for a pen or pencil, but there was none, except for an eyebrow pencil, which she threw back in. *Maybe in my desk*, she thought. The desk drawer stuck at first, but she was finally able to open it halfway. She moved her hand around until her hand felt fur. A loud scream erupted from her lips. A mouse!

Cal rushed in, concern on his face. "What happened?'

Lainey was speechless. She pointed over to her desk as she ran to wash her hands in the classroom sink.

Cal walked over to her desk and spied the culprit. "My, oh my." He retrieved a pair of work gloves from his pants pocket, put them on, then picked up the gray mouse by its tail and quickly dropped it in a nearby trash can. "I'll get this out of here. From the looks of him, he's been dead about a day."

Lainey's eyes grew wide. "How do you know that?"

"Around here, they call me the mouse whisperer."

She laughed. Of course mice didn't talk to him, but Cal's joke calmed her from the shock of feeling that awful fur. "So, if I had decided to come here yesterday, I could've saved that little mouse's life?"

Cal laughed. "I don't know if it has actually been a day, but I sure see a lot of those critters in my job. Dead and alive."

Lainey shuddered. "Gross."

"Don't worry Mrs. Pinewood." He picked up the trash can and placed it outside the room. "The exterminators will be here next week."

"That's good news." She looked up at him after having sat back down in her chair. "Thank you so much for helping me."

"Part of the job." Without further word, he grabbed the trash can and was gone.

Three hours later, Lainey had her designs ready for the new year. She was excited about the bulletin boards she would create. Her plan was to have all 3D bulletin boards with positive messages for learning and teamwork. She couldn't wait to order supplies for her hands-on math and science stations.

She had been so engrossed in her planning that she didn't notice the looming storm outside her window. She hated to admit it, but she was scared to death of lightning and thunder. Her room was no longer lit by the outside sun, but now a dark glow had settled within the classroom. She was surprised that Cal hadn't been by to ask her to leave. The school felt eerily silent. She didn't know why, but her senses went on high alert. Something felt wrong. *Time to go*, thought Lainey. She lifted her purse off the desk. A rumble of thunder sent chills up her back. Rain began pounding against the classroom window as if wanting to get in from the storm. Menacing lightning strikes lit the sky, booming thunder gave it a voice, and swirling wind rocked the trees. Where was Cal? She looked out into the hallway. No Cal. She had to get to her car. Her heartbeat quickened. She eyed the distance from the lobby door to her car. She wished she could run but she didn't trust her legs. If she went between the lightning strikes, she might make it. Boom. Boom. Now was her chance. She took two steps before her world went dark.

CHAPTER 41

CONTACT

Lainey could hear Rachel's voice, then Cal's. They were calling her name, but her eyelids felt heavy. Pain pounded against her forehead. What in the world had happened to her? She forced her eyes open to see Rachel's concerned stare and Cal hovered behind her with the same troubled expression.

"I was so worried about you!" Rachel exclaimed.

Lainey felt bewildered. "What do you mean?"

"I found you lying on Martin's couch and couldn't wake you. We were just about to call nine-one-one."

Cal came closer to the brown leather couch. "I had to pick up my grandson early from soccer and when I got back, here you were."

Lainey groaned. She tried to remember, but all she could recall was her apprehension about the thunder and lightning. She felt her heart drop into her stomach. Something bad had happened to her. An unpleasant odor and the pressure of a gloved hand pressed against her mouth came to the surface of her mind, but just as quickly flashed away.

Someone had knocked her out and purposely placed her on Martin's couch. Why? Lainey coughed as her heartbeat seemed to jump into her throat. Had she gotten in the way of a theft? Where was her purse? She gazed over at Rachel. "I think I left my purse in my classroom."

"I found your purse in the hallway near your classroom," Cal said, adding, "It's on Mr. Lopez's desk." He retrieved the purse and handed it to her.

Lainey sighed. "Thank you." She rummaged through her purse but didn't find anything missing. Whoever had done this was not after money.

Rachel raised her eyebrows a bit. "So, what happened?"

"I'm not sure." Lainey frowned. "I think someone drugged me or knocked me out." Lainey wasn't sure Rachel would believe her. She had said some strange things since she started taking the steroids.

Rachel leaned closer. "What are you saying?"

"I'm saying I didn't walk to this couch."

Rachel appeared distressed. "Explain, please!"

"Maybe I got in the way of a robbery. Maybe someone meant to steal the new school computers but then encountered me in the hallway." Lainey didn't know if she believed this or not, she had no plan to alarm Rachel.

"But how did you get on the couch?" Rachel asked.

"Actually, I don't know. Whoever it was came from behind and pressed a cloth against my face. Now that I think of it, there was a smell to the cloth." Lainey paused. "I guess it could have been a man or an athletic girl who moved me after I was knocked out."

"Knocked out? I'm so glad you're okay." Rachel hugged her. "We need to call the police."

Lainey's head hurt and she no longer wanted to talk about what happened. Time to change the subject. "How did you end up at school?"

"I was jogging in the neighborhood when it started to rain. Your car was in the school parking lot, so I thought I'd hitch a ride with you." Rachel sighed. "I'm glad I did."

"Me too."

"Did you get much done?" Rachel asked, pointing to Lainey's left hand and smiling. "I see you were playing around with the stampers."

"Stampers?" she asked in confusion. Her hand began to tremble when she followed Rachel's motion and saw the letters 'MM' stamped on the back of her hand in red ink.

"What does 'MM' mean?" Rachel asked.

This was bizarre. Lainey had no idea what 'MM' meant. "I don't know; I didn't put it there."

Lainey told the police everything she remembered and was relieved when they left. Her head was still woozy. She hadn't left the couch during the police questioning but now she was ready to leave. Rachel came over to help her get up and offered to drive. Lainey always kept her car keys in her front pocket when she wore her jeans. When she slid her hand into her pocket to feel around for the keys, she realized that today's nightmare was not over yet. She felt a small furry body and stringy tail. She steeled herself and lifted out her hand without saying a word. *I should get an academy award for this performance.* She wiped her hand on her pants and checked her other pocket. Relief. She handed the keys to Rachel and they climbed into the car. Who had done this to her? It haunted her that the furry thing in her pocket was probably the dead mouse from her desk. Someone was sending her a message but who and why? It scared her that the evil in the world had made its way to her precious school. *And what in the universe does 'MM' mean?*

CHAPTER 42

BACK TO SCHOOL

The first day of school had been both exciting and exhausting for Lainey, but it had also put that troubling assault at school behind her. There had been no more break-ins at school and the police seemed to have put the incident behind them. She had been surprised that Kate hadn't heard from the police the details of her encounter with that thug. She thought everyone at the station knew Kate was her daughter, but she had to admit she had never seen those cops before that showed up to question her.

Lainey finished the last bite of her chocolate chip ice cream at Seiman's as she and Rachel sat outside on the restaurant's patio. She never missed this ice cream tradition with Rachel on the first day of school every year.

She wanted to be happy and share her tales about the first day, but her mind was elsewhere. She listened politely while Rachel told her about her first day, and hoped she wouldn't notice her disinterest, but Lainey couldn't stop thinking about the changes in her body since she started taking steroids. And then there was Agatha. She didn't seem to be getting better. No wonder Lainey had lost some interest in finding Randy's killer. It was so unlike her, and she knew it wasn't okay. But somehow, it had happened.

"Lainey, you've been giving me lip service. Are you okay?" Rachel asked.

"I'm fine," Lainey answered, watching a wasp close in on her face. She backed away, saying, "Except for this bee." She wished they were inside now and not outside on the terrace in September where the bees thought they were in control.

"Really? You haven't heard a word I said, and you wore ankle braces on both your feet at school and you're still wearing them. I thought you were getting better," Rachel said.

"Lately, both ankles are hurting."

"You're also using your cane now," Rachel added.

"It's just a precaution." The screeching of tires startled Lainey and she turned her head to see a blue car barely missing hitting another vehicle at the intersection. She also noticed that Rachel seemed unaware of the near calamity.

Rachel scratched her head. "It's odd that you were getting better during the summer and now you seem to be worse."

"And look at my face," Lainey said. "It's bigger. It feels like I'm looking through a tunnel."

"That's the steroids," Rachel reasoned. "I guess it can't be helped."

"My class must think I look like a monster. I can only imagine what their parents must be thinking," Lainey said.

"Second-graders just love their teachers. You could look like a kangaroo and it wouldn't matter. I'm sure the parents understand that you're coping with an illness."

"I hope you didn't just offend the kangaroo-lovers of this world. Kangaroos are kind of adorable. My look is not adorable. You're right, though, that my students do act like I look normal."

"I'm glad you still have your sense of humor, but I know something else is bothering you," Rachel said.

"I feel awkward talking about it," Lainey said, then pressed her hand against her face. "Do you think I look a bit furrier?"

"Of course not!" Rachel exclaimed.

"I feel like I am becoming a furry beast."

Rachel leaned forward in her chair. "Why in the world do you think that?"

"Google says that a side effect of steroids is excess body hair."

"Google doesn't say anything. It's a research tool. Plus, you can always wax." Rachel said.

"Wax! We're talking about gorilla hair. I can feel each hair growing as we speak."

"Get a grip," Rachel sighed. "At least you can walk. Count your blessings."

Lainey cringed at her behavior. She must have sounded so foolish and vain, hyperventilating about side effects. "Thanks for the tough love."

"Is anything else going on? I sense a sadness about you," Rachel pressed.

"Agatha is getting worse. She didn't eat her food today or yesterday. I stayed up with her the last few nights."

"I'm sorry. I know how much you love that dog. But you need to get your sleep. It's no wonder you're a mess."

"I can't. Agatha needs me."

"How does Max feel about your staying with the dog every night and not with him?"

"He tolerates it. I think I'm wearing him down." Lainey

noticed that all the outdoor tables were filled now by the patrons of Seiman's, and the excessive chatter was making her body tense. She didn't understand why she was feeling agitated. Was it her medication making her feel this way? "First, my mom moved in with us, and he never complained. Then, he's having to deal with my sudden health issues — the falls, the steroids, and everything else. My late nights with Agatha could be the last straw."

"Lainey, it's hard to keep up with you. Max loves you. I'm sure he understands."

"Sometimes I feel like he's holding it all in, and one day he will explode."

Rachel smacked down on her napkin before it blew away, commenting, "It sure has gotten windy." She gave Lainey a gentle smile. "Try not to worry so much about everything."

"I'll try." Lainey grabbed her napkin before the wind carried it across the outdoor table to the grassy area surrounding the cement patio.

"Why are you being so hard on yourself? Max is fully committed to you, illness and all."

"I guess my commitment issues stem from my sister abandoning me when our Dad died. I thought we were close too, loving sisters, but where is she now?" Lainey took a breath to quell the heaviness in her chest. "It's been over a year without a word, and I can't help but think of her when everything else is weighing on me too."

"She's misguided right now. Everything you did was out of love for your mom and for her. It's her loss." Rachel's words were comforting. She then picked up her small, gum wrapper-designed purse, and pulled out a tiny, orange book. "I want to give you something that I think will help you deal with all those hurtful thoughts you have." She handed it to Lainey. "It's a small Bible of the New Testament. You'll find words to bring you guidance and comfort. It has helped me through hard times."

"Thanks," Lainey said. She opened it and a brisk wind flipped through the thin pages before she closed it and placed it in her large, black leather purse.

"You promise me you won't just let it lay at the bottom of your bottomless purse?"

Lainey nodded.

"Just read it."

"I will."

CHAPTER 43

WRONG DIRECTION

The hot, humid, early September day seemed to add to the tepid mood inside the Lorianne Falls police station. Kate and Will's investigation into the Watkins and Sparks murders had hit a dead end. The only good news was that there had been no third murder. They had spent the last month going over all the evidence, the interviews, and miscellaneous leads that surfaced out of the blue, and it all seemed to support Lily as their killer.

Kate curled her top lip. She closed her folder containing the interviews associated with the two murders, then took a sip from her cold bottle of lemonade that she purchased five minutes ago from one of the station's vending machines. It felt so good going down her throat and refreshed her weary mind. She glanced over at Will. She noticed the sweat pooling above his brow and the tension in his face. *When will maintenance fix the air conditioning in this room?*

Will seemed to be aware of her gaze. He lifted his eyes and peered into hers. "I really wish we could stop thinking about this case. Sergeant Rodriguez wants us to work on our other cases."

"He does have a point. The grand jury has already indicted Lily, so it's the prosecutor's baby now."

Will raised his brows. "You don't really believe that, or you wouldn't keep helping me probe into the possibility of other suspects."

"You're right. There's a part of me that finds the murderer's MO inconsistent with Lily's profile." Kate shifted her gaze to her feet and back again before continuing. "However, I think Rodriguez may be right. It's time we tried to solve these other cases that deserve our attention."

"You sound just like him."

Kate heard the disappointment in Will's voice. Over the last few weeks, they had bonded in their determination to find the killer. For the most part, both questioned if they had the right suspect. Now, to Will, she must sound like she was giving up. "I'm just saying that we need to spend more time on the other cases; not stop working on this one."

"Kate, you're right," Will agreed. "Let's work together to come up with a plan to address our other cases and still find time to determine if we really do have the right 3D Killer."

Time seemed to stop as Kate's mind settled on Will's mention of the word together. Being together with Will had become increasingly the way she liked to spend her day. She looked forward to coming to work, particularly since his attitude had become friendlier, and she hoped their relationship would continue in a positive direction. "We may need to work smarter. Maybe we just need a fresh look at all this evidence; find a new angle."

Will's posture turned rigid. "Are you saying *I* need to work smarter?" he challenged.

Kate realized she'd made a step backwards. Damage control was needed. "I said *we* and I meant *we*. If *we* keep coming up with a dead end, *we* need to think or do something differently. That's all I meant."

Will relaxed and then after a pause, he shrugged. "Any ideas how to do that?"

"Maybe we should broaden our net. We have only focused on the immediate players."

"You're right. I've had the feeling I should've spoken

with more of the teachers at Lorianne Falls Elementary," Will said.

"Exactly. I'll talk to new people at Holotech and see if anything turns up. Are we on the same page now?"

"Yeah, we're on the same page," Will agreed. He hesitated a moment before saying, "I'm done for today. See you tomorrow." He stuffed his files in his briefcase and gave a slight wave as he drifted out the door.

That was abrupt, thought Kate. He may be done for the day, but she was ready to find some new leads. She decided she'd compile a list of the employees at Holotech and visit them before week's end. Had anyone talked to Adler since his first interview? He had motive but he was dropped off the list of suspects. Maybe that decision had been a bit premature. Funny how Adler's name popped into her head. Maybe it was because he only had a connection to the first victim that he was dropped off her list. Perhaps she'd go back to interview him one more time. She felt new inspiration to find the killer. She hoped she would follow her own advice and check on her other cases, but, for today, that wasn't going to happen.

CHAPTER 44

THE FILM DIRECTOR

Lainey stood outside a small brick ranch house located just outside of College Park near the University of Maryland. It was 8 A.M. The sidewalks were filled with students carrying backpacks; some walked, biked, or hopped into cars as they headed to the campus. She felt a little weird wearing her ankle braces after her talk with Rachel, but she didn't really understand; and besides, no one could see them under her pants.

She had chosen the early morning time to catch Matt Adler at home. Martin granted her personal leave from school for a half-day. It allowed her to combine her investigation with getting her teeth cleaned. Now she didn't have to feel guilty about skipping out on her students. She was sure no one would have a problem with her taking off to go to the dentist.

A cool September breeze brushed the back of her neck as she rang the doorbell. Low voices spread through the closed door before she heard footsteps landing on wood floors. A young blonde woman opened the door. She wore a purple robe, which barely covered her Pink Panther see-through pajamas. The smell of lavender and jasmine filled the outdoor air. She recognized the fragrance immediately. This woman had double dosed herself with Ambush cologne. Only, it couldn't be. She remembered they no longer made her favorite cologne. If she got the chance, she might just ask this woman the name of her copycat fragrance.

The woman raised an eyebrow as she tugged at her robe, tightening it around her waist. "What do you want?"

Lainey leaned on her cane and answered, "I need to talk to Matt Adler."

"He's asleep. He don't want no visitors."

The woman started to retreat into the house, but Lainey pushed at the door to keep it open. She shocked herself by that move. Her fear that steroids would make her aggressive grew. The woman stopped, apparently shocked too at the brazenness. It gave Lainey time to press her point. "It's important. It's about his friend, Randy Watkins."

"Please go away. He won't be happy with me if you stay," the woman said.

"Well, I won't be back. I'll discuss this with the police instead." Lainey saw the expression change on the woman's face, but she turned around to go back into the house. Obviously, she wasn't worried about the police, but she was worried about upsetting Adler.

Standing in the now fully opened door was a short, black-haired man wearing a skimpy black robe that barely covered his Pink Panther speedo. He looked irritated and his expression had a hint of disgust. "Angie, just go inside," he said. "I'll deal with her."

The woman stammered. "I tried but . . ."

Adler pushed his hairy hand towards her face. "Zip it! Go inside." The woman cowered and disappeared into the house. Adler rubbed the back of his neck. His eyes appeared intense and not in a good way. "Alright, Fatface, who the hell are you?"

Lainey felt her face flush at his words. She had forgotten her puffed face. She felt diminished by his comment and that fueled an anger she didn't realize was lurking under the surface. It wasn't just an anger against Adler, but also against herself. He body-shamed her by referring to her face. But hadn't she done that to herself? Repeatedly? Every time she saw her reflection in a mirror?

The raucous voices of children waiting for a school bus caught her attention. She thought of her student Marcus, last week, feeling embarrassed by his stuttering and shying away from other students. His eyes had lightened when she shared that she stuttered as a child too. He had been comforted by her words. She could still see his face and that's when she realized the most amazing thing. She remembered his adoring face looking at her fat face but not seeing a fat face. He just saw his teacher; the condition of her face didn't matter. Marcus helped her to realize what Rachel had tried to tell her when she didn't want to listen. Her body relaxed and she turned her focus back to Adler. "My name is Lainey Pinewood, Detective Consultant with the Lorianne Falls Police Department," she said, feeling a little guilty about the title she gave herself, but rationalizing that she did consult with Kate, the actual detective. "I have a few questions about your relationship with Randy."

"I told the other detectives everything. You're wasting my time."

Lainey liked hearing the words, *other detectives*. Adler did think she was a detective. She would clear that up later. Right now, she was in interrogation mode. "When was the last time you saw Randy?"

Adler rolled his eyes. "That's it!" he exclaimed, "I'm done. I've answered all these stupid questions before." He turned and placed his hand on the doorknob. In a flash of furry, white, black, and brown stripes, two stubby-legged chipmunks scampered across the doormat to a nearby burrow. Adler stopped. He seemed to let his guard down as he turned to Lainey to share his delight at that playful display. "Did you see that?"

Saved by the chipmunks, Lainey thought. "Wait. I only have one more question. Your answer could cement you as the cops number one suspect or take you off their list. It's up to you." She was rolling with these lies. She'd scold herself later, but right now she was in the zone.

"Lady, you must think I'm an idiot," the man said. "The cops already have someone in lock-up for Randy's murder. What are you trying to pull?"

Lainey shuddered inwardly as another lie was created. "I have inside information that the current suspect is being let out of jail. I think you're the next one in. Apparently, your talk with the detectives didn't go as well as you thought."

Adler frowned. "Okay, I'll bite. I didn't do this, but I don't wanna be framed for it either."

Lainey didn't know if her next statement was true or an all-out lie, but she pressed forward. "The police feel you do have a motive for Randy's killing. Just tell me if there's any reason why you might have wanted Randy dead."

"Randy turned out to be a jerk; messing with my wife and lying to me. I dealt with him, but I didn't need to kill him. He got my message."

Lainey didn't know this detail about Randy and Adler's wife. She knew why he didn't care. The evidence was the woman in the Pink Panther pajamas. She wondered how many others there were. "So, there's no love lost between you and your wife?"

"She knows her place." His face twisted. "I'm done talking."

The coldness in his voice annoyed Lainey. She felt sorry for any woman that crossed his path. The police may not know this piece of information and think Adler's motive was jealous revenge. There's no jealousy here.

He couldn't be ruled out as a suspect yet because she hadn't had a chance to ask him about Holotech. She didn't really think there was a connection, but she wished she had more time to talk to him. "Thanks for your time. That's all."

"I wanna know something before you go."

"What's that?" Lainey asked.

He smirked. "What's with your face?"

He had answered her questions, so she stared into his eyes. "I'm on steroids for an illness. It's only a temporary condition." She wanted to say his condition was anything but temporary. He was an abusive jerk and that would never change.

Adler shook his head as he looked down at her ring. "I don't know how your husband goes to bed with that face."

It should have stung, but his comment rolled off Lainey. Her relationship with Max in the bedroom was just fine. Adler was a jerk. She pitied him for judging people for their physical appearances. She thought again of Marcus and knew she would never again judge herself harshly because of how she looked. She watched Adler turn his back on her as he went back into his house. She felt a few drops of rain on her face as she reached to check her cell phone. She had exactly twenty minutes to get to the dentist. Lainey used her cane to quicken her pace. As she walked down the sidewalk to her car, she heard a familiar voice.

Not far from her stood her daughter, gaping as she asked, *"Mom?"*

Lainey's mouth dropped open. She had to think quick. "Can't talk. Late for a dental appointment." With those few words, she hoisted herself into her car and sped away.

CHAPTER 45

A DOG'S LIFE

Lainey had meant to go home and jot down some notes about her visit with Adler, and then work on her part of the second-grade open house presentation, but those plans were changed when she stepped into the front door of her home. Agatha lay on top of a sleeping Max, but her glazed eyes and lethargic tail wag told Lainey that her precious dog was not doing well.

She reached over and patted her head. "Please get better. You're such a good dog," Lainey pleaded, holding back tears. She picked up Agatha and held her tight.

Max woke from his nap in his overstuffed recliner. "Sorry honey, but I'll probably have to take Agatha tomorrow."

Her tears flooded down her face. "Are you sure?"

Max planted his arms around Lainey. "Yeah. It's not fair to her to keep on like this."

"I know, but I don't want her to go," Lainey said, snuggling closer to Agatha.

Max held on to Lainey's hand. "She's thirteen years old. She had a great life with us. She was always loved."

Lainey whimpered. "She gave us unconditional love, even when we didn't deserve it."

"That's what unconditional love is."

"Yes, and I'm going to miss that when I come home every night." From the look on Max's face, Lainey could tell he felt slighted by her words. She hadn't meant to do that, but little Agatha never judged her, and quite frankly, Max did.

"Well, I'm going to bed," he said. "Good luck tomorrow with your open house. I'll probably be asleep when you head out to school tomorrow."

"Thanks. I love you, but Agatha is my priority tonight. It's my last chance to thank her for all the love she gave me."

"Good night, Lainey." Max kissed her and headed upstairs to their bedroom.

Lainey cuddled with Agatha, but her dog's listless response saddened her. She became thirsty and started to retrieve her water glass off the end table when she noticed her purse next to it. A thought occurred to her, and she opened her purse. She felt around until she found what she was looking for: the small, orange book. She pulled it out and flipped to the front of the book, where she saw a table of contents that looked very much like an index. She found a section called Facing a Crisis, Matthew 6, verse 34.

"Agatha, listen as I read from Matthew six, verse thirty-four. 'Therefore, do not worry about tomorrow, for tomorrow will worry about its own things.' See, we're not going to worry about tomorrow. You and I have tonight," Lainey said, then patted Agatha and rubbed her little tummy. The verse was comforting but she would not go to sleep anytime soon. If she went to sleep, it would be like time lost with Agatha. The longer she could stay awake, the more time she would have with her. Lainey felt her eyes tiring but she wouldn't give in. Not tonight.

On the upstairs steps, Max sat with his head buried in his lap. Lainey wasn't the only one whose heart was broken by Agatha's illness. He dreaded the trip to the vet tomorrow. He had done this job one time too many, but prolonging Agatha's life wasn't good for her, and it wasn't good for Lainey either.

Lainey had been acting strangely. He wasn't sure why and he didn't like it. He had dealt with her illness the best he could, but her behavior was worrisome. What had happened to the woman who just five months ago was normal? He wanted her back.

CHAPTER 46

THE OPEN HOUSE

Lainey leaned against the wall of the crowded auditorium and observed the flow of parents welcoming one another before taking a seat in one of the few metal chairs left. Bright fluorescent ceiling lights lit every corner of the room. At the back of the room, she noticed three volunteers serving punch and distributing donated cupcakes: Carla, one of her second-grade substitutes, Mel, and Jerome, a second-grade parent. Wall murals displayed the phrases *Welcome Back* and *Our Students Are Our Future*, the spaces filled with their big, bold letters. Most of the other teachers had already taken their seats at the front of the room.

Her face dripped with sweat. The room wasn't that

warm; certainly not warm enough to cause all this sweating. Her legs felt weak. She wanted to sit down but was afraid she wouldn't be able to get up. Why had she decided to stop taking her steroids again? She leaned closer to the wall as she saw Carla approach her with a paper cup of punch and a paper towel.

"Mrs. Pinewood, you look like you could use these. Are you alright?" Carla asked.

Lainey wiped the sweat from her face and sipped the punch. "Thanks. Yes, I'm fine."

"Why don't you sit down? I think it will start any minute."

"I like standing. I'll wait until Mr. Lopez calls my name." Lainey glanced around the auditorium, seeing all the metal chairs filled with parents chatting while loose children went running down the hallway. She couldn't wait for this evening to be over.

"Mrs. Honeycutt has been trying to get your attention to sit down next to her," Carla said.

"Would you please tell her I can't sit with her?" Lainey asked.

"Okay," Carla said, then left to whisper Lainey's words to Rachel before she went back to serving punch.

Lainey felt stupid standing there, particularly with her sweating issue, but she saw no other option.

Rachel approached her a short time later. "Carla said you wanted to stay here," she said. "Come with me and I'll help you get up when it's time. I noticed you had difficulty getting out of the car earlier."

Lainey steadied herself before she left the comfort of the wall with Rachel. She felt like all eyes were on her as she plopped herself down in a front row chair. *Let's get this over soon, please.*

Mr. Lopez stood up and headed to the podium. He had a lanky sway to his walk and a big smile on his face. Lainey estimated that she had about two minutes before she would have to make the long, four-foot walk to the stage. Normally, it was a breeze, but now, it felt like four miles. Mr. Lopez called the second-grade teachers to the stage.

Lainey made her way with the other second-grade teachers. She felt Rachel by her side as they both took the steps to the stage. She hadn't intended to look into the auditorium, but her eyes caught Sara's staring back at hers.

Mr. Lopez's voice began to boom throughout the auditorium. "Our second-grade teachers are the best in Lorianne Falls, and I'm pleased to introduce them to you tonight. First, we have the team leader, the fabulous Mrs. Donaldson; second, our awesome Mrs. Kernel; third, our wonderful Mrs. Honeycutt; and finally, our talented Mrs. Pinewood. Let's give them a hand."

Mr. Lopez dismissed the teachers to their classes so they could get ready for the parents to visit their rooms, and he informed the parents they would discuss the results of the last year's state test before they would meet with their child's teacher.

Lainey had made her way back to her room without incident and was relieved that Carla offered her a chair. It was evident that Rachel had put the word out that she was not quite herself. *Or is it the sweat dampening my hair that gave that impression?* Either way, she was relieved when Mrs. Donaldson said she'd do the presentation.

CHAPTER 47

THE LAST WORD

Lainey took a deep breath as Rachel pulled out of the school parking lot. Normally, she would have spoken at the presentation about the Second Grade Star-Gazing Show and the Science Fair, but Danielle did an awesome job generating enthusiasm for the highlighted projects of the year. All in all, the open house had been a success, and even her students' parents stopped by to say hi. It reminded her that parents care how you treat and teach their students, and not how you look.

"Are you feeling better?" Rachel asked. She put on her left turn signal.

"Better, yes. It was thoughtful of Carla to get me that chair to sit on during our presentation." She leaned back against the car seat. "She's a great sub too. My class loved her last year; even Bobby."

"If you can please Bobby, you're something special," Rachel laughed. She made a left onto McBluff Drive. "I can't help but worry about you, though. I've never seen you sweat that much."

Lainey didn't want to admit that, maybe, it was because she had stopped taking her steroids again.

"Are you still having trouble sleeping? I use something that helps me sleep. Maybe you need a sleeping aid too," Rachel said.

"Thanks, but no thanks," Lainey said. "I don't even like taking the steroids."

Rachel made a left, drove into Lainey's cul-de-sac, and stopped her Honda in front of Lainey's house. Lainey sat for a moment before getting out. "Thanks for driving tonight," she said. "I really appreciate it."

"You're welcome," Rachel replied. "I was surprised you asked me to drive. Usually, you like to drive."

"I felt distracted driving earlier today," Lainey said, not wanting to mention she just missed hitting a biker. "I was afraid I might get into an accident." She hesitated before continuing, "I guess my doctor would tell me if it wasn't okay for me to drive." Lainey grabbed her purse from below her seat and then zipped her coat.

"I'm sure he would tell you," Rachel agreed. "See you tomorrow, Lainey."

"See you tomorrow. Thanks again for driving." Lainey stepped from the car and was about to close the door when she glanced up at her front porch. Her heart ached as she mentioned one more thing to her friend. "Agatha died today."

CHAPTER 48

THE HAND

The hand rested on the wide metal desk before a twitch manifested in the fingers. The hand grabbed a nearby red lead pencil. The mind thought, so the hand wrote:

> *Mischief Maker*
> *Mischief Maker*
> *Dosed the wife*
>
> *Mischief Maker*
> *Mischief Maker*
> *Caused great strife*
>
> *Mischief Maker*
> *Mischief Maker*
> *Twist the knife*

Mischief Maker
Mischief Maker
Take the life

The hand stopped.

CHAPTER 49

A SENSE OF DOOM

Tossing and turning did not make morning come any sooner. The open house had gone well, thanks to the other teachers on her team, but Lainey couldn't stop thinking about her own strange behavior. Her body had betrayed her and now her behavior scared her. Her students needed a focused teacher right now, and that wasn't her. She had to make a change. First, she'd have to stay on her steroids without stopping so she'd get back the strength in her muscles. Her behavior was another matter.

As soon as it was 6:30 A.M., Lainey made a call. She informed Martin Lopez that she was taking sick leave immediately. He could use her emergency plans for now until she could prepare plans for the rest of her undetermined leave duration. Martin, being the kind and understanding principal that he was, told her not to worry about anything and that he would handle it. She felt very blessed to be a teacher at Lorianne Falls Elementary School. She yearned to be with her students, but she was in no state to be the kind of teacher they needed. She hoped she'd be better in a week.

She sat down on her couch to try to get some sleep. An hour later, she gave up. As an unexplained agitation crept over her body, she thought of one thing that might help: a Big Breakfast and a large diet soda from McDonald's.

Lainey maneuvered through the winding drive-thru, placed her order, retrieved it, and then parked. She was surprised when her Big Breakfast was gone and she didn't even remember eating it. The evidence was the empty platter. All kinds of thoughts flooded into her mind as she sat looking at it. Tears welled up in her eyes as she relived the months following her dad's death and the betrayal that followed. She slumped down as she mourned Agatha's loss. A growing sense of gloom invaded the small interior of her car.

Lainey needed to call Dr. Barnes. Something was

terribly wrong. She pulled out her cell phone and started to make the call, but then she stopped. The McDonald's lawn crew was mowing around the parking lot, right where she was parked. She put her seatbelt on and went around the parking lot to find a spot away from the mowers. It seemed quiet, so she began dialing the number. She stopped pushing the buttons, seeing another mower approaching. Totally frustrated, she pulled out of that parking spot to find yet another. The mowers seemed to be everywhere. She found a different spot but decided to wait it out for a few minutes until the mowers were done. She sipped from her straw and thought about her diet soda for a moment. Maybe I should give up diet soda, she thought. Maybe it's the caffeine that's making me feel hyper.

As soon as the mowing ended, Lainey made her call to Dr. Barnes. In rapid-fire hysteria, she screeched out all her worries for the last five months, starting with her huge face and ending with her anxiety about her strange behavior and crazy thoughts. She felt like crying when the voice mail cut her off. She had just told all of that to an answering machine. Tears flooded her eyes as she put her head, face down, on the steering wheel. She jerked when she heard the ringing sound of her phone. She grabbed it and almost dropped it on the car's floor.

"Hello, Mrs. Pinewood. What's wrong?

"Hi Dr. Barnes, I'm so glad you got my message. My face is getting huge and fuzzy. Is this normal? I'm also feeling very agitated."

"You're on a high dose of steroids and that could be your problem. You need this dose, so I'm going to put you on another medication to help calm you."

"The new medication won't make it worse, will it?" Lainey asked, worried.

"No, it will calm you down and help you feel better. Is your drugstore still the same?"

"Yes." Lainey felt ashamed of herself for not confessing that she had taken herself off steroids and that could be some of the problem but since she had restarted them last night that point was moot. She only hoped she would take the new medication consistently so that she could calm down.

Without thinking, she went through the drive-thru and ordered another diet soda.

CHAPTER 50

PRE-BIRTHDAY JITTERS

An ambulance siren sounded eerily outside the Baltimore Research Hospital. How in the world had Lainey gotten into the predicament that she would find herself, the day before her birthday, in a hospital? She guessed she should blame Rachel for telling her to calm down. *Just get to your birthday and things will seem better*, she had said. With those words, Lainey's birthday became the most important date on her calendar: September fifteenth. She saw and heard the date everywhere. It seemed that every time she turned on her television, she saw her birth date. She watched the news and it was interrupted with a voice stating the time and weather. Of course, the time was 9:15. The closer it got to her birthday, the more desperate she became. She didn't know why she interpreted Rachel's words as she did, but she was convinced that something bad was going to happen on her birthday.

This morning, she frantically called her neurologist, Dr. Barnes. She had called her a lot this week, catching her when she was in a conference, in an airplane, and dining in a restaurant, so this call wouldn't be a surprise. In no particular order, Lainey told her everything that was going on. She thought Dr. Barnes was just going to tell her to rest, like she had before, but she asked her a question instead. Dr. Barnes asked her if she was having negative thoughts from her childhood. She wasn't, but she said yes. She needed the doctor to take her more seriously. She was tipping over the edge. Dr. Barnes gave her the response she wanted: she suggested that she go to the emergency room. But getting to the emergency room would not be an easy task.

First, she needed to sell Max on the idea that she warranted a trip to the emergency room. Quite frankly, she didn't think he would believe that she really needed to go, so she knew she had to be as convincing as possible. That proved a bit difficult immediately, since he was all comfy on the couch, a tray of cheese and nacho chips sitting in his lap while he watched a Washington football game on television. If she was bleeding profusely, he'd have no problem. He would just call an ambulance to pick her up, then he would check on her after the game. She had no doubt that he loved her, but he was a bit irrational when it came to football. In his mind, no one would miss a football game. Also, she had known that he would use the excuse that he needed to stay home with her mom, but there was a problem with that logic: she wasn't even sure she wanted him alone with her mom. Recently, the thought kept taking root in her mind that Max wanted to harm her mother. She felt foolish for thinking it, but in her current state of mind, this nagging feeling had her thinking that this situation had arisen and become so bad that she was on the path to sending her own husband on his way to jail. She had to push those thoughts aside for the time being, though, to focus on getting to the ER.

Another issue plaguing Lainey, in terms of convincing Max, was that she felt her credibility with him had taken a hit recently. She reasoned that it's hard to take someone seriously when they have a marshmallow head, but Max had never made any negative comments about her plump face; that was all on her. The real problem was that she hadn't been herself for months, and it was her erratic behavior and the sharing of some of her crazy thoughts that she thought affected her credibility with her husband. She chided herself for not keeping those thoughts to herself and for not monitoring her behavior better. She didn't and couldn't do those things, so now, her credibility with Max was suspect. With that in mind, she decided that taking care of the "mom excuse" was her best bet until she figured out how to get Max on board with the ER trip. She had to think of something to take care of that excuse before he could make it.

Lainey made another phone call after speaking with Dr. Barnes. This time, it was to Max's best friend, Josh. She told him she was calling in all the chips. She was holding him accountable for all the times her husband was late coming home. Now, he owed her big time. She asked him to come right over and stay with her mom. Normally, she would never have called Josh and made this demand, but she was now bold and desperate. Time had been running out. Next, she needed to plead with Max before half-time was over.

In the end, she was only able to get Max to take her to the hospital because his best friend had been on their doorstep. Doris hadn't been happy to be left with Josh, but Lainey didn't care. She had known that Max didn't really believe she needed to go, but she wanted him to be with her because, in truth, Lainey felt like she was on her way to the gas chamber.

So here she sat, the day before her birthday, in the cold,

overcrowded emergency room. Faces seemed to stare across at her like she was a specimen in a jar. She stared back at all the people in the room. An old man in a wheelchair moaned as a woman rubbed his back. A young teenager, wearing a dirty black softball uniform, held a blue ice pack to her forehead. Slumped in a chair, a blonde-haired, middle-aged woman pressed a blood-stained washcloth over her wrist. The one thing they all had in common was that they seemed to have forgotten their maladies to watch her. She was sure they were there to observe her every move and report back to the doctors who wanted to put her away. Although, she didn't really know why she thought they would put her away. Maybe it was the nagging feeling that she was going crazy. She felt heat waves and then chills flowing through her body. One wrong move and the white coats would descend upon her like cats chasing down a mouse.

Lainey tried to calm herself, but she couldn't quell the fear that she was being watched; that everyone in the crowded waiting room thought there was something wrong with her and they didn't like it. She closed her eyes to shut out their faces, but the restlessness in her mind forced them wide open. In the back of the waiting room, someone caught her attention. *Why is* she *here?* Lainey thought. She rubbed her eyes, but the image remained.

There the old woman that had pelted her at the Main Street Festival sat, knee over knee, in the same dress and the same yellow sweater that she'd worn that day. Something about her seemed sinister, but then everyone here seemed sinister to Lainey. It was certainly an odd coincidence, but despite the odd feeling she got about her, she hoped the old woman wasn't seriously ill. They were both just having a bad day.

Lainey watched Max as he sat next to her, reading the sports page, unaware that, at any moment, she could cause him to be dragged from his chair and plummeted into the world of prison inmates. It would only take a few words from Lainey and all hell would break loose. She knew she would tell the doctors about her husband's plan to murder her mom. She wanted to tell a doctor first, before the police, because she wanted to believe, with all her heart, that somehow she was wrong about Max's plans. If her mind had fabricated those thoughts, then she was, most certainly, going crazy. She heard herself repeating the same numbers in her head over and over again: 911, 911 . . . She felt like her life was spinning out of control, and all she wanted was for someone, anyone, to come and help her out of her misery.

She decided to call Kate. Her daughter would know what to do if Max got arrested. Kate would be shocked by the news, especially since Lainey had never breathed a word about Max's plan. She whispered to Max that she was going to the bathroom. When she found an empty stall, she stood and called Kate. The call went to voicemail, so she left a message, then looked down at the white toilet. *Might as well take care of business.*

Five minutes later, she was back sitting with Max. He was still reading the sports page and crunching on potato chips that he had gotten out of a vending machine. The girl in the black softball uniform had disappeared from her seat, now replaced with a gray-haired man trying to control a nosebleed. Being no easy task, Lainey was relieved that he appeared to have no interest in staring at her. However, somehow, he touched her heart and left Lainey no choice but to act on his behalf. She rushed up to the registration desk and approached the medical assistant, then shared her concern that the elderly man needed immediate assistance for his nosebleed. The assistant looked across at the elderly man and nodded in agreement. An orderly was called over and soon administering aid to the elderly gentleman. She felt pleased with herself, mainly because it was something her 'normal' self would do. It felt great, if only for the moment, to feel a little less crazy.

A long hour passed before Kate walked into the emergency room and sat in an empty seat next to her parents.

Lainey could see the stress and puzzlement in Kate's eyes. She told Max that she and Kate were going to the cafeteria, then asked him if he wanted anything. He said no, so she grabbed Kate and hurried her along to the cafeteria. She didn't want to be anywhere near Max when she talked to her daughter.

Lainey waited at a table while Kate went through the cafeteria line. Kate returned with a tray of grilled cheese sandwiches and drinks, which she placed in the middle of the table as she pulled out a chair and sat down. Kate handed Lainey one of the sandwiches and a diet soda before serving herself. Lainey watched Kate take a few bites and a sip of green tea, noticing the worry in her daughter's eyes, but there was going to be no easy way to coat this. Either Lainey was going crazy, or Kate's dad was about to murder her grandmother.

"Mom, what is it? Why are you here?" Kate finally asked.

Lainey's blue eyes darted around the cafeteria before answering. It seemed like everyone was trying to listen in. Their stares seemed to be frozen in time, their food only props to hide their true reason for being in the cafeteria. They were there to spy on her, just like those in the waiting room. She pulled herself over the table a bit to move in closer to Kate.

"Mom, you're scaring me. You look white as a ghost. Please answer me, what is wrong?" At first, Lainey said nothing. Her eyes refocused from the people in the cafeteria to her daughter, who was now holding both of her hands. She felt the tears pool in the corner of her eyes, a feeling of dread filtering through her mind. Then, as if given an electric shock, she heard herself pouring out her soul to her dear Kate. In an explosion of words — sometimes coherent, sometimes not — Lainey unloaded all her worries and anxieties over the last weeks, her weird thoughts about the people in the emergency room, and, most importantly, her fear that Max would kill her mom. She pressed her palms to her eyes, then looked to see both sympathy and horror in Kate's eyes.

"Mom, this has got to be your medication. There is no way Dad is planning to kill Nana. We need to get you back to the waiting room. I need to talk to Dad."

She felt herself go rigid. There was no way that talking to Max would end well.

Five minutes later, the emergency doctor asked Lainey to remember five words and he would check with her later to see if she remembered them. She spent the next half hour repeating those words over and over in her head. She was convinced that if she couldn't remember them, it would be one more indication that she was going crazy. The doctor completed his exam and told Lainey that she had steroid psychosis. He explained that all her strange thoughts were a result of the steroids. Max did not have plans to kill her mom and Lainey was not going crazy. The doctor told her she should talk to Dr. Barnes about lowering her steroid dose and that the effects of the steroids on her mind were just temporary.

She should have been happy, but the steroid part of her mind thought this was too good to be true. Was this just a conspiracy to make her believe that they thought she was normal? It was their decision to keep her overnight that aroused this concern. The doctor, and even Max, had said she could go home the next day, so she tried to hold on to that bit of encouragement. She had been able to tell the doctor the five words he asked her to remember, too, so that should count for something.

Had all her crazy thoughts really been the result of steroid psychosis? Had she created a crime thriller in her mind? Why had she believed that Max could kill her mom? As she rested her head on the white hospital pillow, Lainey heard the 911 call center greeting in her head. It was going to be a long night.

Max leaned over Lainey and placed a tender kiss upon her forehead. He squeezed her hand gently. A soothing thought slipped into her mind: *Tomorrow is my birthday. Thank God, my birthday is tomorrow. I just need to get through tonight.*

CHAPTER 51

THE BIRTHDAY

It felt surreal to Lainey, sitting in her living room waiting for her family to arrive for her birthday. Her birthday. She thought it would never come. It had been a relief last night when the doctor explained she had steroid psychosis. The only problem was that knowing what was wrong didn't stop her fears. The word "psychosis" scared the hell out of her. She felt consumed by the fear that she would hurt someone. She had heard stories of people on steroids who heard voices and killed people. She wasn't even sure she should be with her family today. Her doctors assured her she was not at the point that she would hurt anyone. But could they guarantee it? They must have been a bit concerned, because she had to sign a paper that she would not teach until she was cleared by a psychiatrist. She was all in for that. Her students came first, their safety paramount. When she was well, she'd be back.

The knock on the door and the friendly call-out signaled that her son, Steve, and his wife, Margo, had arrived with her granddaughters, Chloe and Kailey. Max came in from the family room in time to give Steve and Margo warm hugs. He grabbed the two squirrelly little girls as they squealed in delight to see their PePa. Kailey was the first to notice her grandmother. Lainey saw the slight hesitation in her granddaughter's expression, but it quickly faded as she climbed onto Lainey's lap.

Kailey small fingers circled around her grandmother's face. "MomMom, what happened to your face?"

Lainey held her breath and smiled, then answered, "It's just an illness, it will get better."

"MomMom get better," Kailey said, then hugged her grandmother's face and jumped down to play with Bailey. Sam arrived with his fiancé, Jennifer, the couple full of excitement about their upcoming wedding next year. Within an hour, all her family was present, even Kate. Lainey felt her anxiety lowering. When Rachel and Jake arrived, she realized that everything would be okay. At least for today.

CHAPTER 52

ON SECOND THOUGHT

The Lorianne Falls Steakhouse on Main Street was sparse now. This would not last, but it provided a quiet background as Kate sat musing over the last week. She couldn't get over the craziness of seeing her mom in the emergency room raving that her dad planned to kill her Nana. *So surreal*, she thought. It had been such a relief when the doctor diagnosed her mom with steroid psychosis. He assured them that, once the steroids were slowly stopped, her mom would regain her normal mental state. It did concern her that the doctor was worried about the effects of stopping the steroids too soon. If her immune suppressant drug wasn't ready to take over after the steroids were withdrawn, her mom may continue to have difficulty walking. How strange it all was. The doctor had shared his surprise that her mom had steroid psychosis from the dose she was on. While it was high, that dose usually didn't create this reaction.

Kate thought of her dad's reaction after she'd told him her mom suspected him of wanting to kill Nana. She realized too late that it wasn't the right time to say anything. Understandably, his words conveyed disbelief and concern, but it was the hurt in his eyes that had surprised her. He had always kept his emotions hidden, but not that day. Her dad shared his anger and disappointment at her mom for thinking such a thing and, oddly, he blamed her Nana for creating the crisis when she had nothing to do with it. Thank goodness the doctor had come just in time to calm things down. After hearing about the diagnosis, her dad seemed relieved to finally know why her mom had been acting so strangely. However, her mom would still have to deal with her dad when he confronted her about his "murdering ways."

Kate's mind stepped back into the present. Where was Will? It was her day off, but she had agreed to meet with him for lunch. How important could it be if he was late? *Fifteen* minutes *late*, she thought. She noticed the onion petals appetizer on her table and grabbed a few with her fork, then dipped them into the accompanying sauce.

Delicious. Well, if he takes much longer, there will surely be no onions left to share. Too bad for him. She was about to take another forkful when she saw him standing behind the chair across from her. Except for his tousled hair and bloodshot eyes, she almost thought he looked handsome in his tan khaki pants and blue plaid shirt.

Will sat down, rolling his neck and shoulders. "I'm so sorry I'm late. I didn't sleep much last night and had a hectic morning."

"I can see you were up all night by those bloodshot eyes. What's going on?"

"I spent the night going over all the evidence against Lily Proctor. The evidence seems to support her guilt, but her history says 'model citizen, well-liked in the community.'"

"Come on, Will," Kate said. "You knew she was a model citizen before we arrested her. What made you look at this again?"

At that moment, the waitress showed up and took their orders. Without looking at the menu, they both ordered a pulled pork sandwich and the restaurant's famous potato salad. Kate already had an iced tea, so Will added an ice water with lemon to his order.

In frustration, Will grabbed a handful of onion petals and smashed them into the orange sauce. After he wiped his soiled hands on his cloth napkin, he focused on Kate. "To your question, I looked at this again because of you."

"Because of me?" Kate asked, surprised.

"Yes, I was reading over your interviews with employees of Holotech, particularly the interview with Lily's supervisor that you did a couple days ago," Will said.

"Say no more," Kate cut in. "I think I know what's troubling you."

"Do you?"

"You learned from my interview with Proctor's supervisor that her skills with holographic technology were minimal and that they planned to fire her, but she quit before they had a chance. I thought this shed light away from Lily's guilt."

Will groaned and rolled his eyes. "Man, Kate, I stayed up all night for nothing. Just one word from you after your interview could've saved me all this time." He moved closer, gently pushing the onion plate out of his way. "You couldn't take one minute after your interviews to share what you found out? Communication, Kate."

Kate felt heat in her face and a weird sensation down her nose. "First of all, Will," she started, but Will interrupted.

"Don't flare your nostrils at me."

"I'm not flaring my nose," she contended. She realized

that she *did* flare her nostrils and it irked her that he saw it too.

"Honestly, just share your thoughts without all that nose action," Will said, wiggling his fingers toward her face.

She didn't know if it was his intention, but she felt herself calm down. Their whole conversation had taken a humorous turn, but she was still ready to fire back at him. "As I was saying, first of all, I have a life outside of work." She waited, but he let her continue. "I had the whole weekend off and I took it. I had planned to communicate with you about the interviews before the weekend, but my mom went into the emergency room. Between that and my busy weekend, I had no time. I can't really believe you think I didn't communicate. It was my report on the interviews that you read. I'd call that communication."

A slight red flush appeared on Will's face. "Sorry to hear about your mom. I hope she's okay."

"She'll be fine, but we were worried we would lose her." She knew her mom wasn't going to die, but she didn't want Will to know that her mom had gone psychotic. Inwardly, Kate's reasoning for her phrasing was that if Lainey kept acting so weird, she would no longer be the mom that Kate knew, and that was just as real a loss.

"I'm so sorry for talking to you the way I did. I can

only blame the lack of sleep. You did send in your report, and you deserve a weekend away from work."

"I forgive you." The food arrived and Kate was silent as they ate their meals. Occasionally, she'd glance up at Will, but no one said a word. She realized it wasn't intentional, but that they were both just very hungry.

CHAPTER 53

IMPROMPTU CHASE

The beautiful sunset of red, blue, and purple stretched before the woman as she steered her red Camry down the Baltimore-Washington Parkway before making a right on Route 32 heading west. The woman's face twisted into distortion as anger fueled her mind.

Maniac. No one calls me a maniac. Absurd. With the beautiful aura of sunset fading, a dark, shadowy gloom of clouds surrounded the speeding car. The woman's hand throbbed and blood oozed out as she pressed on the steering wheel. With a swipe, the blood smeared across her pant leg. She didn't notice the young woman cross the dark street pushing a baby carriage at first and swerved just in time to avoid hitting that crazy lady and her child. One less second, and mother and baby would be dead. *Who takes their baby across a dangerous intersection at night? They're the maniacs.* The thoughts followed with disbelief as she barely missed hitting a black car that crossed in front of her.

The only thing out of kilter from the near crash was the body in the back. It was no longer in the back seat but had rolled onto the floor. *Too bad.* The victim in the car was already having a bad day, so one little tumble wouldn't matter. The only thing that made all this worthwhile was the payday. Before night's end, there'd be money in the bank.

The time on the car's dash said it would be almost an hour before arrival at her grandfather's abandoned trailer. Thanks to her dearest mommy and daddy's procrastination, they had never sold the place when her grandfather died.

A moan in the back seat startled her but wasn't totally unexpected. The drug would be wearing off soon. She needed to step up her speed or she'd have to deal with a squirrelly girl.

The more the woman's mind raced about the night's dangerous plan, the more her foot pressed against the accelerator. A lone deer jumped in front of her car. Her heart rate quickened, and her foot smacked on the brake as the deer raced past her. Her foot stayed heavy on the pedal as two more deer crossed quickly before her. She knew the law of three where deer were concerned. She sighed in relief. Ever since she watched her dad shoot a defenseless rabbit, she promised herself she'd never hurt another animal.

More moans sounded from the back floor, but she ignored them. She returned her foot to the accelerator. Time was of the essence: she had been warned that she needed to deliver her package on time and not a minute late. She was five minutes ahead of schedule, which was just enough time to prepare, and all the supplies she needed were in the trunk. She would be glad to be done with her part of the plan. This had been all business to her, and she'd get paid and be out of the country before authorities wised up. But she'd make this the last time she partnered with a psycho and definitely the last time he'd call her a maniac.

She parked her Camry next to the run-down, double-wide trailer. An owl hooted in the night as she stepped out of her car. The closest trailer was about 25 yards away. No problem. She knew old lady Esther: she was likely deaf and, by now, fast asleep. No one would notice her. She dragged the limp bag over to the front door, unlocked it, and pushed hard to get the stuck door open.

She dragged the body bumping up the two steps into the trailer. Now all she had to do was wait.

Why did I give in to Lainey's request to help her investigate these awful murders? Rachel thought. She was a teacher, not a private eye. Now here she sat in her black Honda in the middle of nowhere on this scary dark road in front of this creepy-looking trailer wishing she was home grading papers.

Rachel thought back to earlier when Lainey asked her to follow the red Camry. She hadn't wanted to do it, but she saw the urgency in her friend's eyes and her tone of voice resonated its importance. She'd agreed, and Lainey left to go in the library without telling her who she was seeing. She just told her to wait in the car and if the Camry with the darkened windows moves, follow it. Her only job was to write down the destination address. That done, she would then go back and pick up Lainey. It sounded easier than it turned out to be.

First, she didn't see who got into the red Camry until it was in motion. Her daydreaming halted as she started her own car. Then, there she went in steady pursuit of a driver that had the pedal to the metal. She had never driven that fast. It was all a bit terrifying, particularly when the car stopped suddenly to avoid hitting a woman with a baby stroller. She had almost collided with the Camry while making sure her own black car swerved out of the way.

Keeping up with Camry was another matter. The driver seemed a master at quick right turns and sudden lefts. Rachel was proud of herself for jotting down the license plate number while she had waited for the car to move. There were more red Camrys on the road than she had imagined and, if she hadn't had the tag numbers, she surely would have lost it. It didn't hurt that the major roads became one single road. The only problem with that was it was dark, and she felt very alone. Her heartbeat raced as she considered that fact. What would she have done if the car stopped and someone got out?

Now, Rachel sat staring at the worn-down trailer. She hadn't recognized the person that went into the boxed home; it was too dark. She wasn't even sure if it was a man or woman. She watched as a satchel, apparently heavy, was being dragged up a couple of stairs and shoved into the trailer. Rachel had an uncomfortable feeling about what she saw, but she told herself it was probably heavy laundry or something like that. She only needed to get the address and get herself out of this trailer park. The only problem was that there were no numbers on the front of the trailer. She would have to get out to check the mailbox or slowly drive by it. She felt her body tense. She chose to drive by it. She turned on just her parking lights, which revealed a rusty, black number sixteen on the mailbox. Now she needed to find the street name. The roads between each trailer were gravelly and narrow and in the dark, it was obvious she wouldn't find any street signs. She looked at the time on her cell phone. It had been over an hour since she had left Lainey.

Surely, Lainey must have come out of the library by now, wondering where she was. Rachel tapped Lainey's number on her phone but got no answer. She tried again. Nothing. Rachel's mouth felt dry. She wrote a short text. Lainey almost always answered her texts. Rachel waited. She texted again asking her to please respond as an unknown fear gripped her thoughts. Why wasn't Lainey answering her phone?

The wind howled outside her car. It felt spooky to sit in the car alone. The battery on her iPhone was getting dangerously low and the rustling of tree branches against the car startled her. What if someone was out in the dark and she couldn't call for help? Her fear for herself faltered as her fear for her friend grew. She should have gotten back to her by now. Then a thought occurred to her: she could use her phone's Find a Friend feature to see where Lainey was!

Her heart leapt into her stomach as she saw where Lainey was located. Terror crept so deep into her soul that her heart pounded against her chest. Something was terribly wrong. According to the locator, Lainey was just yards away from her. And then she remembered the heavy satchel being dragged into that old trailer.

CHAPTER 54

CHAIR-BOUND

A sharp pain in the back of her head and a whiff of cigarette smoke aroused Lainey from her unwanted deep sleep. She wearily opened her closed eyes. Alarmed that her world remained dark, she blinked again. She couldn't see! Panic shot through her veins as she realized that the darkness was caused by the presence of a tight blindfold, and something pressing against her upper body felt as if a ten-pound bag of potatoes had fallen on her chest. She tried to move her hands to rip the cloth covering her eyes, but they were unmovable. The more she tugged, the more the tight restraints tore into her skin. Her heartbeat quickened and her foggy mind couldn't quite remember how she'd gotten there.

Lainey remembered walking into the library to investigate who owned the red Camry in the parking lot. She had noticed the car following her last night and she had become suspicious when the same car showed up parked next to hers after she left the grocery store this morning. She had been sure it was the one following her the night before.

Another sharp pain pierced the back of her head. *Oh my god*, she thought. *What had happened to Rachel?* She had left her waiting in the parking lot. Memories came crashing back. That awful blow to the back of her head had felt like someone had put all of Agatha Christie's mysteries into one volume and then slammed it into her head. She had no clue how someone had managed to get her here. But where was 'here?'

How foolish she had been in her openness with the library patrons. No one in the library had been any help in identifying who owned the Camry. Her questions probably put the person who did this to her on high alert. She had been so careless that it was her own fault she was in this predicament.

Who had done this to her? But more importantly, how would she get herself out of this mess? Her instincts told her to calm her nerves. Nothing was impossible. Face the fear. In her early days with the FBI, she had felt danger and dealt with it, so she would do that now. Relief filled her body as she remembered she had taken her steroids earlier in the day. She would need all her strength to deal with whoever had done this. She moved her legs but felt them bound to the chair as well. Smoke from a cigarette tickled her throat. She coughed. Then felt another puff of smoke enter her airways. Someone had purposely blown smoke into her face.

"The lady awakens from la-la land," said a hard, raspy voice with mirth in its tone.

The voice chilled her. "Who are you?" she dared to ask.

"For being former FBI, you're clueless. The blindfold isn't for your beauty sleep." A gun jabbed into Lainey's left side.

Lainey suppressed her pain from the muzzle of the gun. "Why are you doing this?"

"You've gotten on somebody's wrong side." The gun was shoved back into Lainey's left side.

Lainey jerked with the pressure of the gun, but this time the jab had not been too bad. She thought about the voice. It sounded familiar; not every day familiar, but it was someone she had encountered more than once. She was convinced this voice belonged to a woman. If she kept her talking, maybe the name for the voice would come. "What do you want from me?"

"Like I said, I don't want anything from you."

Recognition wasn't coming to her. "Are you going to hurt me?"

"Not unless I'm instructed to. But if I were you, I'd say my prayers."

A cold tremor invaded Lainey's body. Her voice cracked. "Instructions from who?"

"You'll find out soon enough," came the reply.

She hesitated before she repeated her earlier question. "Why are you doing this? What could I have possibly done to you that I deserve being bounded up like this?"

"Money," the woman said, raising her voice. "Now shut up."

Lainey heard the woman move away but she came back within seconds. She recognized the ripping sound inches from her face. Her mouth felt dry. There would be no more talking. She cringed inside as the duct tape pressed against her lips. She scolded herself for going too far with the questions. She couldn't breathe. Her heartbeat pumped against her chest as her nose summoned urgent congestion. Any second, claustrophobia would engulf her. *Face your fear*, she repeated to herself. She knew Rachel would say, "pray," so she did. Her heartbeat slowed and she felt her body relax a notch. She didn't know if it was the chant, or prayer, or the combination of the two, but she grew stronger in her belief that claustrophobia had released its grip. Something else released itself in her mind as well, for the woman's name had settled on the tip of her tongue. She had the beginning letter; she was sure of it. And then it came.

CHAPTER 55

STAY OR RUN

The chilly night air surrounded Rachel's car, sending a quick freeze throughout her body. She pulled her coat closer around her, even though she sensed that the cold feeling had nothing to do with the night air. It was painfully obvious that Lainey was inside that trailer. Every brain molecule in her head said, *Run! Go for help!* But her emotions, her love for her friend, said *Fight*. Lainey could be in danger; most likely was. Waiting in the car was not an option. *Think smart.* She needed a weapon but hoped she wouldn't have to use it. She searched inside the car. Nothing. *Maybe in the trunk.* She looked out the car window nervously, the dark night appearing more ominous than it had a few hours earlier. It didn't matter.

She had to get out of the safety of her car and make her way to the trailer.

She opened the trunk. A small light sent a soft glow over the contents. She sifted through loose papers, folders, a twelve-pack of bottled water, and a bag of newly-bought black and red pens. She lifted the hatch containing the extra tire to find what she needed: the L-shaped lug wrench. After shutting the trunk, she pulled her phone out of her pocket. It looked like it had about half a percent of battery left. Why hadn't she thought to charge her phone while she was driving? Too late now to worry about it. She hoped it had enough juice to make one phone call. She phoned the number. Voicemail. She was able to leave a partial message before her phone finally went dead.

CHAPTER 56

COLD SOUP

An unmistakable whiff of chicken broth filled Lainey with hope. The heaviness in her chest subsided a bit and her desperate thoughts changed from inevitable to hoping there was a way out. She wasn't hungry but thought perhaps the woman would take off the tape to give her something to eat. Obviously, she didn't want her dead yet. Lainey's hope proved true as pain crossed her lips and the duct tape was ripped from her face.

She pressed her lips together to attempt to lessen the pain. Her voice stammered a bit as she said, "The tape . . . I couldn't breathe." She heard the familiar sound of duct tape being pulled off a roll and moved her head back. Her body tensed and she pleaded, "Please don't."

"Tape's going back on." With that, the woman placed the tape back on Lainey's mouth but, this time, there was a small hole in the middle.

Lainey had no time to react as a plastic straw was jammed through the small hole, piercing her tongue. She tasted blood in her mouth.

The woman cackled. "Enjoy the soup!"

Lainey sucked on the straw and cold broth filled her mouth. She gagged; she did not like her soup cold. On second thought, she reasoned that she might need this bit of nourishment and resumed sipping slowly.

Lainey eventually heard the bubbly sound that told her she had finished the soup. She pushed the straw out hoping the small hole would give her more air, but the hole closed in. Now she wished she had kept the straw in her mouth. Panicked, she pushed on the opening in the tape with the tip of her tongue. The opening only grew wet and closed in more, while the tip of her tongue grew sore.

The woman coughed a smoker's hack. Lainey was sure she knew who was holding her captive and couldn't believe it was the same woman. It didn't make any sense. Chills washed through her body as she realized she had left her students alone with this dastardly lady.

She felt a cold breeze cross her head and shoulders. A door creaked and a man's voice grumbled incoherent commands to the woman. One thing for sure: his savage tone meant that Lainey's introduction to him wouldn't be pleasant. Her hopes that she could sweet-talk him into letting her go were crushed.

CHAPTER 57

A SIGN OF COURAGE

The trailer, hidden by trees and bushes, appeared ominous in the dark of the night. Rachel needed a grip on her emotions if she had any chance of saving Lainey. Fear pounded her fluttering heart against her chest as she contemplated her next steps. The thought of walking into a dangerous situation frightened her but staying in the car was not an option. She had to go in. She glanced over at the L-shaped wrench next to her in the passenger's seat. It scared her that she might have to use it, but it frightened her more that it might not be enough. She felt nauseous. The enormous responsibility of life or death lay at her feet. Was she brave enough? Was she willing to give up her life for her best friend if necessary? Tears pooled in her eyes. She wished she had told Jake one last time that she loved him.

Rachel shivered in the ever-increasing coldness and dampness of her car. She fingered the sterling silver cross around her neck and prayed. She prayed the captor would have a change of heart and just let Lainey go. Students and grading papers were in her wheelhouse, not becoming part of a crime scene.

Slowly, a plan crept into her mind. Lainey had always said that surprise was always best when dealing with enemies. She was happy she had listened to Lainey's tales of the FBI. That knowledge would hopefully help her now. First, however, she had to find out what in the world was going on in that trailer. How could she find out without alerting Lainey's captors?

The spraying rain and howling wind sent a chill up Rachel's spine as she stepped outside her car with the wrench held tightly in her hand. She took a deep breath to control her nerves. The crescent moon provided minimal light, so her eyes focused on the light coming through the small window on the left side of the motor home. Her movements were sloth-like as she stepped on damp leaves covering the rocky path. Even with her slow steps, she barely kept herself upright when her shoe hit an old tree stump hidden beneath a pile of fallen leaves.

The window was open just enough for the homey smell of chicken soup to permeate her senses. Not the smell she'd expected; perhaps she was wrong about the danger. She was about to move closer when she froze. What was that sound? It was not of wind or rain. At ground level, not far ahead, she saw the reddish-brown, horizontal hourglass pattern across a long tubular body, and glistening cat eyes shining from a triangular head. Even in the dim light from the window, it was unmistakable: a copperhead. Her body stiffened. Once it sensed her heat, it would come her way. She moved back slowly. To her immense relief, the copperhead moved away as if in pursuit of a closer prey. *Thank you, Lord.* She would have to be quick. Under this window was no safe place to stay.

Rachel stood up just high enough to see through the bottom half of the dirty, glass window and swiped away a spider's web that was covering most of it. Maybe she was gaining some courage. She was usually scared to death of spiders. *Thank you, Lord.* She felt a small burst of confidence. She placed the wrench in her back pocket to free her hands so she could grab hold of the ridge of the window to get a better view.

Her jaw dropped when she saw Lainey blindfolded, her mouth taped, and her hands and feet tied to a chair. Rachel didn't need to see Lainey's eyes to know she was distressed. Lainey was very claustrophobic. She was no doubt practicing her calming mantra: 'Face your fear.'

Rachel gazed through the window again. Where were the captors? She had not seen them when she first peered through the window. As if hearing Rachel's thoughts, voices erupted from the blind corner of the room. It was strange but she thought she recognized the woman's voice. She couldn't stay underneath the window, not with the copperheads in the area. She lowered herself back down and nearly slipped on a protruding wet rock. The rain had turned to a drizzle, but the wind still howled. With careful steps, she went back to her car.

Inside the car, she assessed the situation. She was relieved to see that Lainey was still alive. The fact that she was tied to that chair meant they were keeping her alive for a reason. But for how long? She felt a tightness in her chest and told herself to breathe. Wasn't she too young to have a heart attack? She inhaled. She exhaled. The feeling of tightness subsided, giving her a chance to refocus. How was she going to get Lainey out of there? What weapons did the captors have? What if that trailer was booby-trapped? She calmed herself down. She was overthinking this. And then it hit her like a rock through a window. She knew exactly what she would do.

CHAPTER 58

A CLUE

OMG, thought Lainey as the voice penetrated her ears, igniting a wickless flame inside her brain. She'd been given the clues so early in the game. She remembered the day she stopped by Kate's office at the police station while she was reviewing a video from the Jesse Sparks murder. Kate had relented and allowed her to observe the holographic projection of Jesse Sparks being killed by a murderous robot. How could she and Kate have missed this? The clues to the killer's identity were right in their face. They had interpreted that strange stare in Jesse's eyes as the awareness of his impending death, but realized now that it was recognition that he was being murdered by someone he knew, perhaps even trusted. They had thought Jesse's last word, "I . . ." meant that he was trying to say, "I need help." So stupid. The video was looped to make it sound like the "I" came first, but in fact, it was the last thing the victim was saying. If Jesse Sparks could have lasted one more second, he would have named the killer. That one letter was the clue to the name: I.

She wanted to scream the name as loud as she could, but the tight tape around her mouth muffled her outrage. The smell of whiskey and cigarettes invaded her space.

A deep voice whispered into her ear. "Hello, Mrs. Pinewood."

Lainey's stifled voice came out as a moan. She felt sick to her stomach being so close to evil. She wanted to push the voice away, but her bound hands stopped her.

"I'm going to take the blindfold and tape off. If you scream, I can guarantee you'll regret it."

Her heart leapt into her throat as she felt the painful rip of the duct tape. She felt his rough hands untie the blindfold before he threw it to the floor, and then squinted as her eyes adjusted to the bright lamp light in the small room.

There he stood before her, in a black Nike sweatshirt and gray jeans, a wide smirk on his unshaven face. It was evident that he enjoyed letting the cat out of the bag. He was flaunting his power, but it only empowered hers. She stared straight into the killer's blue eyes. "You won't get away with this!"

His creepy laugh filled the air. "Oh, I'll get away with this. My plan has gone beautifully, thanks to your ignorance. You're more teacher than FBI."

"Well . . . you're more of a jerk."

The slap across her face stunned her.

"Add foolishness to ignorant." He pulled a small flask from his back-jean pocket and took a swig before replacing it.

She knew that she'd been foolish to risk agitating this creep. If she kept the conversation going, she might have time to figure out how to get out of this mess. "Why am I here?"

"Catnip. Pure catnip."

Lainey's eyes narrowed. "What do you mean?"

"You're drawing my prey to me."

She shifted forward. "Stop being so cryptic."

His eyebrows raised in amusement. "So many questions . . . and demands. My dear, it's your husband I'm after."

"Max?"

"Only one you got, right?"

Silence. What in the world did Max have to do with this man? She had prayed Max would find her, but now her greatest hope was that he would stay away. He was heading into this psychotic's mousetrap. There was no way her children would lose both of their parents tonight. She had to do something before Max came through that door. Lainey stammered, her nerves betraying her. "Why?"

"Enough!"

"Max never did anything to you," Lainey pressed.

He wrapped his arms around his head. His face twisted. "He took everything from me." He lowered his head before staring straight into her eyes. "That's why I started toying with you."

"Toying with me?"

"Well, it was Max I was after. Tormenting Max with your mysterious illness was my goal." He laughed. "I hadn't expected your psychotic, paranoid behavior." He laughed again. "It only enhanced my plan. I must say you were an easy target."

Lainey cringed. "What do you mean?"

"You're starting to get annoying with the same questions, but I delight in my masterful manipulation, so I'll share just a bit." He paused before continuing. "You no doubt know by now, I have no plans to let you see the light of day."

Lainey interrupted, "I'm not stupid. I know your kind."

"Not stupid, but very naive. And so trusting, Mrs. Pinewood. Shall I continue?"

Silence.

"Didn't you ever think it strange that a substitute you barely knew would bring you your diet soda so faithfully?"

"Kindness?"

"*Don't take candy from strangers.* Isn't that what you tell your students?"

Silence. The realization of what the words meant crushed her. She felt unable to breathe. He was the reason she had CIDP.

CHAPTER 59

THE DELAY

Max pointed the flashlight down at the flat tire. He frowned. This was a heck of a time to have car trouble. It must have happened when he went past the road construction site earlier in the day. A darn nail for sure. He tightened his black jacket around his chest to seal out the cold night air. This was turning out to be a bad night.

It started with that strange call a half-hour earlier. Someone phoned to tell him a package had been delivered to their house by mistake and that it had to be picked up. Max was fine with picking up the package tomorrow, but the caller was insistent that it be picked up tonight. Something about needing to catch a plane and the package wouldn't be safe on the porch.

Now, as he lifted the trunk hood, he was dismayed, and a bit angry, to see the spare tire missing. He knew who was responsible for the missing tire and he'd let her know about it when he got home. Surely, Lainey had needed the extra room for her school stuff, but that was no excuse for not putting the tire back.

Max wanted to forget about the package, but he was fairly sure it was his new golf clubs for the tournament next week. He stepped around to the side of the car to take a second look at the tire. If it wasn't too flat, perhaps he could ride on it a few more miles to a gas station. He pressed the tire, then decided it wasn't smart to risk it. He would ruin the rim, too, if he went any farther. A few drops of rain fell on his nose. He could deal with bad weather, but this tire problem was another matter.

He wished he had taken down the phone number of the caller instead of just the address. The sound of rustling leaves and whistling wind caught his attention, indicating an approaching storm. He slammed the trunk hood down. Rain speckled his glasses as he made his way to the driver's side of the car, then closed the door as he sat behind the wheel. He found a McDonald's napkin stuck in the cup holder and used it to wipe his glasses dry, quickly realizing that it was a mistake as ketchup smeared across his right glass lens. *That's it. Lainey will not be driving my car again.* He glanced in the back seat to see one of his golf towels and grabbed it. It will have to do. Max needed his golf clubs, so he grabbed his cell phone, tapped some numbers, and left a voice message for the recipient of the call. He felt a chill sitting in the car and turned on the heat. Waiting was not something he did well, so he did what he always did with idle moments and pulled out his iPhone again. With the Candy Crush app calling his name, he navigated to level 2058 and settled in.

CHAPTER 60

EYES WIDE OPEN

Lainey smelled the alcohol and tobacco breath of her captor before she heard his words. It had been two hours since he had gagged and blindfolded her again.

His gruffy voice moved closer to her ear and she heard, "Good news and bad news."

Silence.

"The good news is . . . I'm taking off your blindfold." He snickered, then continued, "The bad news: I'm still going to kill you."

Lainey's head jolted forward with the yank that released the blinding black cloth. Her eyes blazed against her heinous captor, becoming more enraged by the smirk that awaited her. She felt the burning pain at the pull of the tape as it ripped across her defenseless mouth. She wanted to spit her disgust, but her saliva was nonexistent.

"Thirsty?"

Lainey didn't answer, but instead watched him walk over to a side table and pour a small glass of water. No sign he added any poison this time. She couldn't wait for that moistness to soothe her throat.

She hoped he would help her drink it since her hands were still bound to the chair. Instead, he stepped forward and threw the cold water into her face. Tears filled her eyes; not because of the loss of the drink, but because of the way he demeaned her by throwing it. He was despicable and she wanted to curse at him, but the twisted look on his face scared her.

"Where the hell is your husband?" He hurled the empty glass across the room, sending sharp, clear pieces splattering in all directions, then turned to his accomplice and bellowed orders. "Clean that up!"

Carla appeared to want to protest, but Lainey suspected she recognized the anger on Isaac's fiery face. She left and, within a minute, came back with a broom and dustpan. With a bit of mumbling, she soon had the mess under control.

Isaac turned his attention back to Lainey. "You heard me. He's late."

Lainey hoped Max never showed up. One of them had to remain safe. She tried to create saliva so she could talk. "How would I know? You made the arrangements."

"You imbecile!" His distorted expression did not prepare her for what came next. He sprayed her face with the foulest projectile of tobacco-infested phlegm and spit. She felt sick to her stomach as it rested upon her nose and began to slowly slide down her face.

A cell phone rang in the back room. Isaac grabbed his pack of Marlboro cigarettes and then he was gone.

Carla grabbed a damp, used washcloth and wiped the spit from Lainey's face.

"That's disgusting," Lainey said.

"You need to keep your mouth shut," Carla said as she threw the cloth into a wastebasket.

Lainey would have thanked her, but the washcloth had its own unwanted assortment of foul, moldy dampness. She took in a deep breath, relieved that Carla had not remembered to blindfold and gag her again.

CHAPTER 61

A LATE ARRIVAL

The Lorianne Falls police station seemed quiet for a Friday night, except for the irritated voice of Sergeant Rodriguez scolding a rookie for late report filing. Kate didn't miss her rookie days. Rain sprayed against the conference room window, interspersed with blasts of wind. She had spent the last two hours going over the files related to the Sparks and Watkins murders again. Details nagged at her. No matter how she spun her theories, she couldn't see her current list of suspects committing these murders. The motivation was not strong enough for any of them. Somewhere in the police files was a connection she had missed. Someone had gone under her radar; under Will's radar.

She opened one of the files again and tried to concentrate, but her brain felt scrambled. She absentmindedly snapped a pencil in half, nearly cutting herself with the ragged edge. Where was Will? A tension headache was taking a spot in the corner of her forehead. Will was supposed to be here after his softball game. Surely it had been canceled with all this rain. She rubbed her forehead hoping to ease the throbbing of her temple.

Two hours later, Will leaned in the open conference door with a Baltimore Orioles baseball cap turned backwards on his head. Mud covered his cleats and stretched halfway up his blue-striped softball knickers. A hodgepodge of splattered mud and grass stains covered his team shirt, rendering the team's name, Lorianne Falls Dingers, barely readable. His head lazily slumped against the frame of the door, a wide smirk extending across his face. "Am I late?"

Kate sat back in her conference chair and stared at the sight before her. She had never seen this version of Will. That goofy grin was, somehow, charmingly disarming. Her irritation at his lateness was muddled by something . . . a feeling. Whatever. She had to put that feeling in check. She had to put *him* in check. "It's nice of you to show up," she greeted.

With a swagger, he moved from the doorway and slid into a seat next to her. His brown eyes stared into hers. He edged his way even closer. "Will you forgive me?" Not waiting for a reply, he leaned back and gave an uncomfortable laugh. "Of course not." He took off his Orioles cap and threaded his fingers through his matted hair. "I'm really sorry I'm late."

She caught her breath at the scent of his: a mixture of alcohol and Tic Tacs. His closeness stifled her response. She wanted to be mad, but his apology did seem sincere. After all, it was his day off. A part of her didn't want him off the hook so easily. "Why were you late?"

Will put down a pencil on the wood conference table. "I'm sorry Kate. Just before the game got canceled for rain, I blew the hell out of the ball. A home run." He smiled. "A Lorianne Falls Dinger." He picked up the pencil again, swinging it like a bat. His face glowed. "You should have seen it. Way past center field! Everyone was out of their seats for my nail-biting slide into home plate."

"That's awesome, Will." Kate grabbed her water bottle and turned the cap. "But Bill's on your team and he was back an hour ago."

Will shifted in his chair. "Bill's a bench warmer. The rest of us wanted to celebrate." He rubbed the back of his head. "Honestly, Kate, in all the excitement, I forgot about meeting you. I guess I was basking in the glory of my home run. We beat our greatest rivals, the Fallsville Super Cops." He picked up one of the red files sitting on the table. "What progress have you made?"

"I've reviewed all the files again. I know there's a clue right in front of our faces." Kate was worried that the important clue she was looking for would remain undiscovered and hoped Will's analytical mind would unravel this puzzle.

Will leaned closer to Kate. "At least we've ruled out a few suspects."

Kate took a deep breath. "After we looked like fools, booking two innocent women. I had to eat crow for my mom."

"In my mind, they won't be completely innocent until we find our killer. You've eaten crow prematurely."

Kate wasn't amused. "Most likely, they didn't do it," she said with a sigh. "That's not what's really bothering me."

"What is?" Will hopped up and retrieved a bottle of root beer from the staff refrigerator. He grabbed a glass from the cupboard, and ice from the refrigerator's ice maker, and poured the contents of the bottle into his cup before tossing the bottle in the recycling bin.

Kate frowned. "We're dealing with a psychopath. A psychopath, that right now, has the upper hand."

Will sipped his drink before responding, "and let's not forget the possibility of an accomplice."

Kate nodded. "It's more than a possibility. The creepy holographic show at the Jesse Sparks murder couldn't be done without help."

Will shrugged. He took one of the extra coffee napkins and wiped up the condensation off the table before placing a dry napkin under his glass. "Yes, I kept that thought of an accomplice on the back burner, but it's time to consider it as a real possibility."

Kate shuffled through the files until she came upon the Interviews. "Let's go over these again. I have to believe there's a clue there we've missed." She handed Will a green file covering all the interviews regarding the Jesse Sparks murder.

"I'll look at the interviews for Randy Watkins," she said, taking the yellow folder covering the interviews with the teachers at Lorianne Falls Elementary.

Without a further word, they read each interview transcript thoroughly. Will got up after an hour and made a pot of coffee. Within minutes, the smell of fresh-brewed coffee attracted two uniformed police officers. Kate barely noticed; her mind intent on finding the truth. She inventoried each interview. There were thirty-eight interviews. Something about that number didn't seem right. She counted the principal, his administrative staff, teachers, even the cafeteria workers. All their interviews were accounted for. It was then that she understood the problem. Where was the statement from the custodian? Or the nurse? Where were the interviews with the Special Ed teachers and the substitute teachers? She was sure *everyone* had been interviewed. If she or Will didn't interview witnesses, then Ryan handled them; the same rookie the Sergeant chastised for late paperwork. She thought her blood pressure spiked when she made the connection.

She couldn't wait to share this with Will, the breakthrough finally within her grasp. A police siren sounded outside the conference room window. Will lifted his head, hearing the siren too. Kate stood up. "Will, this is a game-changer."

"What do you mean?"

"Some of the interviews conducted at Lorianne Falls Elementary are missing."

Will frowned. "You mean, we screwed up?"

She shrugged. "Not us; Ryan."

"Ryan?"

Kate frowned. "That darn rookie. The Sergeant was right to blast him earlier. He never turned in our interviews."

"If he's still here . . ." Will walked to the open door. "I'm going to kill him."

Kate watched Will leave. It was the first time she noticed the soiled path created by his muddied cleats. She'd have him clean that up later. After they dealt with Ryan's blunder. No, their blunder. She hated to admit it: they should have noticed the missing interviews sooner. Like last month.

Kate went to refill her coffee cup, only to find about half a cup left. Oh well. The noise in the police station had risen since earlier in the day. Marvin, a local drunk, protested loudly that he was not drunk and that he did not hit Sal. Another voice, slurring his speech, screamed that he was hit by Marvin.

Kate was glad to see Will come back but dismayed by the absence of Ryan. She was about to ask for an explanation when her eye caught a message notification on her cell phone. A voicemail from Rachel? She never called her unless it was about her mom. Kate picked up her phone and listened, then looked up at Will with alarm. "Something's wrong. We need to get out of here. Now."

CHAPTER 62

THE RESCUE

A light drizzle and calmer winds brought comfort to Rachel as she approached the small trailer window close to the three cement steps leading up to the back door. At least now, the outdoor elements wouldn't add to the obstacles she faced. She figured it must be about 10 P.M. In October, night starts early and stays late. It certainly felt like it had been about three hours since she first started tailing that woman. An artificial outdoor green carpet provided a semblance of a patio. Two rusted lawn chairs sat straight up, held down by large rocks resting on their seats. A small white mucky wood table nestled between them. *Perfect*.

She slid the table under the window as quietly as she

could and steadied herself on top. For once in her life, she was thankful she was petite.

She moved her trembling fingers in a circular motion to wipe more of the dirty film from the glass and peered through, surprised and relieved that Lainey was no longer blindfolded and gagged. Her hands and feet were still tied tightly to the chair though. Rachel eyed the bruise marks around Lainey's wrists and ankles. Her mouth felt dry, but her palms were damp. She searched the dimly lit room for signs of the man or woman. No physical presence; a brief relief. A gas flame under a cast iron frying pan on the stove caught her attention.

It was a gamble and surely risky, but Rachel's mind was racing, her actions ramping ahead of her thoughts. She tapped sharply on the window to gain Lainey's attention. Within seconds, they were eye to eye through the window. Lainey seemed stunned to see her, and not in a good way. She watched as Lainey's head jerked to the left with her eyes pointing towards an apparent bedroom door. She knew immediately that Lainey was trying to tell her that the captors were behind that door. Not both, as she saw Lainey put up one finger towards the front door. It was clear one of the kidnappers was outside. Lainey's mouth seemed to be in rapid repeat, mouthing strongly for her to leave. Leave now.

A whiff of cigarette smoke nearby heightened Rachel's urgency to open the window. She tried to lift it up, but it stuck in place. Going through the window was not an option. She looked at Lainey, who frantically tried to tell her something. Lainey's wide eyes and waving fingers were starting to scare her. Why was she acting like that? Maybe she thought someone would come out of the bedroom door and find her. Just in case, Rachel ducked down from the window. The intense odor of cigarettes and the jab in her side told her exactly what Lainey was trying to say.

"Get down!"

Rachel felt the hairs stand up on her neck. *Dear Lord, help me.* Her knees shook as she carefully climbed down from the table. The woman she faced, now recognized, stood coldly expressionless. Rachel was too shocked to speak. She felt the L-shaped wrench pressing against her back pocket. How would she get the courage to use it? She stared at the gun in Carla's hand. If she didn't use it, she'd be dead.

Carla grabbed her and pushed her onto the sidewalk next to the porch. Rachel clumsily lost her footing and tripped, her arms swinging and accidentally knocking the gun out of Carla's hands. Without thinking, Rachel pulled out the wrench and hit Carla in the back of the head as hard as she could. Instantly mortified with what she had done, she scrambled to aid her, but Carla was out cold. *My Lord, what did I do?*

Rachel ran up the steps and pushed her way through the door. She rushed to Lainey and hugged her dear friend. She could have clung to her friend forever, but Lainey warned her to hurry. Country music played behind the walls. Maybe time was on their side.

Rachel struggled to untie Lainey, as her hands were sweating and her long, perfectly manicure fingernails were getting in the way. She had one hand undone, but she needed scissors or a knife for this tough rope. She could hear a Willie Nelson song coming from the bedroom. She went in the kitchen and found a small paring knife. She moved quickly across the room to finish untying the other hand. Rachel knew there was no time to lose but that didn't stop Lainey from asking a question.

"What happened to the gun?" she asked in a hushed, but urgent, whisper.

Rachel's mind went blank. She hesitated before answering. "It's outside."

"You always get the gun!" Lainey exclaimed, exasperated and trying to keep her voice low.

Rachel understood the implications behind Lainey's words and hoped her mistake would not be the death of them. A part of her wanted Carla revived, but just not yet. She cut the last rope from Lainey's right foot. Relieved that her friend was freed, her thoughts went to the woman outside. Her conscience couldn't ignore how she had hurt Carla with that wrench. She needed to call for help. "Where's your phone?"

With a wobble, Lainey stood up. "Let's worry about my phone after we get out of here."

Rachel had taken a few steps towards the door when she heard the flush of a toilet in the back room. The front door was three feet away. By the time he washed his hands they would be outside. She heard the country music stop as they made it safely out the front door.

CHAPTER 63

UNEXPECTED CONSEQUENCES

Lainey's worst fear materialized as she stepped outside the back door and found a gun pointed to her chest. Ever since Rachel admitted she'd left the gun outside, she worried the gun would find itself back into the wrong hands. Here she stood, in the same predicament, but now Rachel's life was at stake as well. Could things get any worse?

Rachel whispered at her back, "What are we going to do?"

"Whatever the woman with the gun wants us to do." Lainey thought they would choose the path of least resistance, at least, until she could figure out what to do next.

Lainey felt the damp chill of the night as she waited for Carla to make the next move. The yellow glow of the bulb lighting the back porch accentuated the evil she saw in the woman's eyes. She felt Rachel trembling behind her. It troubled her that her friend was unraveling. Focus, she thought. *Assess the situation.* True, Carla had the gun, but also true, she stood on a very narrow step below them.

Lainey plowed her right foot into Carla's lower body and sent her plummeting down the back steps onto the concrete sidewalk. "Run Rachel, run!" she screamed as she grabbed the loose gun and ran out into the graveled parking area. Rachel stayed ahead of her. The sound of gun blasts quickened their pace. The car was just a few feet away now. Suddenly, rifle shots blasted past them, shattering the windshield of Rachel's car. They froze.

Isaac's voice bellowed through the dark night air. "If either of you make one move, I'll shoot right through Rachel's back."

Lainey should have stayed with the path of least resistance. Fury erupted within herself as she regretted taking forcible action. She had overestimated her ability to escape and underestimated the amount of evil she was facing; a mistake that could cost Rachel her life. She had no doubt he would shoot her, regardless of what he said.

"We're not going to resist." Lainey's voice quivered. "Please let Rachel go. I'm the one you want." Her heartbeat jumped in her throat as she watched him walk closer, the shotgun still pointed at Rachel's back.

"Shut up!" He shoved the shotgun into Rachel's back. "Now head back to the house." He motioned to Lainey to get moving.

The tears in Rachel's eyes revealed that she was barely holding on. Lainey glared at Isaac. "We'll do what you want, so you don't have to strong-arm us."

"Shut up," he commanded, giving Rachel another shove.

Carla appeared and grabbed the gun Lainey had dropped. The gun now pointed at Lainey. "You heard him. Move."

Isaac glared at his accomplice. "You're a waste. How did you let this happen?"

Carla mumbled an incoherent answer. Her demeanor showed submission, but her eyes revealed a glimmer of defiance.

CHAPTER 64

DEAD RELATIVE

Back in the double wide trailer, Lainey cringed at being tied up again, but was relieved she hadn't been gagged or blindfolded. Across from her, Rachel looked like she was in time-out, as her chair faced tightly against a dull blue wall. Her friend's slumped-over appearance should have alarmed her, but the faint whispering she heard reassured Lainey that Rachel was handling the situation in the best way she knew how: through prayer. However, Lainey wanted to be saved now. She had hoped someone had heard the ruckus outside with the shots Isaac fired, but from how it looked when she tried to escape, the area was deeply wooded and there was no telling whether there were any other residents nearby.

As she observed Rachel, Lainey noticed a gold-framed photograph on the wall above Rachel's head. The longer she stared at it, the more it seemed to highlight their predicament. An old man in a red-and-blue-striped flannel shirt, and a young girl in a green jumper, smiled broadly as they held up their captured fish. Their smiles seemed to reflect the relief Lainey felt when she thought she had escaped her captors. But unlike the fish in the photo, they had no hope of catch and release. It wouldn't be long until they were tossed into that deadly frying pan.

Carla sat in the small kitchen systematically devouring a pile of Skittles. On the round wooden table, the Skittles had been divided into piles by their color. Lainey had watched her eat the green Skittles first and now she was on to the red. She was disgusted by what she saw. Her life was in danger and this woman sat eating Skittles. How could she be so heartless?

Lainey noticed another odd thing about Carla: she kept watching the shut bedroom door. Was she afraid to get caught eating the Skittles? Were they his Skittles? No; if that was true, she wouldn't have touched them in the first place. Lainey frowned. Why was she thinking like this? Was it a function of her conscience to ease her mind from the imminent danger of her situation by letting her obsess about Skittles? Well, it didn't work.

Lainey glanced over at the bedroom door. Reggae music slipped out into their space. What was he doing in there? More importantly, when was he coming out? She owed it to Rachel to get them out of this mess. When he did open that door, she'd better have a plan.

She turned her thoughts back to Carla. The gun rested in the woman's lap, but she appeared less formidable than she had earlier. Maybe it was her candy routine or her eye twitch that had developed over the last fifteen minutes. Lainey figured Carla was not too happy about the way the jerk treated her outside. She wondered if Carla realized that her life had no more value than theirs. It would only be a matter of time before he'd reel her in. Hook, line, and sinker, she'd be caught too. She just didn't know it yet.

Rachel's sudden cough brought Lainey's attention back to her friend, who appeared okay, but it also brought her attention back to the picture hanging on the wall above Rachel. She noticed that the girl in the picture was about fourteen. It was the second look that intrigued her. She knew that girl. She wasn't sure how she would use it, but it might be her only chance.

Lainey's eyes turned to Carla, who had already turned in her direction and appeared to notice her interest in the photo. "That's you in the photo?" Lainey asked.

The woman narrowed her eyes towards her. Silence. Her hand rubbed her pant leg in a back-and-forth motion. More silence.

"It's just that you look so happy." Lainey caught something in Carla's eyes. Weariness? Sadness? She needed to explore this. "Is that your dad?" she baited, not really believing that the man in the photo was her father, but if he meant something to her, she would not tolerate this mistake.

Carla drooped back in her chair but held firm to the gun. "My grandpa."

Lainey saw the tears well up but not burst from her eyes. This hardened woman had a tender spot. "Do you get to see him often?" Lainey asked softly, hoping her questions seemed genuine.

"He's dead," Carla replied, a tear falling down the side of her cheek. "If it wasn't for my mother . . ." She stopped as if she realized that she was about to tell too much.

The way Lainey saw it, this was more than a tender spot with Carla. Like an onion that caused one to weep, warning unheeded, the protective fleshy leaves were forced to relinquish their delicate bulb. Lainey had stripped away Carla's custodial layers with just one word: Grandpa. In those two syllables, her layers peeled away to reveal her hidden pain. Lainey felt for her. She had her own triggers that tore at her heart. Amazingly, she saw that the woman's eye had stopped twitching, its focus now in alignment with the heart. If Lainey was going to make a connection, now was the time. It wouldn't be long before the woman's protective layers guarded her emotions again.

"I'm sorry about your grandpa. I lost mine too," Lainey offered. She thought she saw a flicker of connection, but it didn't last as Rachel threw up all over herself and the wall. Lainey shouted, forgetting for the moment the danger she was in. "You've got to help her!"

If Carla planned to help, there was no telling, as the bedroom door burst open. The man's hands clinched as he took in the scene. Isaac focused his attention on Rachel before he bellowed towards Carla. "Clean that crap up!"

The callousness in his voice should have alarmed Lainey, but it was the sight within his bedroom that terrified her. On the bedside table rested a huge can of gasoline with large matches protruding over the edge of its lid. In her mind, those items had only one use: he planned to burn them alive. Her mind spinning, she realized there was no time to get Carla on their side. Calm down, she willed herself. Most likely, they'd be dead before he set the blaze. Her body shivered. That thought wasn't any more helpful. He had threatened to shoot Rachel in the back, but dead or alive, he'd strike the match. Her time for action had to be now. Plan or no plan, she was getting Rachel out of here.

CHAPTER 65

THE CHASE

Kate waited anxiously in the Ford police cruiser while Will changed from his softball clothes to his work attire. He had persuaded her that since they didn't know what situation they would find, he didn't want to be hindered by his softball cleats. She reluctantly agreed. The phone call from Rachel had worried her.

Kate tried calling her mother several times but there was no response. With great relief, she watched Will come down the steps at headquarters before taking his seat on the passenger's side.

"Do we know where we're going?"

She started the engine and stood her phone up in the cup holder. "Rachel tried to tell me, but she was incoherent." She backed out the car before she noticed that Will was unbuckled. "Seatbelt."

He snapped it. "Okay. So where to, then?"

"I've pinpointed her location to be about forty minutes from here."

"Pinpointed her location?" Will asked, confused at what information Kate would have to be able to do that.

"Yeah. She's on our family's iPhone tracker system," she explained as she turned onto Route 32 and increased her speed to 50 miles per hour. The slower speeds in the Lorianne Falls district were now behind her.

"That sounds invasive. I don't need someone knowing everywhere I go."

Kate was in no mood for chitchat. She let his comment go unanswered as her mind focused on her mother. Who did her mom know in rural Glenwood, Maryland? What in the world was going on with her? Why was Rachel so worried? Was Rachel's imagination getting the best of her? She couldn't take that chance.

They had left the station a little before ten o'clock, so traffic was light. Kate checked her iPhone to confirm the arrival time. They would arrive five minutes earlier than she expected. Will had asked many questions on the drive but she had kept her responses to a minimum. One question, however, did leave her with misgivings. He asked her if she had called her dad. Kate had decided not to worry him until she found out what was going on with her mom. Now, she was second-guessing that decision.

No longer on Route 32, Kate's directions sent her along narrow, graveled roads into what appeared to be a trailer park. Most of the trailer park looked abandoned except for a few scatterings of lighted porches, which made reading roadside signs difficult. Kate tightened her grip on the steering wheel when her headlights finally shone upon Rachel's parked car on the side of the road. She parked behind it and she and Will exited the car.

Kate shone her flashlight onto Rachel's car. Her fear level heightened at the sight of the shattered windshield where a hole from an apparent gunshot had passed through. Who was the intended target? She caught her breath. She prayed it wasn't her mom or Rachel. What happened here? It scared her to think of the possibilities. She was surprised to find the car unlocked with the keys lying on the passenger's seat, and so relieved that there was no blood anywhere. She tried to remember Rachel's voicemail. She hadn't revealed where she was at the time, only that her mom was in a stranger's home and wasn't answering her cell phone. What happened that triggered shots being fired? The amount of danger her mom could be involved in multiplied with every consideration.

Will signaled to Kate that the trunk was empty. She blew out a breath. Thank God. No body. At least one of her questions had been answered. She surveyed the area in the limited light of the crescent moon and her flashlight. Most of the trailers they'd seen were hidden under the privacy of forest trees, undermining potential threats. Now the only question was: did she have time to call for backup?

CHAPTER 66

FINAL ATTEMPT

After Rachel's anxiety attack, the stench of vomit lingered. Cigarette smoke and alcohol added their own foul combination, exacerbating Lainey's dire situation. She had not come up with a plan that she thought could work and, if she didn't find one soon, she would have to take her chances with the plan that had the best shot.

The only good thing since the vomiting incident was that now she and Rachel were within one foot of each other on the same wall. She had thought it an odd strategy for Isaac to choose, but his speech since then had indicated that he wanted to look both of them in the face. He had even removed their blindfolds and gags. He had, however added more rope across their chests and tied their arms tighter to the chairs. He had ranted on about them being more trouble than they were worth and was particularly upset that Max had not shown up. Whatever he blamed Max for was fueling this man's madness. What did Max do? She may never know, and she didn't care. She knew Max. This man was out of his mind.

Lainey looked over at Rachel, whose lips were still moving with the words of her prayers, though she had become silent as she mouthed them. She appeared calm, so apparently her faith was getting her through now. When Lainey thought Carla wasn't watching, she mouthed, "I'll get us out of here," to Rachel.

Rachel saw and nodded in understanding.

Lainey glanced over at Carla, who was pacing in the kitchen. The ashtray on the kitchen table contained ten cigarette butts. Five empty Skittles bags also lay on the table among four Snickers' wrappers. The calm coolness that Carla wanted to portray was mitigated by her smoking and eating behaviors. Maybe it was time to try again. She'd wait until Carla sat down so they'd be eye to eye. Whatever happened next, she had to reach this woman's heart.

It was fifteen minutes before Carla sat down in the white rocker across from Lainey. She held the gun tightly in her hand and directed it towards the two bound women.

Lainey sent a reassuring glance to Rachel, but she felt far from calm. Her eyes turned to the closed bedroom door and she felt a quiver in her body as she thought about the man behind it. It may be only moments until he was out again to end their lives.

It was during the wait for Carla to sit down that she had gotten an idea on how to reach her. It was in something Bobby had said about Carla being a substitute last year for her class. In a second-grader's way, he understood another side to Carla.

It wasn't going to be easy to start this conversation; Carla's stern expression didn't set the right tone for any kind of productive conversation. Lainey gathered her courage, then said, "Carla, I want to tell you something."

"Not interested."

Lainey had to get past this answer, so she cut to the chase. "What do you think Bobby would think about this?"

Carla leaned forward and furrowed her brow, then taking the bait she asked, "Bobby, the second-grader?"

"He's in third grade now, but yes. He told me that you were his favorite substitute."

"He did?"

"Yes," Lainey confirmed. She glanced over at Rachel, who had directed her attention to their conversation.

Carla closed her eyes, but her fingers held tight to the gun in her lap. After a moment, she opened her eyes and said, "Bobby's a sweet boy."

"He really likes you," Lainey added. She saw Carla give a cautious smile. She didn't know how long she could keep this conversation going before it annoyed Carla, so she asked her final question next. "How do you think Bobby will feel if his favorite substitute killed his favorite teacher?"

Carla knocked over a lamp as she jumped up. "Shut up!"

It wasn't the response Lainey wanted, but she had successfully struck a nerve. Had she said enough to reach the woman that Bobby had seen? Lainey wouldn't have time to think about it as the commotion from the fallen lamp and Carla's loud outburst had brought the beast back into the room.

CHAPTER 67

THE BEAST

A sudden blast crossed the living room of the small mobile home, leaving no question as to the intention of the shooter. Carla fell to the floor with a thud and then there was an eerie silence, which was almost as deafening as the roaring explosion. Lainey watched Isaac brazenly holding the gun in his hand. She had seen that same cockiness in the thugs she dealt with while in the FBI. It sickened her to see the pleasure behind his dark, deviled eyes.

Rachel, trembling and wide-eyed, was not handling this new commotion well. She had cowered back into her chair as far as she could while hampered by her bound limbs. It was obvious that she was trying to shield herself from Isaac's wrath. Lainey's heart sank that her friend was suffering and she couldn't do anything about it. She whispered, "It'll be okay," but she doubted her own words. She only hoped Rachel believed her. The sound of moving feet rerouted her attention back to Isaac. He stood close, evidently to exert his power over her.

When Isaac cast his eyes on her, she felt an unsettling emotion, but anger arose stronger than the rest. If this was going to be her last day, she'd go down fighting. As long as she could speak, she'd speak her peace. "You didn't need to kill Carla."

"I do as I please."

"She was on your side," Lainey insisted.

He chuckled and said, "Idiot. She's not dead." He walked over to Carla and kicked her in her side. "Get up!"

To Lainey's relief, Carla wobbled to her feet, obviously shaken by the near miss. Isaac had extended his arm to help her up, but Carla shook it away. *I would have done the same thing*, thought Lainey. Even when Isaac helped, he was up to no good.

Once seated again, Carla turned her attention to Isaac, her voice agitated. "Why did you do that?"

"To use your own words, you needed to understand the situation."

Silence.

"Come on, Carla. Every time I leave you alone with these women, something goes wrong."

"Not every time," Carla argued.

"Who knocked over the lamp?" He pointed over to Lainey and Rachel. "They're tied up."

Carla cast her stare onto Lainey and nodded her head toward her. "That one annoyed me."

"I didn't know you had such thin skin," Isaac taunted as he took a cigarette out of a pack on the table and lit it. He took another puff, then placed the burning bud on a makeshift ashtray. "By the way, we're leaving tonight. Pack your bags."

"I thought we'd be here for a few days?" Carla asked, confused.

"Change of plans."

"What about them?"

"Different timetable, same fate," Isaac answered, plopping down into a brown chaise chair and pointed his gun at Lainey and Rachel before turning back to Carla. "Go pack. I'll sit on these two."

His words, *same fate*, cemented what Lainey had known all along: he had no plans to spare them. The smug way he sat in the chair staring her down disgusted her. The way he treated Carla, his partner in crime, showed how he really felt about women. How did he get like this? She tried to imagine him as a second-grader, with a second-grader's joyful innocence, and she wondered what happened to him along the way that he became this violent creep. Her curiosity won out over common sense, and she posed him a question. "Why are you so abusive towards Carla, your ally in this?"

"You're a nosy one. She's nothing to me. Nothing more than a hired hand."

"You didn't answer my question."

"Carla's right. You're annoying," Isaac said, then turned to Rachel, whose eyes revealed that she had been lost in her own thoughts. "Is your friend always this annoying?" Isaac asked her.

Rachel's reaction was slow as she looked over at Lainey. "No."

The answer was apparently not quick enough for Isaac, who stood up and ripped the silver cross from around Rachel's neck. "If I speak to you, you answer!"

Lainey was horrified. That cross had been given to Rachel the day before her mother died of cancer and she had worn it every day since. Lainey felt her face tighten. "Rachel did answer you."

"She can speak for herself," Isaac admonished, then turned his attention back to Rachel.

The disturbing sound of Rachel's coughing and raspy

breathing worried Lainey. Rachel glared at Isaac. "I said no. May I have my cross back?"

Isaac flipped the cross up in the air until it landed back on the palm of his hand. He then placed it in his front pocket. "Nope," he said with a smirk. "What are you going to do about it?"

There was a strange calmness in Rachel's voice as she answered, "Everything you do tells me that you're one of God's lost sheep. I'll pray for you, and I hope my mom's cross comforts you the way it did for me." With that, tears began to roll down Rachel's face.

Her words must have caught Isaac by surprise or struck a nerve because he said nothing in response. He rubbed the back of his head and paced back and forth, glancing back at Rachel as he did.

Lainey was proud of Rachel for staying true to her faith, even now, but thought her bold words would fall on irreverent ears.

Isaac stopped pacing and pulled a chair over to sit next to Rachel. He looked her right in the eyes and, his voice unusually civil with a deadly calm, he said, "I don't get you. And I'm gonna kill you."

Rachel's damp eyes leveled to his. "I know. And I trust in the Lord. I know he wants me to forgive you before you take my life."

"You're a fool. He wasn't there when I needed him."

Rachel responded softly. "He was there. You weren't listening."

"Enough." Isaac stood and lifted the cross out of his pocket and tossed it onto Rachel's lap. "Here! Take it to your grave."

He stormed across to the kitchen and grabbed a Coors Light from the small refrigerator. He drank from the can before returning his gaze and gun on Lainey. He scowled at her. "What are you looking at?" He took another sip of his beer. "Where the hell is your husband?"

"He's probably sound asleep by now." Lainey felt sure it must be past eleven. Max was usually in bed by nine-thirty these days. It was obvious that whatever Isaac had said to Max, it didn't arouse any urgency. She knew Isaac wouldn't like her answer, but she no longer cared. She'd keep him talking until she could plan their escape.

"Well, he's gonna wake up to a nightmare," Isaac said.

Her body stiffened as dread filled her mind. Their dead bodies would lay in wait until Max stumbled upon them. The only good thing was that his body wouldn't be one of the discovered corpses.

The sound of Rachel's coughing worried Lainey. Moldiness and cigarette smoke fouled the air; not the ideal conditions for Rachel's asthma. Without an inhaler, Rachel wouldn't be able to breathe. Lainey couldn't let her be any more uncomfortable than she already was. A thought came to her and then she remembered something Max said: *If you don't ask, the answer is always no.*

She looked over at Isaac, who was sitting at the table eating a Payday. "Do you think we can open the window?"

Isaac smirked. "Is it too warm for you in here?"

"I'm worried about Rachel's asthma."

"I'm okay," said Rachel.

Lainey continued to address Isaac. "They give a special dinner to prisoners on death row the night of their execution. Isn't this our night? I'm just asking you to open a window."

He unlocked the window and, with some force, moved it up about two inches. "That's high enough and now you both have gotten your last request."

The look of relief on Rachel's face warmed Lainey. The crisp night air, with the brisk breeze coming through the window, aerated the room with nature's beautiful aroma of forest smells. A night owl and nearby crickets sounded their own song, while a lone fox seemed to provide a high pitched, yippy solo. *If I get out of this,* she thought, *I'm going to keep my windows open much more often.*

Lainey felt herself inhale, but then her throat tightened and she exhaled. The realization hit her that it wouldn't be long before Carla came out and Isaac's plan would be put into motion. Lainey felt her heartbeat skip. She didn't have to look at Rachel to know she was feeling the desperation. "Surely, you could let Rachel go. She has done you no harm."

Rachel chimed in, "Lainey, no. I won't leave here without you."

Isaac turned his eyes toward Rachel. "How sweet, but nobody's leaving here except me."

Lainey wondered why he hadn't included Carla in those who would be leaving. Did he misspeak or did he have other plans for Carla, too? He was becoming more dangerous by the minute.

The second bedroom door opened, and Carla wheeled out a large, blue, hard-sided luggage bag and sat it near the front door. "I'm ready."

"It took you long enough," Isaac said. He took his last swig of beer. "I have some last-minute preparations, but I expect to be done with this mess within the half-hour. It's your turn out here. Don't let them get to you," he warned.

Carla nodded, then Isaac went into his bedroom and closed the door. Lainey sighed inwardly. The guards may have changed, but their dire situation did not.

CHAPTER 68

THE HAND

The bass-shaped lamp shone dimly on the scratched pine desk in the small trailer bedroom and lit the open, lined journal. The hand's grip was tight around the pencil, and it nestled on the paper. The hand wrote what the mind thought, so the hand wrote:

Mischief Maker
Mischief Maker
I spied the cop

Mischief Maker
Mischief Maker
Can't wait to stop

Mischief Maker
Mischief Maker
Tick Tock Tick Tock

Mischief Maker
Mischief Maker
Up goes the clock

The hand twirled and then wrote again. *Welcome to the party.* The hand stopped.

CHAPTER 69

BACKUP

Within minutes of finding Rachel's partially hidden car, Kate discovered a red Camry parked in a small, gravel driveway. Even though it was hidden by holly bushes and the night's dark shield, the high beam of Kate's flashlight had lit the way. She eyed Will, who, moments earlier, had escaped being shot by a frightened elderly woman who had pointed a shotgun out her trailer window. He'd gone to survey the surrounding area and come close enough to her trailer to hear her calling out her intentions to blow whoever was out there to smithereens. Situation under control, the woman sat inside their police cruiser as Will questioned her about whether she had seen anything suspicious besides him.

Kate approached the car cautiously. She pulled out her iPhone and snapped a picture of the license plate before sending it to dispatch. The car was unlocked. The issue of probable cause crept into her head, but her mom's disappearance and Rachel's ominous phone call gave her strong incentive to carry on. She opened the driver's side and found the front and passenger seats empty except for snack-size candy wrappers and an empty soda cup littering the floor mat. She felt an irritation in her throat, most likely, from the stench of cigarettes permeating the interior air of the car. The odor took her back to fourth grade when she cried and begged her dad to stop his heavy smoking. From that day on, her father credited her for saving his life.

She checked the compartment between the front seats. There, she found hand wipes, about two inches of assorted coins, an unopened box of toothpicks, and a small switchblade. She pulled a small plastic bag from her pocket and carefully inverted it to pick up the knife with the bag, so she didn't touch it and leave her own fingerprints on it. She opened the glove compartment, but only found a family-size bag of Skittles.

She opened the door to the back passenger side and steered her flashlight's glow onto the back seat, where she discovered two long hairs clinging to the back of the left passenger's leather seat. She leaned over to retrieve a toothpick from the box she'd found, pulled the last plastic bag out of her back pocket, and then used the toothpick to gently put each hair into the bag. It was the collection of the hair samples that sent a sudden chill through her body. Her instincts as a detective were leading her to treat this car as a possible crime scene. She didn't want to be investigating a crime. Why was her mind creating this kind of scenario? She chastised her thoughts. This was all going to be a misunderstanding. Her mom was acting the way she always did; never telling anyone about where she had gone. Kate could see the future events play out: her dad would call to ask if she knew where her mom was, then her mom would scold them for assuming the worst. *Well Mom*, she thought, *I'll assume the worst one last time even if it kills me to hear your wrath later.* And she deeply hoped that she heard her mom's wrath later.

Kate held her breath as she opened the trunk and exhaled when it appeared that someone had just stopped at Costco. Large quantities of candy, junk food, and an eighteen-pack of toilet paper lay packed into the back corner of the trunk. *Nothing suspicious about that.* An owl hooted in the night as if trying to warn of her presence. She gently closed the trunk.

Kate needed to talk to Will about what he had learned

from the neighbor. She was about to approach him when she spotted a black sedan. It was partially hidden by a dilapidated storage shed. This time she found the car locked. She snapped a picture of the license plate and sent it to dispatch.

Kate's apprehension about her mom's disappearance grated at her. She leaned impatiently against the police cruiser to question Will. "Did you find out anything?"

"Yeah, more than I thought I'd get from an eighty-year-old."

"Come on. Any information that could help us?"

"Yeah, she was able to tell me that a man showed up over three hours ago and a middle-aged lady opened the door to the trailer near where we found Rachel's car. Based on her description, the woman didn't look anything like your mother."

"What else?" Kate wanted to get to the good part; the part that would help save her mom.

Will shrugged. "She told me about hearing voices and a gunshot."

"That explains the windshield but doesn't tell us when it happened or who was involved." Kate's mind sprung into overdrive, and she didn't like the conclusion she was coming to.

Will rubbed the back of his neck and furrowed his

brow. "There's more, and I may have a clue as to who was involved."

"Will, what is it?"

"When I questioned her about the voices, she thought they may belong to multiple women. She definitely heard one man's angry voice."

Kate wanted to believe that this was a local domestic quarrel with a hotheaded husband, but her gut knew differently. "Was she able to understand what they said?"

"She heard a woman's name: Rachel."

Kate's body jerked. "Is she sure?" At Will's nod, Kate said, "Did she see anything?"

"No." Will brushed a loose hair off his face. "Not at that point. What did you find out?"

"Nothing that will help us right now. I took a small knife and two long hairs from the red Camry." She could see from Will's reaction, the sudden crease on his forehead and the downward turn of his eyes, that he had the same question she did: what if those hairs belonged to her mother? She stopped leaning against the car and found herself pacing in an erratic circle.

Will moved closer and gently touched her arm. "We got this." He narrowed his eyes into hers. "We know there are at least three people, and one has a gun. We can handle this."

"And one of them may be Rachel," Kate said, pushing Will away. "I'm done talking."

"Agreed. We know what to do."

Kate looked down the graveled road. "Where's our backup?"

Will threw his hands up into the air.

"We can't wait."

CHAPTER 70

UNEXPECTED BACKUP

A familiar voice came out of nowhere. Kate turned around to see her dad's quizzical look. She melted into his arms. "Daddy." She wanted to linger there but pushed herself away and fought back tears. She had to be strong. Her dad would expect her to be a professional. Especially, when he found out who was at stake.

He took her hands in his. "What's going on?"

"Dad, why are you here?" she asked instead, knowing it was no coincidence. Somehow his presence was connected, but how?

"Jake brought me here to pick up a package." His concerned eyes held hers. "But I don't understand why you're here."

"When did you talk to mom last?"

"This morning," he answered, arching his brow. His eyes tightened. "What does your mom have to do with this?"

"We think Mom and Rachel may have been abducted." Kate's heart stopped while she waited for his response. His voice said nothing, but his darkened eyes said everything.

Jake stepped forward with alarm in his face. "Rachel's been abducted?"

Will stared over at Jake. "Who are you?"

"I'm Rachel's husband."

Max interrupted. "Why are we standing around?"

"Waiting for back up," Will answered.

Max turned his attention towards Kate. "And this waiting is okay with you?"

"Of course not, Dad."

"Good." He stepped closer to his daughter. "I'm your backup. Tell me what you know."

Will said, "While you get your dad up to speed, I'll search the area by the trailer." He looked at Jake for a moment before instructing, "You stay by your wife's car and keep an eye out for the rest of our backup."

Kate had no intention of talking things over again, but her dad was ex-CIA. She'd be a fool not to take his counsel. One mistake could cost her mom everything, so Kate and her dad stood by the patrol car while Kate shared all the information she knew. Her dad explained about the phone call that was apparently meant to lure him there. They agreed that her mom's disappearance was somehow connected to the anonymous caller.

Ten minutes later, Will stood before them. Kate saw the urgency in his eyes. "What is it?" she asked with dread.

"We have a ticking time bomb."

"Crap," Max said.

CHAPTER 71

THE COMPANY

The appearance of Isaac was chilling enough, but what Lainey saw on the green luggage he rolled out of his bedroom stunned her. In bold black letters were two letters: 'MM'; the same letters that had been stamped across her hand the day she mysteriously blacked out at school. It was no mystery now. Even the dead mouse found in her desk had probably been put there by this evil man. How long had this plan of his been in play? Would she ever really find out what this had been all about?

He glanced over at her, so she spoke up. "What does 'MM' stand for?"

With an exaggerated wave of his hand, he dragged his words. "Mis . . . chief . . . Mak . . . er."

"What?" The weird expression on his face confused her.

"My dear, it's a tale of parental love." His expression hardened. "My mother called me mischievous and found me adorable," he explained, his mouth twisting, "and my father beat me for it. Apparently, I was a very mischievous little boy."

"I'm sorry."

"Don't be." His lips twitched. "It's my badge of honor."

She said nothing.

"Don't give me that teacher's look and think you can make it all better with a smiley face sticker."

Rachel coughed.

Isaac frowned and turned his apparent agitation towards her. "Do you have something to say, preacher lady?"

"I'm sorry too."

His face turned red. "I've had it with you two and your better-than-thou judgments." He pulled his fingers through his hair. "Ruin my wonderful mood, hell no!" And then he stormed towards the kitchen.

Isaac stared them down before he got into a deep whispering conversation with Carla as they sat huddled around the kitchen table. Their bursts of giggling were frightening. *Two heads perpetuating evil, while their current victims lay in wait.* She shuddered at that thought.

Lainey was complicit in this waiting game of theirs. Why hadn't she acted yet? She shifted her weight in the chair as pain spread through her body from sitting in one position too long. She looked over at Rachel, who appeared sullen, her eyes suggesting she was deep in thought. Maybe she was thinking of Jake, just as Lainey's thoughts had gone to Max. When she wasn't thinking of Max, her mind went to her children. She longed to be with them one more time. She still had a lot of advice left in her, but they would be on their own now. She wanted to hug her precious grandchildren one more time. Tears welled in her eyes as she thought of all the events in their lives she would miss. She glanced over at those two wicked souls still discussing their fate. How could she just sit here again and let them have their way? How many times had she told her students that the word, can't, should be struck from their vocabulary? Sometimes, she was so disappointed in herself. Since she had gotten into this situation, she was always taking one step forward and two steps back.

There had to be a way out. Surely, the FBI had taught her how to get out of a situation like this. She almost laughed to herself as she thought of another possible solution: maybe she'd treat Isaac as a behavior problem. She had dealt with a few classroom bullies in her day, and he was certainly a bully. She gritted her teeth. But what if these ideas only led to one step forward? What was it going to take to get further?

Isaac suddenly grabbed Lainey's chair and turned it around to face him. His eyes seemed to glow with an inappropriate twinkle that unnerved her. Whatever Isaac and Carla had been discussing, he was happy about it.

"I'm feeling good tonight, Mrs. Pinewood." He twirled her chair around as if she were a lightweight, his mouth in a full grin. "Company's coming."

"Company?"

"So sorry I won't be here long enough to entertain them, but I plan to give them a smokin' hot time." He laughed and danced in place. He grabbed Carla's hand and twirled her around.

Carla's tight mouth displayed no pleasure at being whisked into Isaac's madness. His quick release of her hand sent her flying into the kitchen table, scattering the Skittles everywhere. If looks could kill, he was a dead man.

"I've not forgotten you, Mrs. Honeycutt." He tipped Rachel's chair on its hind legs and twirled it around. "Enough frivolity." He moved his luggage near the door and sat back down at the kitchen table, his eyes still on Lainey and Rachel. "I'm going to be leaving you two shortly, but we haven't even kissed . . . yet." He wiggled his eyebrows. "Something you both can look forward to."

Lainey gave him a disgusted look, while Rachel flinched.

"I guess that means I won't be teacher's pet." He chuckled as he grabbed a beer from the refrigerator.

This was not the man we dealt with earlier, thought Lainey. Isaac appeared almost giddy. His anger at them had turned into devilish glee. Was he on drugs? His behavior seemed manic. "Why are you acting this way?"

"Maybe I'm in the mood for love." He licked his lips and stared into Lainey's eyes before he took a long sip of beer.

Lainey felt her skin crawl and her stomach curdle as she gripped the arms of her chair. She needed to get him off this train of thought. "Who's this company you're expecting?"

"It's better you don't know."

"You seem so happy about these unexpected visitors."

"It's because I get a twofer for my efforts."

"A twofer?"

"You *are* a nosy one."

Isaac's tone had changed, making him sound more like himself, but it set Lainey back for a moment. But, her curiosity aroused, she was more determined to find out who these visitors were and why her inquisitiveness evoked this anger towards her. "What will it hurt? It's not like we'll be able to tell anyone."

"You're going to wish you kept your mouth shut." He slumped his head over but then stood tall. "Let's just say your sweet Max will find two family members dead instead of one."

Silence. Her heartbeat raced even as her body stiffened. Not Kate . . . but who else could it be? Her body numbed as she looked over at Rachel. Her friend's face seemed to indicate she'd found a place in oblivion. No one existed in the room to her except for Lainey. An unsettling thought crept into Lainey's mind. It simmered at first as if expecting her to fight back but instead she held tight. Her scalp prickled and the fuse of her anger caught fire. Damn Max. What had he done to this man? Now Kate was caught up in all of this. Her beautiful Kate. She heard Isaac's voice in the background of her thoughts, but her troubled mind obsessed over the danger Kate was in. She did hear his next words, though, as he raised his voice.

"Wife, daughter, kaboom! Is that clear enough for you?"

Silence.

Carla stepped forward towards Isaac. "You're being cruel."

Isaac's face tightened at her boldness. He moved to hover over her and bent to face her. "Hypocrite. You're knee-deep in this," he said dismissively.

As Lainey watched the scene, it made her sick.

Carla moved towards Lainey and touched her hand. "I'm sorry he told you all that."

"Don't you think it's ironic that you volunteer at a shelter for abused women? You're no better than he is." Their eyes met and then Carla walked away.

Lainey gazed over at Rachel, who stared back at her. She noticed Rachel's left-hand trembling, even while tied tightly to the armchair. She thought of her dear Kate walking into a death trap. They were living through a nightmare. *Living through* played back in her mind. She felt a glimmer of hope. A thought flickered in and out and then settled in. Somehow, her subconscious saw a way out. They would *live* through this.

Kate was nearby; most likely, right outside if Isaac saw her coming. Kate was not hasty and analyzed any situation before she proceeded. If she was here, she'd be preparing before she rushed in. If Lainey had any chance to save her, she'd need to escape before Kate ever made it to the front door of the trailer. The hope strong in her heart, she believed this time that she would take two steps forward and no steps back.

CHAPTER 72

THE PLAN

Kate's heart stopped at the word *bomb*. Could things get any worse? A cumulous cloud drifted across the moon, darkening her spirit as it shadowed out the light. She needed to call the bomb squad, but she worried they wouldn't arrive in time. It didn't stop her, though. Five seconds later, she made the 10-45 call. That done, she drew her attention back to Will and Max. Her dad was on a fact-gathering mission with Will. She listened intently as he fired one question after another.

Her dad's gaze targeted Will as his voice demanded, "Where did you find it?"

"Under the trailer."

"Did you see the countdown?"

"We've got twenty minutes."

Silence. He stared up at the moving clouds as if seeking guidance from a higher being, but his question proved more practical. "What about make or model?"

"It's heavily smudged . . ." Will's forehead wrinkled as he contemplated, ". . . maybe Russian — or maybe German — made."

"I can't work with *maybe*."

Kate's eyes widened with realization. "Dad, do you know how to disarm a bomb?"

"Yeah, but it's been years." He stood straight against the police cruiser. "We need to know who we're dealing with before we rush in half-cocked." He leaned in closer. "What information do we have on the kidnappers?"

Will said, "We're waiting on dispatch."

"I've heard from them." Kate pushed a wisp of frizzy brown hair off her face.

"Why didn't you tell us immediately?" Will asked, exasperated.

Max interrupted. "Tell us what you've got."

"The two parked cars I found . . ."

Max yanked an oak leaf hanging near his face. "Kate, give us the short version."

"I'm trying, Dad."

Max raised an eyebrow but said nothing.

She looked over at Will, who appeared uncomfortable. She sensed her dad judging her and she wanted to be angry, but the sight of her dad's glazed eyes changed her mind. This wasn't easy for either of them. He was right. She needed to be quick. "Their names are Isaac Taylor and Carla Swipes. Two substitute teachers from mom's school." She shook her head. "It doesn't make any sense." Even as she said it, a thought nagged at her. A discrepancy in a comment Isaac made during a police interview . . . he had contradicted himself from an earlier interview. It was what she was going to mention to Will when she'd gotten the phone call from Rachel. If she had only found this file earlier, perhaps this awful night could have been prevented.

"That is odd." He paused. "Picture ID?"

She held her phone over to him so he could see the response from dispatch. She was not prepared for the shock she saw in his eyes or the alarm in his voice.

Max's expression darkened. "I know this creep. He's changed some facial features but those eyes, I would know anywhere. His name is *not* Isaac."

His revelation was unsettling, but Kate needed to know more. "What?" She searched his eyes. "How do you know him?"

"No matter. This guy is deadly."

Will interjected. "What's his name?"

"Walter Kidwell." Max rubbed the back of his neck. "How long has your mom been in there with him?"

Kate took a deep breath. "Based on Rachel's call and other factors, I'd say around five hours." The distressed look in her dad's eyes scared her.

"Hell, we may already be too late." She watched his face change; she assumed it was because he saw the alarm in her eyes. "What do you know about the accomplice?"

"Not much. Her license is from Texas." She raised her eyebrows. "Dad, we don't have much time." After she said it, she knew it was the wrong thing to say, especially to her father.

He kicked some gravel beneath his shoes. "You think I don't know that?"

"I agree with Kate. We've already lost almost five minutes," said Will.

She thought about the fifteen minutes that Will speculated they had. If there were only about fifteen minutes left, then Walter and Carla would need to escape before the bomb went off. It was the only thing that made sense. "We need to guard the exits and enter the trailer within the next five minutes."

Max said, "I like the plan so far."

"We could use another person," said Kate.

"I'll ask Jake." Will shrugged, his eyes scanning toward the road. "And maybe our backup will be here soon."

"Don't count on it."

"We're here. Count on that." Max continued. "We need a one-minute playbook to decide how we tackle this rescue." He rubbed the back of his neck. "Any ideas?"

Kate was used to coming up with instant ideas as she faced difficult decisions every day, never knowing if an encounter with a possible suspect might prove deadly. The only problem was that this time, her mom's life was at stake. She prayed her fear wouldn't muddle her brain. Within one minute, they had a plan. If it worked, her mom and Rachel would be rescued. If the odds were with them, they might even catch Isaac and Carla in the bargain. They each had their part. The decision to have Jake participate was dropped. He had become an emotional wreck, while being able to do nothing but stand by and worry, and his involvement would only add to the risk they would be taking.

Kate took her place twenty feet from the front door, hiding behind a huge oak tree, while her dad stationed himself ten feet in front of her next to a holly bush. Will was around the other side of the trailer. It had started raining again, adding to her feeling of trepidation. In minutes, she would either have her mom back or lose her forever.

Max signaled with his left hand that he was going in. Kate was to wait thirty seconds and then follow. Twenty seconds into the count, her body stiffened. Even though it was dark, and a drizzling fog had set in, she saw the large rock hit the back of her dad's head and his body drop. Before she could pull out her gun, a dark figure dragged her father's body across the gravel yard and into the forest underbrush. Panic riddled her body, rendering her motionless, even as her mind reacted in a frenzy. The blood pounding against her head felt like the ticking time bomb urging her forward. Tick Tock, Tick Tock. Only a few minutes left. Tick Tock. Tick Tock. Dad? He needed help. She called Will. No answer. Tick Tock. Where the hell was Will? She shivered. Was it the cold, damp drizzle, or the feeling that she was in this alone, or the wicked ticking in her head that caused this chill all over her body?

Kate pulled her hood over her head as if that would protect her from what lay ahead. It did do one thing: it calmed her. It reminded her of how her first day in the police academy had caused her so much stress, but then on graduation day she had a sense of supreme peace. The kind of peace that comes from purpose and heart being in alignment. The ticking of the clock in her mind was no less urgent, but instead filtered by her determination and that undeniable feeling of hope. She'd get her mom out. Her sureness sent adrenaline to unlock the paralyzing forces — that enemy within — that had held her body captive.

She'd follow their plan even if she had to do it alone. The whirling sound of a police siren blaring in the distance answered that one question she had fretted about all night: when will they get here? Too little, too late. Her body tingled and her heart fluttered. She looked around one last time for any unknown dangers before she crouched down. Her gun was steady in her hand as her thoughts were in full police rescue mode. She raced forward, reaching within a few feet from the trailer, when a loud explosion blasted her body through the dark misty air.

CHAPTER 73

THE BLACK RAINCOAT

Glass, smoke, and debris torpedoed her back as Lainey dragged Max away from the burning trailer and across the gravel and overgrown grass. Sweat poured down her back from the burning heat and from the heavily weighted black raincoat that she had grabbed out of the old trailer to disguise her presence in the night. A fear of a second explosion forced her to move quickly, despite Max's heavy weight and her own weakening muscles. His face was dreadfully pale as she maneuvered him behind a big oak tree. Coughing filled the air as she fought back the smoke trying to invade her lungs. She checked Max's wrist and found a weak pulse. What to do? What to do? She looked over at Kate, who lay motionless not far from the burning trailer. She checked his pulse again. Stronger. If Max could talk, he would send her to Kate.

Lainey raced over to her daughter after the second explosion sent her to the ground. Panicked deer darted through the space beside her as the eerily human sound of a fawn cried in the distance. More debris filled the air, but it didn't stop her from reaching Kate. She felt her heart racing as she bent over her. Her breathing was shallow but that was a good sign. Lainey gently slapped her face once, twice, three times before her daughter opened her mouth and put her hand to her face.

Kate's eyes grew wide and then teared up. "Mom!" She trembled as she moved forward to hug her mother. "I thought I'd never see you again."

Lainey pulled her closer and hugged her. Her own body trembled in her daughter's embrace. "Me too." She wiped her own tears and met Kate's eyes. "I couldn't live with that."

"Did they hurt you?" Kate asked.

"No, they were just bullies."

"Mom," Kate said in a warning tone. "Don't protect me."

"Mental cruelty kinds of stuff," Lainey allowed. She looked down. The last thing Isaac had done was kiss her. It felt like the way a water hydrant must feel when a dog pees on it: humiliated and disgusted. Luckily for the water hydrant, it doesn't have feelings. She looked back up at Kate. "I survived."

"Mom, something's happened to Dad."

"I know, but he'll be okay." She pulled Kate's hair out of her eyes.

"But how could you?"

Lainey watched her daughter stare at the black raincoat she was wearing as awareness filtered into Kate's eyes.

"Mom, you're the one that hit Dad with that huge rock."

Lainey swallowed guiltily. "I had no choice."

"Didn't you realize it was Dad?"

"I knew. That's exactly why I had to throw the biggest rock I could find." There was no telling when the bomb would explode but she had known there wasn't much time left. Isaac had whispered *Tick Tock* in her ear after he gave her that disgusting kiss. Her heart ached as she remembered that difficult moment when the rock left her hand and Max collapsed to the ground.

Kate tilted her head as her eyes widened. "That doesn't make sense."

"The bomb was about to go off."

"Why didn't you just yell for him to stop?"

"I couldn't be sure Isaac wasn't still in the area." Lainey

knew that if Isaac heard Max's name, he'd be back to finish the job. Her one regret was her bad aim. She never intended to hit him, just get his attention before he got to the trailer.

"Where's Dad?"

She pointed to the dark foggy area about ten yards away. "Over there."

"Are you sure he's okay?"

"I wouldn't be here if he wasn't." She pressed her lips together as she remembered his shallow breathing. Perhaps she should have stayed there a little bit longer.

"Mom, where's Rachel?"

"She was behind me when I ran out." Her heartbeat quickened. "I've got to go find her now that I know you're okay."

"Be careful, Mom. I'll check on Dad." She paused. "Then I need to go after Isaac and Carla."

"Are you okay to do that?" Lainey said.

"Mom, I just got rustled." Kate brushed off soot and debris before she stood up. "Do you have any idea where they went?"

"No, but they mentioned having motorcycles hidden nearby."

"That was a smart move on their part. Will and I were watching their cars, so they're long gone."

"Isaac bragged about how he'd make fools of you."

"Isaac's real name is Walter. He'll be the fool when we catch up to him." Kate hugged her mom. "See you in a few." Before she left, she turned back and said, "I love you. Stay safe," and then she was gone.

Kate's quick departure left Lainey's, *I love you*, floating in the misty air, each sound landing on a drop of mist for only the night's animals and birds to hear. The firemen's water hose came close to her as they flooded the trailer with water. A police officer yelled out to seal the scene as other cops moved to surround the trailer rubble with yellow tape.

Lainey's head throbbed as if the weight of what she had been through etched itself on her mind. Her legs felt the weight of the moment, slowing her down, but her determination pulled her through as she stood up. She was relieved the steroids were keeping her moving. She hoped Rachel was just hiding somewhere, but she couldn't be sure. Had Isaac and Carla left right away? She suspected Carla was long gone since money was her only motive. But Isaac, where was he? Her breath quickened. The night air suddenly seemed ominous as a wind blast sent chills down her spine. What if Rachel was with him now?

CHAPTER 74

THE MEN IN HER LIFE

Her mom had said *over there*, but with the lingering smoke from the burning trailer dispensing itself in the already dark fog, Kate found herself a bit disoriented as she searched for her dad in the unfamiliar brush. She remembered him being dragged to the right of the trailer, but the right of the trailer had no meaning now as most of it lay in rubble. The yellow porch light that had lit the way smoldered beneath the trailer's black debris.

It was the moan that she heard rising above the crackling sounds of the burning trailer that finally led her to her dad. Max's head rested against the bottom of a tall oak tree. His eyes were closed, but he was moving his legs as if to prop himself higher against the tree.

He opened his eyes when she knelt next to him.

"What happened?" he asked, rubbing the back of his head.

"Let me take a look." She noticed a large bump and touched it lightly.

"Ouch!"

"Sorry, Dad. You have Mom to blame for this."

Max's eyes brightened. "She's alive?"

"Yeah, Dad." She hugged him tightly for a moment, then let go. "Are you okay?"

"Where is she?"

"Looking for Rachel." She stared back at him. "You didn't answer my question."

He winced. "Yes, except for the throbbing on the back of my head."

"Dad, I need to find Will."

"I want to find your mom." Max shook his head and sat up but leaned back again in apparent pain. "She needs me."

He was in no condition to even move, much less chase after her mom. "I got this." She took off her windbreaker and put it over her dad's shoulders. "I'll find Mom. You may have a concussion." She kissed him on his cheek. "I'll send the paramedics over." She gently held both his shoulders. "Just stay put."

Satisfied that her dad would have help soon, she resumed her search for Will. She'd worry about her mom once she found him. Her mom had a way of taking care of herself. The fire department and paramedics had arrived along with the backup, so she sent the first paramedic she saw over to her dad.

Kate finally found Will sitting on the back of an ambulance, a blood-stained bandage wrapped around his forehead and ash covering half his body. The sight alarmed Kate, but the big smile he gave her as she approached put her mind at ease. If Will could smile, he would be okay. The weird part was how that smile made her heart skip a beat. She told herself that it was just happiness that they had both survived the blast. Nothing more.

"Boy, am I glad to see you. I thought you were a goner," Will said.

"You look like you took a hit."

"Just some flying debris," he said, waving it off, then frowned. "I'm so sorry Kate, but I haven't seen any sign of your mom or Rachel." He looked down and then back up. "They're looking through the explosion area now."

She could see the pain in Will's eyes, and it warmed her heart that he cared. "I found my mom." She felt herself exhale. "She's fine."

"Where is she?"

"She went to look for Rachel." She watched Will's downcast eyes as he looked back over at the smoldering ashes. "Mom said she got out." She relished the relief she saw in his face. "We're just not sure where she went."

"And your dad?"

"Fine." She knew he didn't know her dad had gotten hurt, and she didn't have time to talk about him. "We need to help find Rachel and go after Walter and Carla." She frowned. "I'll put out an APB. Walter and Carla escaped on motorcycles."

"I'm going with you."

After finding a motorcycle track leading to Route 32 east, they headed east. Oddly, they only found one set of motorcycle tracks. Kate could only guess that the suspects had separated, but there was no evidence as to where the second motorcycle had gone. She wasn't sure if she was following Carla or Walter, but one was better than none.

Kate kept her eyes on the road but glanced over at Will, who was checking his phone. "Any news?"

"Nothing to help us."

"How's your head?"

"It looks worse than it is."

Kate noticed that the gas level on their police cruiser was close to empty. Within five minutes, she spotted a small convenience store with one gas pump outside and was relieved that it was still open, since, according to her phone, it was nearing one in the morning.

Will hopped out and pumped the gas while Kate called to check on her dad. He sounded better, but he hadn't found her mom or Rachel. She put her phone down when she caught sight of something at the back of the store parking lot: a motorcycle partially splattered with mud above the tires. Coincidence? Maybe. She slipped out of the car and let Will in on what she suspected. With the caution only good detectives would use, they pulled out their guns and slowly opened the delivery door of the store.

CHAPTER 75

FOR THE SAKE OF A CHILD

The trailer park had come alive in the fifteen minutes since the rescue vehicles had arrived, as the few sleepy residents of the small, mostly deserted, trailer park realized the ruckus happening within their isolated community. Four residents in pajamas and robes had arranged their lawn chairs around the burning trailer. The firemen's truck and huge hose blasting water through the air, and the numerous policemen invading their quiet neighborhood provided rare entertainment for this impromptu gathering. Only the screeching cry of a baby provided any clue that there was more going on here than met the eye.

The farther Lainey moved from the burning trailer the more noticeable became the sounds of chirping crickets and small animals roaming the path with her. An owl screeched its hoot from time to time. Fatigue had settled in her left leg, and it dragged a bit, but her determination to find Rachel kept her moving. She had missed her night's dose of steroids, but, until she knew what happened to Rachel, she'd keep pushing herself. In hindsight, she probably should have requested help in her search, but she had acted impulsively, like she always did when she felt alarmed about something . . . someone.

Her feet ached from the cold dampness of the fallen leaves that covered her canvas shoes with each step. Each splash and splat caused an agonizing reminder that this terrible ordeal was not over. The flashlight that she had grabbed from Jake grew dim. He had wanted to help search, but she convinced him to stay where he was in case Rachel showed up.

The dimmer the flashlight got, the more she depended on her hearing. Every rustle in the night stirred her with apprehension that it was Carla, or Walter, or with anticipation that she was closer to Rachel. The random owl hoots sent her eyes upward each time, but she never did catch sight of that nosy night owl always wanting to know *who* was about. It probably asked that same question to Rachel, and for some unknown reason, that gave her comfort.

Before Lainey realized it, she found herself walking

on gravel that led out of the trailer park and into an open field. The fog and smoke were no longer a barrier to her search as both appeared to have evaporated or ascended to higher skies. It was then that she saw the yellow Harley flat on its side. Her chest tightened but she fought back the feeling and exhaled. Carla or Walter was still in the area, but why?

She turned her eyes around as awareness struck her that maybe she was being watched. The sight of the motorcycle had unnerved her, but only momentarily. She cautiously walked over to it, where she discovered bloodstains splattered among some of the small gravel bits. Upon further investigation, she noticed the separation of gravel indicating that, most likely, a body had been dragged along this path. Her heart sank.

She followed the blood trail and it led her back into the forest. The trees shielded the dim light that had helped her earlier and her flashlight was of no use as the trail of bloodstains seemed to disappear. It was the call-out from the bushes that finally gave her some clarity as to where she needed to be.

The shaky voice repeated itself. "Over here."

Lainey spun around but wasn't sure where the voice came from. Her body froze. What if this was an ambush? It had sounded like a woman's voice. She thought it sounded like Rachel, but was it? Could her mind fool her into a dangerous situation? She hesitated and grabbed a long, thick tree branch that had fallen on the ground.

"Over here, over here," the frantic voice demanded.

Lainey moved in the direction of the voice and soon, her steps came to a halt. Her relief was immediately tempered by the scene before her. With the help of the moon's incandescence, Lainey's mouth went dry and her pulse quickened as she saw Rachel hovering over Carla's pale body. The sight of Rachel's bloody hand as she pressed it against Carla's chest stirred her. She took off her raincoat and placed it under Rachel's hand to help control the bleeding before she took Rachel's hand away and put her own pressure on Carla's chest. She was still breathing, but it was very shallow and weak. "I'll take over," Lainey said, gently.

Their eyes met and Rachel broke down into tears, but just as quickly, she wiped her eyes as if there was more for her to do. Rachel held Carla's hands and prayed. She whispered words into Carla's ear before placing her mother's cross into Carla's hands. From the corners of Carla's eyes, tears fell as she grasped the cross tightly. The flashing of the color red and the accompanying siren's howl came closer as Rachel spoke. "I called nine-one-one."

Lainey continued to press down on Carla's chest,

hoping against hope to stop the bleeding. "What happened here?" She hoped her words weren't accusatory, but she couldn't help but worry that Rachel had something to do with this. She didn't want Rachel to have to deal with the burden of shooting someone. She was sure it must have been in self-defense.

Rachel trembled as she answered, "Isaac shot her and . . ."

They both looked down at Carla as she coughed again, and blood-stained phlegm expelled from her mouth. Rachel tried to reassure her that she would be okay, but Lainey knew differently. There was too much blood and time was running out. If she didn't ask now, it would be too late. "Why did you loosen our ropes before you left with Isaac?" Lainey used his alter-ego because she wasn't sure if Carla knew his name was really Walter.

Carla's eyes flickered open and just as quickly closed. Her breathing became labored as she tried to push her body forward. She gasped for breath as her weak words struggled to make their way into the air. "I did it for Bobby."

Lainey watched as the cross fell from Carla's hand and her body went still. The woman she had wanted to hate tapped at her heart, especially after hearing her last words.

CHAPTER 76

THE PERILS OF FRIENDSHIP

Lainey and Rachel stood solemnly as Carla's body was lifted onto a gurney and taken away. It was a tragic end, Lainey thought, but one Carla had orchestrated for herself when she made the fateful decision to follow Walter along his evil path.

Now that they were alone again, Lainey wanted to know more details. She and Rachel found a huge log that stretched across the forest bed, but crawling ants sent them to their feet as soon as they sat down. The darkness hid the smallest of creatures, but the small light from the moon was enough to lead the way to a nearby picnic table.

Rachel picked up a fallen leaf that she found on the top

of the table and twirled it lazily between her fingers. "I never want to go through anything like this again."

"I shouldn't have involved you in it."

Rachel sighed and added a weak smile. "You do lead me astray at times."

"I certainly never expected to be a target of this maniac." She grabbed Rachel's hand as the leaf dropped and they collapsed into a long hug. They found relief from the weight of their ordeal in the comfort of one another's arms. After several moments, Lainey moved away and asked her friend, "What happened here?" She stared at her intently, adding, "I thought you were running *from* Carla, not *towards* her?"

"It was dark. I didn't know where I was," Rachel hesitated a moment before continuing. "I heard arguing and hid behind a bush. That's when I saw Isaac and Carla sitting on their motorcycles." She winced and her head fell into her hands. "I don't want to talk about this."

"Please," Lainey pleaded gently, resting a comforting hand on Rachel's arm.

"Isaac was yelling at her and said he wouldn't pay her." She hesitated again as her face flushed. "She told him he'd live to regret that." Tears welled in her eyes before she continued, "He yelled something really foul and then, oh Lainey, he shot her."

Lainey took her hand. "That must have been awful."

"I waited until he left." Her eyes seemed to go blank. She murmured, ". . . blood all over her chest . . ." Rachel covered her eyes for a moment, then turned to stare over at Lainey. "She was still alive, so I dragged her near the tree in case he came back."

"I don't think it's likely. I'm sure he thought she was dead."

"Well, I didn't know that," Rachel stammered. "I told her she'd be okay and prayed."

"You said you called nine-one-one."

"Yes, I found her phone in her pants pocket and called them." She gazed up into the dark sky, then slowly back down towards Lainey. "For a few moments, we prayed together."

"If I know you, you tried to bring her to Jesus."

"To me, that was more important than the call."

Lainey was uncertain about what to say so she remained silent. The sound of familiar voices turned both their heads.

The sight of Max quickened Lainey's heartbeat and, as he approached, she stood up and collapsed into his arms. His hold tightened around her, almost taking her breath away. On an ordinary day, she would have broken away and scolded him for squeezing too hard, but today, her depth of need surrendered to his strong embrace.

Rachel appeared frozen to the table bench, crying as Jake rushed to sit down next to her and pulled her close. She clutched his hand, and he folded his other hand over hers. He whispered something into her ear that seemed to comfort her. A night owl hooted as Jake and Rachel nestled in silence.

As much as Lainey wanted to stay comforted by Max, her mind grew restless. Where was Kate? Had she been able to apprehend Walter? He wouldn't be easy to catch, and his unpredictable psychotic behavior made him dangerous even for the savviest detective. Kate was smart but Lainey feared her daughter lacked experience with a criminal like Walter.

She looked into Max's eyes and melded his with hers. The realization that they were both on the same page stirred her. "Let's find Kate." She wouldn't worry about Rachel now that she knew she was being cared for. The worst was over for her. She, however, had one more obstacle before things got back to normal: Walter.

Max asked, "Are you okay to do that?"

"You should talk," Lainey shot back.

Max threw his hands up. "Let's go."

Lainey asked, "Any ideas?"

He lifted out his phone. "Family tracker."

She nodded.

He looked down at his phone. "She's about thirty miles from here."

They spent a minute deciding how they would get there, and the decision was made to take Jake's car and he could ride with Rachel in her car.

Lainey rolled down the window and inhaled the refreshing night air. Leaving the trailer park sitting up in the seat, and not stuffed in a bag like the way she arrived, was a feeling she never wanted to forget.

CHAPTER 77

NO TIME FOR MISCHIEF

Inside the small back room of the convenience store, Kate hid behind a cardboard storage bin while Will crouched behind a large crate. The room smelled of cigar smoke and musky ammonia. Dust covered many of the boxed grocery items stacked against the walls. Kate was taken aback by the cartons of candy that showed the disgusting evidence of mice having gnawed their way through.

She checked for a camera that might reveal her presence in the back room but saw none. Perhaps there was one in the store front, but by then it wouldn't matter.

The sound of two men arguing caught her attention as she waited and assessed the situation. Not ever having heard Walter speak, Kate wasn't sure if he was one of the angry voices. But she couldn't assume he wasn't. She took a few steps forward while Will stayed in position. The closer Kate got to the front of the store, the clearer the voices became.

She could hear the frustrated voice of the store clerk repeating that he would not lower a price, while the customer complained of the high price for a pack of cigarettes. Obviously, the customer was surprised by the price, so that told Kate it was most likely a visitor and not a local. The arguing continued as she thought about her next move. If it was Walter, there was a chance he had a weapon, and she didn't want anyone in the store to get hurt. But all logic went out the window when she heard a woman scream. Wasting no time, she rushed in while Will moved forward and waited.

Before Kate, a small middle-aged woman in high heels clutched at a tall well-dressed man. Her face twisted as her body trembled. "Kill him!"

Kate looked to see who the woman needed protection from and saw the clerk lift a small rat.

"No need to kill the critter," he said, tossing the rat out the front door, then returning to the cash register. "So do you want the cigarettes or not?"

The man huffed as he paid for the cigarettes, while his female companion tugged at his suit pants to hurry him.

Kate quickly concealed her gun and pretended to look at the refrigerated drinks. In all the ruckus, they hadn't notice her come from the side. Will showed up through the front door and proceeded to walk down the snack aisle.

Kate pointed at the couple leaving the store and gave Will the heads-up to question them. There was no one else in the store, so she went over to the clerk and identified herself. She showed him a picture of Walter and Carla, but he had no recollection of them ever coming to his store. Her instincts told her he was probably telling the truth, so she thanked him. She really wanted to grab a bag of chips, but something about that store made her second-guess her decision.

Will was leaning against their car when Kate asked him if he learned anything from the couple. He responded in the negative.

She glanced around and noticed the empty back lot. "Did they leave on that cycle?"

"Yep."

Something didn't seem right about this scenario. Her mind went back inside the store to when she first observed the couple. What was it about them that didn't make sense? The disconnect came to her when she remembered their attire. It was the woman's high heels and the man's suit that disturbed her. "Did you notice anything unusual about them?"

"What are you hinting at?" Will asked.

"How did they interact with that motorcycle?"

Will scratched his head. "That's funny you asked." He leaned against the car. "They argued about who should drive it. I thought that it must be a new motorcycle."

"Not a new motorcycle; just not theirs." As Kate planted the seed of clarity, she saw it dawn on Will's face in one major *Aha* moment. "It's Walter's or Carla's," she finished.

"Crap, we just missed him!" Will exclaimed.

"Or Carla."

"Definitely not Carla."

"How do you know?" Kate asked, skeptically.

Will held up his phone. "Carla's dead."

In some ways, the news didn't surprise her, especially after Will mentioned that she was shot by Walter. Criminals often ate their own when it served their best interests. Their cohorts were so often robots to directions that they didn't think for themselves. She was glad they'd only have to chase after Walter. "Walter must be in that couple's car. He either paid them off or forced them to give it up."

Will said, "The fact they didn't call police tells me it was a payoff."

"Let's go back in and see if they used a charge card."

"It doesn't seem likely they'd use credit if they just got cash," Will said.

"They might be worried it's stolen or counterfeit."

"Good point."

It didn't take long for the store clerk to share the credit slip with them once Kate showed him her badge. It wasn't much, but every bit of information would lead them closer to Walter. They were about to leave when she thought of another question. "Did any other customers come into your store within the last half hour?"

The man pulled on his small curly goatee before he spoke. "Uh, there was one man who bought a candy bar and a bag of peanuts."

Will asked, "What can you tell us about him?"

"Not much; paid cash and left." He shrugged. "He wasn't much for small talk."

"We were looking more for a description," Kate said.

"I wanna say he was about fifty. Tall, with short wavy black hair. That's all I can remember."

"Thank you for your time." Kate was disappointed that it seemed to be a dead end. Walter was tall but the rest of the description didn't fit. It was possible that he could be in a disguise. Walter had enough time, particularly if it was all part of his devious plan, but without knowing how he changed his appearance, it was of no use to her now.

They were almost to the front door when the storekeeper called out, "Oh he had a smoky odor like maybe he's a fireman."

Kate felt a flutter in her belly and turned around. "No sir, a bomber." The flutter became a lightness in her chest as she smiled at Will and they both walked out the door.

CHAPTER 78

TRACKING THE STORM

Lainey stared down at the red dot on the tracker as Max sped along Route 32. Kate had remained stationary for the last fifteen minutes. What the hell was going on? She bit her lip as her mind created disaster scenarios. Why wasn't there any air in this car? She rolled the window all the way down. The wind howled past the opened car window but shared none of its powerful breeze. She felt like sticking her head out, but the tree branches that cascaded over the dark road held her back. Her mouth went dry. She needed 'nature's refreshment,' as Rachel called it. *There has to be some in here.* She looked in the pouch on the car door to find a bottle of spring water. In quick gulps, she devoured the full sixteen ounces. She knew it did the trick as she felt herself grow calmer. Why had she let herself go into the frantic zone? She had Walter to blame for all her turmoil.

The car roared along as Max maneuvered it down the curving road and through the rolling hillsides. Lainey fought back the motion sickness that had plagued her since childhood by gulping down another small bottle of water that had slid out from under her passenger's seat.

"Are you okay over there?" Max asked.

"Why do you ask?"

"You're hyperventilating." He paused. "And it's a bit distracting."

"Sorry."

Max rubbed Lainey's shoulder. "Hang in there."

Always calm Max, she thought as she tried to believe everything would work out. What if Kate was stationary because she was lying dead? Lainey shuddered and squashed that thought, but not before tears welled up in her eyes. She had to stop thinking like Kate's mom and get herself thinking rationally. Her next glance to the tracker allowed her to focus her attention away from herself. "Max, she's on the move again." Her heartbeat quickened and a thought came to her that surprised her in its simplicity. "Why don't we just call her?"

Max turned to glance over at her. "Hon, don't you

think I thought of that?" He took his right hand off the wheel and wiped his forehead. "We can't be sure what's going on."

Awareness engulfed her. "We might bring attention to her or distract her."

"Exactly." The car screeched as Max barely missed hitting a deer. "Is she still on thirty-two?"

"Watch the road, dear." Lainey tried to calm her racing heartbeat as she focused on the tracker. "Yes."

For about an hour, she kept Max updated as they followed Kate's signal past Annapolis until they crossed the Chesapeake Bay Bridge.

"You just went through the toll booth without paying," Lainey said.

"We have EZPass."

"Jake doesn't."

Max looked at the windshield and noticed the missing tag. He smacked the steering wheel. "Sorry Jake."

Lainey noticed Max had started speeding again but now that they were off the curvy dark roads, she was hopeful they'd make up for lost time. She was irritated that fatigue had invaded her body. She looked at the time on her iPhone to see that it was 2:15 A.M. Her tired eyes rested on the roaming target. Time was passing too slowly. She feared they'd never catch up with Kate until it was too late.

She poked at Max's arm. "We need to speed up."

"Not good timing. We're stopping." He pulled into a Royal Farms parking lot and headed inside the store.

Lainey had wanted to protest but he didn't give her any time for that. It was just as well since her bladder was doing its own beckoning. Two water bottles and no bathroom break under Walter's watchful eye had her running to the ladies' room as fast as her leg would allow. When she came out of the bathroom, Max was in the cashier's line with a box of pain meds in his hand. It was her first reminder that he still coped with the effects of the rock she had thrown at him.

When Max came out, she had already slipped into the driver's seat. She handed him the phone. He didn't resist as he slid into the passenger's side and buckled his seatbelt.

"Thanks, hon."

Lainey turned the key and pulled into the gas station. She got out and filled the gas tank, then slid back into the driver's seat. "Where's Kate now?"

"Somewhere near Bridgeville, Delaware."

Traffic was extremely light as Lainey pulled out onto Route 50 East. She looked over at Max, who had closed his eyes. "Why don't you rest? I can put the phone in the cup holder."

"You know I can't sleep until I see Kate. Besides, something else is bothering me."

"What is it?"

". . . Did he touch you?"

Lainey tried to remain expressionless as she kept her eyes focused on the road. He'd know if she was holding back. If he even suspected Walter had touched her, he'd go ballistic. The thought of that kiss soured her mouth. She kept her eyes from meeting his. "Carla tied me up and pushed me around, but I survived." She held her breath as tightly as she held the steering wheel and waited for Max's response.

"Lainey, did he . . ."

She suddenly whipped the car to the right, barely missing the poultry truck in front of them carrying crates of chickens, ostensibly on their way to slaughter. The truck's sudden stop caused a barrage of squawking and flying feathers. *That trucker should have gone through the yellow light*, thought Lainey. *Those poor chickens.* She raced past the truck just as the light turned red. It was just enough commotion to interrupt Max. She exhaled, "That was a close call."

"And you talk about *my* driving," Max commented.

Lainey's mind calmed. Crisis was momentarily averted as the near accident seemed to have derailed Max's train of thought. It didn't occur to her that Walter might just let the cat out of the bag before a morning rooster crowed.

CHAPTER 79

BREADCRUMBS

Even in hot pursuit of Walter, Kate couldn't help but notice nature's nighttime beauty. Ever since Will turned onto Route 404 near Denton, the windshield became a panoramic view of the countryside featuring the constellations illuminating the sky and the majesty of rural Maryland. Their glow cast beautiful shadows over the corn stalks in the fields, on the apple orchards, and on the vast variety of diversified vegetation that textured the farmland. However, it was the huge, elongated irrigation sprinklers with their towering wheels that created the eerie sensation of a giant black creature in wait for its prey, and the sudden increase of nocturnal insects that splattered their tiny body parts against the unyielding windshield as they sped along, that eventually forced Kate out of her musings.

The knowledge that they were only about fifteen minutes behind Walter exhilarated Kate's mental game. Luck had been on their side when they stumbled on Walter's interaction with the couple at the convenience store and the subsequent information that had put them on his trail. She had no doubt their apprehension of Walter was on the horizon and then this horrible ordeal would be over. Her pulse raced as she thought of him within her grasp.

Kate glanced over at Will, who seemed lost in thoughts of his own even as his hands held steady to the wheel and his eyes were sharp on the road. There was an oddness in his quiet that disturbed her. "Are you alright?"

"This almost seems too easy," said Will.

"Too easy?"

"Like we've been given breadcrumbs."

She stretched her arms in front of her. "It's good detective work."

"I'd like to think that too, but he apparently stalked your mom, and we were never the wiser."

Kate deliberated on his words. "The motorcycle left outside the store was for our benefit?"

"Or an extremely stupid move on his part."

"It doesn't make sense." Her mind raced for answers,

but she found none that were reasonable. What would be the purpose of such a strategy? To kill two cops? What did that gain him?

"We don't even know why your mom was targeted," Will said. "Without understanding Walter's motivation, we're running blind."

"Money and revenge top the list . . ." Kate contemplated, crossing her arms over her chest. "My family doesn't have a lot of money."

"Maybe your mom left bad sub plans," Will said, grinning, and then quickly cleared his throat. "I'm sorry, too soon?"

If her mom wasn't in imminent danger, that comment may have been funny, especially with Will's goofy grin, but not now. "I need the cop in you, not the comedian," Kate admonished.

"Alright. One piece of information is that your father recognized him," Will said, seriously.

"Hmm, you're right. Dad minced no words about this creep."

Will rubbed his forehead. "They have a history, and it didn't sound good."

Kate noticed a car on the side of the dark road up ahead. "Pull over!"

Will swerved to the right and parked a short distance

behind the blue sedan as he turned off the car's headlights. In the darkness, Kate moved slowly, gun ready, as she approached the car fitting the description given by the couple and verified by the DMV.

Kate began to think Will was right about this being too easy. Why in the world would Walter leave the car where anyone could find it? She put her gun into her shoulder holster and focused her flashlight on the interior. The keys dangling in the ignition caught her eye. *He's done with this car . . . or could the dangling keys be meant for a fast getaway? Is he nearby watching us?*

Her body shivered when she saw the card glistening on the passenger's seat as her flashlight crossed over it. A hologram. Walter's calling card and the reason the Sergeant labeled him the 3D Killer. Blotches of red stains covered the card but didn't hide the images of a knotted rope, a small black bottle with a skull's face, a gun, and a Smith and Wesson knife. *All the weapons he had used on his victims*, she thought. *Wait. He never used any kind of knife . . .* Her mouth went dry. A murder yet to be?

With uncertainty, she opened the door and lifted the card, and the movement caused a 3D message imprinted within the red blotches to shine through with silvery evil. The hairs on her arms stood up with rapid alarm as her blood raced through her body. Three simple words were illuminated in 3D splendor: *You are next!* The words were so harmless by themselves, but the redness surrounding them delivered their real intent. The exclamation point sounded in Kate's head like the pounding of a heavy metal rod against a huge brass tam-tam gong. She had gotten the message loud and clear.

Unease gripped her as she wondered why Will wasn't by her side. She remembered that he'd stepped out of the car right after she did. She heard the rustling of leaves and a dog barking in the distance, then more crackling of leaves. It must be Will. She couldn't wait to tell him of her discovery and warn him that Walter might suspect he'd been followed. As she clutched the cryptic card, she was cautioned by a sick feeling in her stomach. It was too late, though, to prevent the blow to her head, and as she began to fall, so did the prophetic card.

CHAPTER 80

MISCHIEF ON THE RUN

Kate collapsed on the car's hood as her body reeled from the staggering blow to her head. She recoiled in agony as her survival instinct told her to run and her training urged her to fight, but those choices became moot as she collapsed backwards. The forceful thrust of a gloved hand came from behind and smashed her lips into her teeth. She steeled against the pain of her now bleeding mouth and dug her incisors into the invading fingers, but the gloves her attacker wore prevented the harm she intended. The reaction was immediate and chilling.

As a gun pressed into her ribs, Walter's words came. "Do that again and we'll end this right now."

Kate knew all along that Walter was responsible for

this foul play, and his sour breath washing over her only served to intensify his evilness. But was there someone else she needed to fear? His use of the word we concerned her. Was there a new threat on the scene or an accomplice they had missed? Was this unknown person responsible for Will's disappearance? She could only hope that Will escaped harm.

Before she could stop him, he blindfolded her and strapped her into the back seat of his car, then bound her hands. He said nothing and then she felt his absence in the car. *Where did he go?* She heard and felt a thump from the rear of the car. Her heartbeat quickened.

Walter's voice cackled. "We're ready to go, my dear."

Kate sensed that they had driven about a half-hour before the car came to a stop. She heard the driver's side door open and moments later she heard the door of the trunk open. The trunk was then shut and five minutes later, the car was set back into motion. *What had Walter been up to?* she wondered.

After a short time, the car stopped and Walter opened Kate's door. She caught a quick glance of Walter's all-black attire and his dark, piercing eyes as he adjusted his hold on her to get a better grip before he dragged her away from the car and into a nearby cornfield. He didn't seem bothered that her blindfold had fallen to her neck, and she concealed the fact that her hands weren't restrained very well either and had come free. She arched her back to defend herself from the rocks, sticks, and corn stalks that surely scraped and bruised her skin as Walter callously hauled her against the coarse earth. She cringed as chirping crickets manically jumped across her face, and her hands flailed frantically to stop their assault.

What was she doing going along with this lunacy? It was time to stop being a willing victim of Walter's madness and turn the tables. But were the odds in her favor? If she put up no resistance, her life would be in Walter's hands, and she knew what he would do with it.

With a sudden jerk, Kate kicked and hurled her body up and down to force Walter to lose his grip, but he yanked so hard at her hair that she thought he'd end up with more hair in his hand than on her head. Her scalp blazed fire at the roots of her hair and, as she let her body go limp, she screamed silently in agony.

Walter stopped and looked down at her. His eyes gleamed. "I was trying to be so gentle and then you had to do something stupid." He laughed as if it was the funniest thing he had ever said before he became silent. He glanced around into the dark field. His tone sober. "If you want to be self-destructive, try that again."

As ominous as his words sounded, they provided

critical information. His earlier words had been a bluff and he had no intention of killing her *yet*. That gave her the precious gift of time. He had won this battle, but victory was up for grabs. Her heart lightened. She'd wear the badge of underdog with honor. Like the brave military dogs that face danger with reckless abandonment, that would be her from this time forward. However, she did need a plan. Fortunately, an idea came to her as she bumped along the ground and realized her phone was still in her back pocket. Walter had taken her gun, but not her phone. She gently pulled it from her back pocket and let it slip onto the cornfield. If Will was searching for her, she prayed he would find it. If not, her only hope would be that her dad would think to use his phone to track her.

CHAPTER 81

BARNYARD FUN

The darkness prevented Kate from seeing where Walter was taking her, but the smell of cow manure and hay gave her a good idea that she wasn't going to a four-star hotel. With an abrupt halt she felt her body slammed to hay-scattered ground. Walter was all about abuse and a show of power; signs in her mind of a very weak man but a very dangerous one.

Kate heard the squealing of pigs not far from where she lay, and the quiet rustling of footsteps a few inches from her body. She felt Walter's rough hands grab hers and bind them together with rope. "Walter, is this really necessary?" For a moment, she feared for her life as Walter's expression turned to astonishment and then anger. She didn't want him to know it was her dad that supplied his name, or he may snap. "You couldn't hide your identity once you kidnapped my mom. You made it personal."

Walter yanked at the rope and tightened it harshly against her skin. "Shut up!"

A panicked thought encroached Kate's mind. "What did you do with Will?"

His devilish grin was followed by his eerie cackle. "He found his resting spot."

Kate felt a tightness in her chest but said nothing while he bound her feet, her mind registering the imminent danger now that she knew Will's fate. *Or is this just a ploy by Walter to destroy my spirit?* She had to believe Will was alive and, hanging on to that thought, she knew she had to get busy working on a way to escape. She regretted not making a move sooner. Why had she been so compliant? What was it about him that was so intimidating that her cop skills were mitigated?

The sudden illumination of a lantern revealed her surroundings inside of what she now saw was a small barn. There was a horse's bridle hanging on a hook but no sign of stalls. A tall scarecrow hung off a hook on the open barn door, its black, drooping triangular eyes giving it a forlorn quality. Its red lips were attached to the face with black crisscross stitches, adding to its marred appearance. As a child Kate loved scarecrows, but this one creeped her out.

She saw the small brown pigs scurrying about in their pens as flies buzzed around them. Her spirits lifted as she realized the presence of pigs meant that this was not an abandoned barn. If she was lucky, the farmer would be around soon to see what was going on.

Her eyes shifted right and met Walter's crazed ones. Her heartbeat quickened. She stared back at him and saw behind his eyes. Evil held her within its grasp. She turned away to break its grip. She had to escape from him before bound limbs were the least of her worries.

Walter laughed. "We had a moment." He rubbed the back of his neck. "Very unexpected." He stared down at her. "Perhaps your demise is not in my best interest." His voice ballooned into a cackling laugh before he lowered his hand to touch her leg.

Kate's eyes widened and her heart raced but she stayed silent. His implied intent sickened her, and she pulled her knees close to her chest. Her fear was heightened by his reckless disregard for the volume of his laughter. In her heart, she knew what this meant: the farmer wasn't coming. Walter had already seen to that.

CHAPTER 82

REST STOP

If only Liam hadn't had so much to drink at Barney's Bar that it forced him to make this unplanned pitstop. He had stopped at two beers, but the additional sodas pounded at his bladder. Pressure building, he stopped his blue Ford truck in front of a deserted rest area and did his business.

The cool night air refreshed him, so he sat down on the dilapidated seat of a lone picnic table and pulled out a cigarette. He recognized this deserted rest stop. It had become a casualty of progress as fast-food drive-ins sprang up to litter the highway to the beaches. Now, it only served as a lover's lane for the local seniors. And he didn't mean high-schoolers, as he remembered finding his eighty-year-old grandmother in the arms of old farmer Higgins. He winced as he recalled seeing his grandma's bare skin in the back seat of Higgins' yellow 1967 Chevy last year. He could still see the shocked look in his grandmother's eyes when he called her name, however, it hadn't stopped her from sending him away with a twinkle in her eye. Then, the added encouragement from old-man Higgins that he would get her home safely highlighted the humorous role reversal. Liam had known his grandmother for thirty-five years and, as this incident emphasized, she did what she pleased. He smiled to himself at the memory and finished his cigarette.

The soft glow of pre-dawn light filtered through the trees and bushy thickets that surrounded the rest area. He closed his eyes and took a deep breath. He had worked hard to get where he was, despite some obstacles, but he had done it. In two days, he would start his new job. He wished he had time for another cigarette, but his tired eyes from working the late shift warned him to get going.

The early morning temperature dropped, so he grabbed his flannel shirt from the back of his truck and slipped it over his gray t-shirt. A rooster crowed in the distance as he hopped back into his truck. He anticipated being home just in time for his mom's blueberry pancakes. He would have to tell her that he had taken a job seventy-five miles out of town and that he would be taking his daughter with him. His mother had been a rock for them ever since he lost his wife to cancer, but it was time for him and his daughter to strike out on their own.

He sat back in the driver's seat and turned on his headlights. As he started to back out, he heard a soft moan, perhaps that of an injured animal. The second moan told him it belonged to a human. He left the headlights on and jumped out of his truck to head in the direction of the sound. As it turned out, the headlights did not help him find the injured man, but it was nature's dim light that shone upon the man's face hidden amid a thicket. Liam spoke gently. "Are you alright?"

"I think so," came the reply.

Liam helped the man to his feet and walked him over to the picnic table so he could sit down.

"I have to get out of here," the man said.

"What's your name? And what happened to you?"

"I don't have time to chat about it. The name's Will. Do you have a phone?"

CHAPTER 83

FLIRTING WITH DANGER

Kate gazed out the barn window, wishing for a change in the sky to let her know what time it was, but she knew that it must still be a few hours before sunrise. She had cringed at Walter's overtures towards her but the more she thought about it, the more she realized it may be her only way to survive. She needed him to believe that she had come around to his way of thinking, that they could mean something to one another — just enough encouragement to distract him; to get him off his game. Then she would turn the tables and escape this diabolical depravity.

Walter moved closer to Kate. "I bet your boyfriend is wondering where you're at."

"My boyfriends aren't in charge of me."

"Boyfriends, heh?" He moved closer. "That makes you a player."

"I don't play with guys who plan to kill me."

"I can change my plans for a woman like you."

Her skin crawled, but she forced coolness upon her face. "If only I could believe you."

"It's you I need to believe," Walter said before he narrowed his eyes. "And I don't."

Kate stayed silent as she shivered with uncertainty as to what to say next. She tried to calm her nerves so her next statement would sound believable. "You can trust me."

"Shut up!" His face turned scarlet. "Do you really think I would ever trust you, Max's daughter?" Walter asked incredulously. "I can trust you about as far as I can throw you." Then his face twisted into a bizarre contortion. "I could throw you around in the hay for a bit though. It disgusted me to kiss your mom, but it was worth it to stick it to Max. At least you're easier on the eyes."

"You disgust me!"

"Like your opinion matters." He turned his eyes to a book resting on a pile of hay under a window of the barn, "I've got some poetry to write."

Finally, Walter left her alone to write what she thought must be really weird poetry from a deranged man. He looked at her a few times from his perch upon the haystack but said nothing and went back to his writing. Nothing surprised her about Walter now, but it did seem weird that in the middle of all this, he needed to journal. What in the world could he be writing?

Outside the barn window a rooster crowed, but it went unnoticed by Kate. Nausea had overwhelmed her body as she realized this foul man had touched her mother. Her heart pounded in her ears as the depths of her mother's ordeal consumed her. In that moment, she believed if she'd had a gun, she would have killed him.

CHAPTER 84

THE HAND

The small lantern shed a menacing glow as it flickered upon the pencil in the open journal and shadowed the man against the barn wall. The hand wrote what the mind thought, so it picked up the pencil and wrote:

Mischief Maker
Mischief Maker
Girl not smart

Mischief Maker
Mischief Maker
Played a fake part

Mischief Maker
Mischief Maker
Aim the throw

Mischief Maker
Mischief Maker
The final blow

The hand stopped. The hand did what the mind thought, so it grabbed the knife.

CHAPTER 85

THE AWAKENING

If it hadn't been for that blessed rooster crowing, Will would still be lying out among the roadside brush and debris. Its boisterous cock-a-doodle-do had broken his drug-induced slumber — he was sure his deep sleep was man-made. The throbbing on the side of his head had caused him to cry out in a distressed screech of agony. He remembered pressing his hand to his head and applying pressure to the injured area. It had helped for the moment, but the pain regained strength when he removed his hand. He'd moaned again and tried to sit up but to no avail. It was then that the good Samaritan in the blue flannel shirt saved the day. It had taken a few seconds after he was helped to the picnic table until one thing became clear:

this was no time to linger over his injuries. Kate was somewhere out there with her life in danger.

The savior's name was Liam. He had lots of questions for Will, particularly being interested in what happened and who did this to him. It felt like an interrogation, and even though Will was grateful for the aid, talking wouldn't get him closer to finding Kate.

His first instinct was to call Lainey and Max to see if they'd heard anything. It turned out they were just a few minutes away and would pick him up. Will had heard the anxiety in Max's voice as they determined their hook-up spot, as well as the panic in the shriek Lainey had given before telling him that she would leave him behind if he wasn't there on time.

Will had thanked Liam and sent him on his way after he dropped him off at the spot Max had designated. Liam seemed hesitant to leave him, but Will assured him he'd be okay. There was no reason to get someone else involved in this dangerous mess.

The wind had picked up significantly, adding its own pressure against his wounded head as Will stood in front of an Arby's restaurant. He figured it must be close to 4

A.M. by now. The longer it took to find Kate, the more likely she'd be dead. His jaw clenched as his mind contemplated the worst. No, he couldn't go there. He grew more anxious with every passing second. Where are they? He paced back and forth, eyes staring down the highway, hopeful for any sign of Kate's parents. Though it was still very early in the morning, cars, trucks, and RVs passed him by as they headed east, speeding past fields and farmland to get to the beaches.

Will felt an uplift in his spirit when he spied a blue sedan in the light from the buildings lining the street, partially hidden behind a huge brown RV. His steps lagged behind his excitement as he tried to rush to the car that had pulled over to collect him. A slight dizziness slowed his movement, but he was able to maneuver himself into the back seat, the door to which Max had pushed open. No sooner had he sat down, his back was plunged against the seat as Lainey sped away from the curb, the abrupt movement being enough to swing the door closed for him. Without delay, he buckled his seatbelt and took a deep breath.

Will glanced up to see Lainey hunched over the steering wheel. Her hands were in a full grip and her eyes laser-focused on the road ahead. Perspiration had matted her hair, even though he could feel that the air conditioner was on full speed. He couldn't get a read on Max, who had kept eerily silent since Will had gotten into the car. There was a bubble of intensity in the air that needed to burst, and it came with Lainey's sudden barrage of questions.

Where did he see her last? Was she okay? He tried to give them hope with his answers, but he was worried too. Eventually, some of the questions put him on the defensive. He knew it was the situation talking, but it still bothered him. The one that hurt the most, 'Why weren't you able to help her?' nudged at his own sense of failure.

Will's mind searched for some understanding of what had happened to him last night. Kate had rushed over to the car they'd found while he stepped out to look for the whereabouts of its occupants. In hindsight, he should have stopped her from recklessly approaching the car. He had to admit that neither had followed police protocol, which might have prevented what came next. He hung his head in shame. He had let Kate down and her parents knew it.

It sickened him that he hadn't saved her and now she was out there somewhere needing him and here he sat, depending on her cell phone to lead them to her. He tugged at his collar and wiped his moist hands across his pants. His mind kept going over the situation. He had messed up and he didn't know what to do about it.

CHAPTER 86

THE HITCHHIKER

Lainey was lost in her own thoughts when Will called out from the backseat, "Could someone please turn up the air conditioning?" As they'd been driving, the temperature evened out so the fan speed had been lowered, but Will suddenly felt a wave of heat wash over him. Without a moment to spare, he rolled down the back window and his vomit scattered into the wind. She heard Will's retching as the foul odor infiltrated the front of the car. She thought she should pull over, but she was too close to finding Kate.

"Are you alright?"

Will's voice was weak. "I'm fine, but I made a bit of a mess."

Lainey had no clue if there was anything in Jake's car

to help Will. If they had had her car, she knew she had a roll of paper towels under the passenger seat but that didn't help her now. "Max, look around in the car and see if you can find anything."

Max passed a pile of brown napkins back to Will. "I'm already on it. There were extra napkins in the glove compartment."

Will took the napkins. "Thank you."

Lainey was worried about Will, and, for that matter, she fretted about Max too. She was now driving the wounded to battle with the evil one. How was she to save Kate when her protectors might collapse at any moment? Both men in her car were suffering from blows to the head that normally would have sent them to the emergency room, but here they sat, heroically, on their way to save her daughter.

Max spoke quietly to Lainey. "Slow down a bit. It looks like she's within a mile or so." He turned around to Will in the back seat. "I'm thinking we should park the car somewhere outta sight when we get within a quarter mile of the phone signal. No sense giving Walter any warning."

Will interjected. "No sense giving *them* any warning. After all, someone had rendered me unconscious and discarded me at that rest stop. We have to anticipate that Walter may have accomplices."

Lainey looked in the rear-view mirror at Will. "You think there are more accomplices?"

"With Carla dead, it's the only explanation."

Max said, "Maybe not." He turned once again to Will. "You said that Kate rushed to the car to check it out without waiting for you, right?" He narrowed his eyes in speculation. "So it's possible Walter was waiting by your car and took the chance to knock you out as soon as Kate was far enough away not to notice. Then, once you were unconscious, he dealt with Kate." Max rubbed his forehead. "I'm not sure how you got to the rest stop."

"Why discard me and keep her?"

"He's not done with my family yet," Max said.

Not a moment later, they all noticed tire tread marks leading into a field on the side of the road ahead. Lainey pulled over behind it, then they all got out to look around, utilizing their cell phone flashlights to see. Lainey soon noticed that the tire path led her to a car hidden by broken cornstalks. She wanted to run and open the car door, but fear that her daughter's dead body might be inside slowed her down.

Will said, "That looks like the car Walter stole."

Max used his cell phone flashlight to observe the car and survey the area. "Stay close together, just in case," he said, not wanting to take any chances.

As they made their way along the passenger side of the car, they inspected the inside, finding no sign of Kate. Then they started surveying the surrounding landscape. Lainey pointed her cell phone light on something at the edge of the cornfield to their right. "Look at how this patch of the cornfield is trampled down. It looks like it goes quite a way."

"Good eye." Max looked down at his phone. "Her phone is definitely not far from here."

Lainey didn't wait for Max and Will; she headed down the trampled pathway looking for clues that Kate had come this way. The first clue came quickly as she knelt to grab a long blonde hair, which had happened to stand out against the dark ground. It wasn't perfect evidence, but it could be Kate's hair. Max examined the hair and agreed.

Will walked a bit ahead and then suddenly stopped and called, "Come here!" He pointed to a cell phone partially hidden at the bottom of a smashed cornstalk. Its slick surface had flashed in the light from his own phone.

Lainey motioned to Max. "That's Kate's phone."

Max pulled a clean, brown napkin out of his pocket. "This will have to do." He carefully wrapped the phone, being careful not to contaminate the evidence.

Lainey moved towards Max and held him close. She

looked into his weary dark brown eyes. "The phone on the ground, the blond hair along the way, I can only assume it's our daughter that's been dragged along this path."

After embracing his wife, Max held both of her hands in his. "Yeah, but it means she could still be alive, otherwise why the need to take her anywhere?" He looked around at the browning corn stalks. "He could have killed her when she found his car."

"He still wants something from her." She looked down at her feet. "I just hope he hasn't got it yet."

"Most likely, he wants me," Max said, hooking a finger under her chin and lifting her face to look in her eyes. With his gaze, he attempted to detract from the thoughts he knew were running through her mind and refocus on his words instead.

Before Lainey could ask Max to elaborate, she noticed that Will was missing. As quickly as she began to panic, she calmed with relief when he almost immediately reappeared. "Where were you?"

"Canvassing. There's an old barn not far from here we should check out." He pointed along the mangled path.

"We have a problem though," Max said.

"What's that?"

"None of us have a weapon."

CHAPTER 87

TARGET PRACTICE

The quietness in the barn and Walter's temporary retreat to journal writing eased Kate's mind for a moment and she struggled to stay awake. The chirping of crickets seemed to support her drowsiness with their peaceful serenade, and her breathing slowed as she surrendered to her body's plea.

Her eyes popped open wide when she felt herself lifted into the air and propped against a wooden pole, which supported the barn's roof. Though weary, her adrenaline-laced body wiggled as hard as it could, but her bound hands and feet provided no defense against Walter's strong manhandling. Within moments another rope tightened against her, and their eyes met as he yanked it across her chest. She saw the controlled fury in his eyes before she recognized the shiny knife he held in his right hand. The knife was so close that she prepared herself for the sharp pain, but it didn't come.

Walter stepped back but his dark eyes penetrated hers as he twirled and tossed the knife in the air before he caught it and then aimed it in her direction. "I'm quite good at this." He twirled and threw the knife back into the air again but this time he thrusted it towards the scarecrow, landing it right in the middle of the scarecrow's left eye. "Just target practice."

Kate shuddered but her voice remained calm when she said, "So, you're planning to blind me?"

"No, injury is not my purpose for you." He pounded at his chest. "With one forceful thrust at just the right aim, I'll pierce your heart." He grinned. "I'm only one of a few that have this special talent, but it's not as easy as hitting a scarecrow's eye."

Kate could feel her heart pounding against her chest, and now her voice trembled as she asked, "Why are you like this?"

His face contorted and that sinister grin appeared. "Ask your dear daddy."

Kate's strong instinct to defend her dad emboldened her. "My dad is a good man." She couldn't think of anything her dad could've done to deserve this kind of wrath, but she didn't care. She knew her dad. "You're just crazy."

Walter's head jerked and his face grew red. "Idiot." He grabbed the knife from the scarecrow's eye and stood a small distance from her but didn't elaborate.

"My dad will find you." With those words she saw venom in his glowing eyes and couldn't help but worry about the sharp pointed edge of his weapon.

"I look forward to it." Walter backed away from her until he stood in front of the open barn door with his eyes directed towards her chest.

Kate stared in increasing horror as Walter placed his weight on his dominant leg and positioned the aim of the knife straight at her heart. Her eyes caught a flicker of movement before the knife left his hand, and she screamed.

CHAPTER 88

A REVERSAL OF FORTUNES

Walter spewed foul words as the car jack slammed against the back of his knees, sending him flying to the floor. Lainey threw the jack to the barn floor while Max jerked Walter up, pinning him against a large stack of hay by the barn door. From the shock on Walter's face as he stared at her, Lainey felt she had also dealt a serious blow to his ego. He was so sure she was dead, but, as he now saw, she was very much alive.

Will shoved a pitchfork at Walter to keep him in place. "You scum," he spat.

Lainey rushed to her daughter and untied the rope against her chest, as well as the one binding her feet. Tears fell from Lainey's eyes as she stared at her daughter before embracing her in a tight hug. "Thank God you're okay."

Max came over to the women. "We need to get you out of here," he said, taking his turn to embrace his daughter. Sirens blared nearby as they held each other tight.

Lainey yanked out the knife protruding from a milk bucket tipped over on the barn floor. She pointed it in Walter's face as her heart raced and her anger grew. "You don't deserve to be alive." She reeled back as his spit blasted into her eyes and she just missed cutting her own face as the knife in her hand grazed it.

Quick to react, Max threw a hard upper punch to Walter's face. "You jerk!" Blood spurted from Walter's mouth and Max stepped back. In the most menacing voice his wife and daughter ever heard him use, Max warned, "If you ever come near my wife or daughter again, I'll kill you."

It was clear to Lainey that Max was seconds from being out of control, as the emotion of the situation was clearly getting under his normally thick skin. The anger in his eyes told her another punch was coming and she gently touched him on the arm. "Let the police handle him." He turned to her, but his eyes only softened a little, giving her no indication of what would happen next.

Walter sneered at Max despite the blood still dripping

from his mouth. He moved closer to Max as much as he could, considering the pitchfork Will still had trained on him, and cackled his next words. "I enjoyed handling your wife."

Lainey froze as her eyes met Max's and then turned away. With a closed fist and powerful punch, Max delivered a blow to Walter that knocked him through the barn door and into a pile of manure. He attempted to get up, but Max quickly shoved him back down.

Lainey grabbed Max's arm. "He's not worth it." She was about to make another comment when two police officers appeared.

CHAPTER 89

HOME AT LAST

It was five-thirty P.M. and the darkness had settled in around the neighborhood when Lainey caught sight of the worn street sign, McBluff Terrace. Lainey made a right and headed up the small cul-de-sac-capped street towards the loop where her split-level home occupied its familiar spot. There were times in the last several hours she'd thought she'd never see home again. The soft glow from the bay window in the kitchen lifted her spirit. Even though she had escaped, the whole experience unsettled her. It felt so good to be home. She looked over at Max as she pulled into the driveway, seeing that he was clearly just as grateful to finally be home.

Once inside, Lainey threw herself down on the couch

and Max joined her. She grabbed a sofa pillow for him and one for herself. "I could stay here all day," she sighed.

Max drew closer. "I was so afraid for you and Kate." He closed his eyes, leaning in to rest his forehead against hers. "I couldn't live with myself if I'd let you down."

Lainey snuggled close to him but then abruptly sat up. "I still don't understand what Walter had against you that caused him to poison me, then try to kill me, Rachel, and Kate. And he would've killed you if you hadn't been delayed with your flat tire." She paused. "I can understand that Randy and Jesse were collateral damage and Carla never had a chance once she made a deal with the maniac." Max's eyes had turned to gaze across the room blankly and he didn't respond. Lainey shook his shoulder. "Don't zone out. Talk to me." She watched him roll his neck and shoulders, always a sign with him that he was anxious. "Quit stalling."

Max looked around the living room and down the hall. "I'll tell you what I can, but this stays between us."

"You're acting like you're still CIA," she groaned.

"Some of my cases are still active despite my retirement and therefore still considered sensitive. Walter is part of a bigger case, but I can tell you why he hates me." He traced his fingers along Lainey's cheek and jawbone before continuing. "It's really tragic because it's all based on a misunderstanding." He pulled his fingers away from her face, then revealed, "He believes I'm the reason his wife is dead."

Lainey sat motionless and confused. "How can this be?"

"You thought I was capable of murdering your mother so this shouldn't surprise you."

"Those were drug-induced thoughts, and now you're being sarcastic. Just tell me."

"I'm sorry. It's hard," Max said, clutching his hands together. "We worked together twenty years ago. He was a subordinate, but we were on friendly terms. When he started to go rogue, making hot-headed decisions, I had to let him go."

"What does that have to do with his wife?"

"She was still with the CIA, and I sent her on a dangerous mission. She was killed and Walter blamed me. It didn't matter that she had volunteered. To Walter, I endangered her as revenge against him."

"There's no way you would send someone intentionally into harm's way unless lives were at stake."

"He didn't see it that way. To him, he lost a wife and his young son and baby daughter lost a mother."

"That's so sad." Lainey felt for Walter, but she couldn't fully understand the depths of what losing a spouse meant to him — she still had her Max — and the poor children losing their mother . . . unthinkable. Being raised by Walter, well, that must have been unbearable. No. He must have loved his children and treated them right. It was the only conclusion she could bear as she thought of her own children. She grabbed a blanket off the ottoman and covered her arms. "You said the case was active. Am I still in danger?"

"No. I don't think so. The agency's case is unrelated to his actions towards me and my family."

"But you can't be sure."

"No, but the agency seems to be. I'll put my trust in them." Max groaned with another realization. "Since we're talking about the CIA, I think it's time you knew the truth about my pool tournament."

"Your pool tournament?"

Max lowered his eyes and patted Bailey on the head as the cat rested on top of the couch. Bailey purred.

Lainey stared expectantly. "You're stalling again."

"It all started with something I overheard Doris sharing with the aide. Your mom was concerned because she saw a scary clown outside her window one night. The aide tried to tell her that it was her imagination. Frankly, that's what I thought too," Max sighed and ran a hand through his hair. "But then weeks later, we had that toilet-paper trashing of our cul-de-sac, so I became suspicious about Walter."

"What does Walter have to do with *that*?" Lainey asked, utterly confused.

"Walter was a bit of a prankster during his days with the CIA. It's part of the reason he was dismissed. Some of his pranks were not harmless, although Walter thought they were hilarious and didn't understand the ire of the other agents." Max grabbed her hands. "Sorry, but I had to lie to you about having a tournament so I could spend a few days investigating Walter's whereabouts. I didn't know how long it would take or if it would lead me anywhere and I didn't want to worry you if none of this ended up having to do with him."

Lainey grumbled, "Well, you know I hate lying, but being married to a CIA guy, I guess I'm kind of used to it." His lies had been the worst part about being married to Max. Sometimes, she was sure he was lying, but she knew if he was lying, most likely he was on a dangerous mission. She couldn't be mad at him because he always came back alive.

"I've never lied to you about how much I love you and our kids."

"I know," she said with a smile. "So what did you find out?"

"Not much. The CIA reported no recent sightings of him. Since he's part of a larger investigation, he's on their watchlist, but he disappeared off their intelligence radar two months ago. He was last seen in Argentina."

"So, you believed we were safe," Lainey concluded.

"Yeah. CIA had no intel that I was a target for Walter. I never had a chance to check with the FBI because you fell and I came home. I felt confident the FBI would alert me, so I let my guard down and your health became my top priority."

Lainey sighed and cuddled closer to Max. "Well, we're safe now."

"Hon, you've got me to protect you. I won't let you down again." He kissed her long and hard before he released her.

The doorbell rang and Lainey glanced at Max. It was still early enough that one of her neighbors may be coming by to sit on her porch and chat. She often did that with Latisha, her neighbor of ten years. "I'll get it. I think I know who it is."

It wasn't Latisha. Standing on the other side of the screen door was Rob with his twin brother, Al. Rob held a yellow envelope in his hand. It seemed to be the same one he carried many months ago when he rescued her from her fall on the porch. The stamp was still missing, if this was the same one. What in the world did this letter have to do with her?

Lainey smiled not knowing how to greet them. She couldn't explain why, but there was awkwardness in the air.

Rob spoke first. "From the first day we rented next door, we have wanted to give you this." He held it close to his chest as if not wanting to part with it. "I know you don't remember us, quite frankly, we don't remember you. We were only five at the time you entered our lives; more importantly, our mom's life. If we hadn't found this letter, we would've never known."

Naturally, Lainey was confused. Nothing about what she heard made sense. "Known what?" she asked, cutting in prematurely.

Rob put his left hand towards her. "Please, let me continue. Our mother died over a year ago." He paused to glance over at his brother before turning back to Lainey. "When we were packing up her things, I came across this letter with your name on it. It later became apparent to me that she meant for you to have it. I say that because I read it."

"You read it?"

Max stepped over to the open screen door but said nothing.

417

Rob continued. "I was just going to throw it out, but after Al snatched it from me and read it for himself, he thought maybe we should find you. It sounded like a daunting and unnecessary task, but he convinced me that our mom wrote it because it meant something to her."

Al spoke up then. "I'm the sentimental brother. Everything my mother treasured, so did I. It's because she kept it in the jewelry box that her grandmother gave her that I knew we couldn't just throw it away."

Rob poked at his brother. "Al can be quite sappy at times, but he was right." Rob slid the letter between his fingers as he talked. "After we read it, we realized why our mother wanted you to have it — it was to thank you."

Lainey stood speechless. She still hadn't heard anything to give her an idea why these brothers thought the thank-you was meant for her.

Rob seemed unaffected by Lainey's lack of response and continued, "She thanked you for helping her get away from an abusive relationship with our dad. She was worried he'd traffic our sister, and that we'd join him eventually in one of his criminal schemes. Apparently, you came just in time."

"What did I do?"

"You arrested our dad."

Finally a clue she could use, she realized that this must

have been a long time ago; before her teaching days. "Who is your dad?" she asked, more curious than ever.

"Four."

Lainey gave a sideways glance to Max. It was clear now who these brothers were. Her mind pictured them thirty-some years ago as they played soccer outside their father's warehouse. She remembered their mother as shy, but they had exchanged words pleasantly. She had wondered at the time how this sweet woman had come to be married to that awful thug. It seemed ironic that, months ago, when she came across her FBI badge, her mind had drifted back to Four, and now here she was with his two sons. "I'm glad everything worked out for your mom and your family, but I was just doing my job," she said, humbly.

Rob continued with his story, saying, "Our lives improved after our dad went to jail. Al and I both went to college. If Dad hadn't been arrested, we would be there with him or maybe dead. We wanted to thank you like our mom did." Rob finally handed her the letter. "Please read this. It's all in there."

Lainey accepted the letter, but she did ask one question, "Why did you wait so long to give this to me?"

Rob shook his head. "I tried the first time I met you, but you had fallen, and the next time, you had just been rattled by that fox, so it never seemed the right time."

"The neighbors said you were medically challenged so we didn't want to intrude," Al said.

Lainey recognized why Al was the sensitive one. His use of 'medically challenged' was code for the neighbors thinking she had gone crazy. Thankfully, the steroids had lost their psychotic effect once the dose was lowered, and her thinking was back to normal. "Why is now the right time?"

"That's simple to answer. We're going back to New York," Rob said.

Al chimed in, "Our rental lease is over, and we miss the city."

Lainey had been through so much in the last week and she was very tired, but she did appreciate the brothers making the trip to give her the letter. "Thank you for coming all the way from New York to give me your mom's letter. And thank you for helping me when I fell. I wish you both the best in life."

"Rob and Al, thank you." Max smiled warmly as he shook both their hands.

The soft pillow felt glorious under Lainey's head as she waited for Max to turn off the bedside lamp. If she wanted to sleep, she had to come clean with Max. She knew the same thing was on his mind and she was the only one who could set his mind at ease, or at least, give him the truth.

When Max turned out the light and rolled over next to her, she gave him a poke.

"I'd thought you'd be too tired, my snuggle bug," Max said.

She'd forgotten momentarily that her poke was a romantic gesture to him, particularly at bedtime. He'd be disappointed, but she couldn't put this off much longer. "Remember when Walter said he enjoyed handling me?"

"Sure. I slugged him." He readjusted his arm to prop his head up in his hand to be able to see her more clearly. "What is this about?"

"I didn't want you to think the worst." She pulled her covers higher. "The only thing he did was kiss me."

"That slime. I'm not done with him."

"Max, calm down. His kiss was slime . . . nasty and foul." She took a breath. "He only did it once, and he meant it as a power play against you. The whole incident was disgusting."

"I'm so sorry you went through that. I can see why you would find it disgusting."

"You can?"

"Because he wasn't me." He pulled her close and kissed her cheek.

Lainey had a new thought, now that he had taken the news so well. She was just too tired and if he got any closer, she knew what would happen next. She flipped the light on. "I need to tell you one more thing."

"You want to wait until tomorrow night to make love?"

"How did you know?"

"You're exhausted, and my headache is back from the rock you threw at me." He turned out the light. "I love you."

"I love you," Lainey responded, then rolled over, closed her eyes, and slept.

CHAPTER 90

BAR GATHERING

Two days after her harrowing ordeal, Kate was ready to relax with some of her friends at Sam's Brewpub and Grub on Main Street. She pulled open the restaurant door to a crowded bar and the familiar smells of fried pickles, burgers, and chili cheese fries. As her mouth watered for some of those decadent fries, she glanced over behind the bar to see Sam give her a smiling nod while he poured a shot of whiskey for Joe Davis. Joe was joking around with the other drinkers at the bar but a few hours from now, he'd be in a fight. It was just the way it was with Joe.

Near the lone pool table, she noticed Kassidy and Lily laughing about something as they shot darts. It relieved her guilt about jailing them to see they had moved on and seemed to be back to their normal selves. She noticed Sergeant Rodriguez sitting with an unfamiliar man that wasn't a regular. She waved at Rodriguez when he glanced up at her, but she could see he was still annoyed with her as he waved back with a flick of a finger. He had put her and Will through the wringer for how they mishandled the case, and even blamed her for being kidnapped. Imagine that! She had been surprised and grateful when Will had come to her defense. Eventually, Rodriguez had to admit that they caught the killer, despite a bit of rule breaking. He had given them a stern warning about following protocol in the future. She figured he'd have a lot more to say when she went back to work on Monday.

Kate was pleased to see her best friend, Riley, sitting at a table far away from the big-screen television broadcasting the Baltimore Ravens game against the Washington Football Team. Kate's dad had made her a Washington fan but over time the Ravens had captured her heart. Not tonight. Football was the farthest thing on her mind. She was here to enjoy needed time with her gal pals.

Riley stood up as Kate approached the table and they both hugged. They had been in the police academy together and became fast friends. Riley had been on an undercover assignment, so it had been months since they were together. The other two women at the table were

Kate's close work friends so she gave them a big smile and sat down.

Riley smiled. "I ordered your favorite drink, Sex on the Beach, and we're still waiting for the cheese fries." She pushed a pink drink topped with whipped cream and a cherry towards her.

"You know me so well," Kate said, gratefully taking a small sip. "So good."

"I heard you and your mom both got kidnapped." Riley frowned. "How are you?"

Kate was about to explain when Will asked if he could sit down. She was surprised, since they worked together but they didn't party together. Somehow, it was a comfort to see him, and she encouraged him to take a seat. She introduced him to Riley as he already knew the other two women at the table.

No sooner had she introduced him, Rodriguez showed up with the stranger from his table. Kate looked him over. He was nice-looking man with sandy brown hair and intense blue eyes. She realized those intense eyes were directed towards Will.

Will jumped up from his chair and extended his hand towards the man who grabbed it in a hearty shake. Will's voice sounded exuberant. "This man saved my life."

"I was just at the right place at the right time."

Kate noticed the refreshing modesty in this man's voice. Even with Will's surprising news, the table stayed silent and even Rodriguez was momentarily quiet before he stated his purpose for visiting their table. "This is Liam Maddox. He's one of the new detectives I hired this week."

Everyone at the table gave Liam a warm welcome before Rodriguez spoke again. "Will, I'm surprised to see you here. I understand there's no drinking while recovering from a concussion."

"I'm here for the fried pickles."

Rodriguez grunted and then addressed Kate. "Liam's going to be your partner for the next three weeks while Will recovers on desk duty. After that, we'll see."

Kate had nothing against this new detective, but she knew exactly what this was. Rodriguez had threatened a break-up of the Will-and-Kate team, and this was his first step. If she had anything to do with it, she'd be back working with Will in three weeks and a day. However, she couldn't deny that she wasn't sure if Will felt the same way.

Loud cheering echoed throughout the bar as Ravens fans raised their fists in victory.

Liam shouted out, "Go Ravens!" His face flushed immediately. "Sorry, I'm a die-hard Raven's fan."

Rodriguez patted Liam's on the shoulder, grinning. "I knew I liked you."

Kate glanced over at Will in his Washington team jersey as he slumped back in his chair. The strikes were beginning to mount against her partner. She'd be sure to wear her Raven's jersey at the next precinct picnic.

After the uproar subsided, Kate took a deep breath and smiled. "Liam, I look forward to partnering with you for the next three weeks."

"I'm honored to be a part of the Lorianne Falls Police Department."

Kate figured Rodriguez had told this detective to come in and whip her into shape. She wasn't worried. *She'd* whip this new *detective* into shape. "Come sit with us so we can learn all about you."

"I'd love to." Liam appeared earnest in his desire to get to know them.

Rodriguez grabbed Liam's shoulder. "You'll have plenty of time to get to know each other on the job. I have things I need to discuss with you." He then steered him away from the group.

After they left, Kate's thoughts soon turned to Will. He hadn't said much as the rest of the table resumed boisterous chatter. The chili cheese fries that had arrived sat untouched by Will. Was he really disappointed that they hadn't ordered fried pickles? Or was there something else?

Riley's voice broke through Kate's thoughts. "How

about a game of darts?" she asked, angling her glass and finishing the last gulp of beer within it. "Any takers?"

Will stayed silent but the rest of the table was all in. Kate decided to hold back a few minutes to check on Will. "I'll join you shortly." She pulled over the plate of chili cheese fries. "I'm going to finish these fries first."

Riley laughed. "So much for your diet!"

"I'll start on Monday."

Kate moved her chair closer to Will. "Are you okay?"

Will stopped twirling the cork beer coaster and seemed to ignore her question. He abruptly stared into her eyes and said, "I've been benched."

"It's only until you recover."

"I'm not so sure about that."

Kate said nothing as she had her own doubts about the sergeant's plan for them.

Will lowered his head. "Rodriguez expected me to keep you under my wing and instead I let you fly out of control."

Kate stiffened. "Don't underestimate my abilities."

"I didn't. I overestimated mine." Will cleared his throat before his eyes focused on her again. "You're a fine detective, but you made rookie mistakes that almost cost you your life. I should have taken you off the case once it was evident your mom was a target."

"We found the killer."

"That's your answer for everything." He ran his fingers through his hair. "You don't understand." He looked away for a moment. "I let my emotions rule over my best detective instincts." His eyes met hers and then he turned away again.

His use of the word *emotions* left her with questions, but the vulnerable anxiety in his eyes took her to another moment in time. She was back on her front porch on prom night when, as an awkward teenager, he'd tried to kiss her, and she made that childish remark that sent Will hurrying away down her sidewalk. She couldn't take that moment away from him, but she could provide comfort now. "Will, you're being too hard on yourself."

Will moved closer before he stuttered out one word. "Kate."

She caught her breath as she felt his eyes searching hers.

"Kate, we're waiting for you," Riley said as she came over and pulled at Kate's arm. "Enough shop-talk. We have a match to win."

Kate felt numb for a moment before she realized Riley was talking about darts. She was about to protest when Will stood up, his face flushed. She didn't know what to say so she looked away. He mumbled a good-bye and left the table, heading for the door. If Riley hadn't interrupted, she was sure they would have kissed. Or was that her imagination? Was it just something she wanted, even longed for, or was she looking for closure to that dastardly prom night? By the look on Will's face when he left, kissing her was the last thing on his mind. Well, there was nothing she could do about that now. Or was there?

Before she knew it, she called out, "Will!" then ran after him and stopped him before he made it out the door.

Will stood motionless for a moment, and then turned towards her.

Boldly, Kate planted a kiss upon his mouth and felt his lips engulf hers before he suddenly pulled away. She stared into his dazed eyes and said, "Will, I've been wanting to do that ever since our prom night."

Kate felt a nudge on her shoulder and reluctantly turned around to see Riley's inquisitive stare. Kate turned back to Will but he was already gone. Her heart sank. She closed her eyes, took a deep breath, and mustered all the merriment she could before turning back to Riley with a smile. "Let's go play ourselves some darts."

CHAPTER 91

A KNOCK ON THE DOOR

It was the first day of Spring break. A cool breeze blew throughout Lainey's kitchen from an open screen window and dispersed the aroma of freshly baked brownies into the living room.

She refilled Rachel's glass with lemonade and then stretched out on her couch with her new apricot-colored cockapoo puppy, Holmes, snuggled on her lap. Bailey purred and then rested on an arm of the couch. Rachel ate the last bite of her brownie before she leaned back in the overstuffed, but comfy, pink rocker that Lainey had purchased for her mom last month after she complained that there was no room on the couch for her. She still remembered her mom's scream of delight when she first sat in her new chair. Lainey smiled, remembering how Max had been the one to suggest the purchase.

The new puppy had softened the loss of Agatha, but it still hurt. The horrible nightmare of Lainey's mysterious illness, her steroid psychosis, and Walter's obsession with wanting to harm her family and Rachel still lingered in her mind. Innocent Randy was just in Walter's way, and Jessie Sparks knew too much about Walter's connection to holographic technology. Kate had shared some details of Jesse's death, and Lainey realized that the outlandish 3D projection of Jesse's last breath was simply meant to taunt the police. The whole idea disgusted her but that was all behind her now.

Rachel had been there for all of it, supported her, and even risked her life. Their bond was so strong that she hoped, when Rachel needed her, she would be there for her too. Lainey smiled at her friend and leaned forward. "Rachel, I can't thank you enough for being there for me this year."

"Of course," Rachel responded, smiling. "You scared me a few times, but we got through it." She sipped her lemonade and placed it back on the coffee table. "And to think Isaac — I mean Walter — was adding a toxic nerve agent to your diet sodas when we thought he was just being nice!" She touched her mother's cross that hung from her neck. "I hope you don't think me callous for saying so, but I'm glad he didn't poison my tea." She seemed to think for a moment. "I guess it explains why you improved over the summer and then got worse once school started again."

"Thank goodness he wasn't able to poison my diet soda in the summer."

"I still don't get why Walter did that to you," Rachel said.

"He wanted to mess with someone that Max loves." Lainey saw the eagerness in Rachel's eyes for her to say more but she had promised Max not to share the full details of his involvement with Walter. Answering Rachel's facial expression, Lainey continued, "I'm sorry I can't say more — CIA thing. But anyway, I do think I surprised Walter with my steroid psychosis."

"You surprised *me* by your behavior and your strange thoughts. Especially thinking Max wanted to harm your mother."

"I think the psychosis from the steroids arose from the guilt I felt from pressuring Max to let my mother live with us. The guilt festered and I, wrongly, thought Max wanted to harm my mom to get her out of our lives." She took a deep breath. "The day before my birthday, Max was putting my mom's pills in her pillbox, like he always did, but in that moment, I believed he may use her medication to poison her. I thought I needed to protect my mom. It was one of the reasons I was so urgent to get to the hospital." She twisted her wedding ring around her finger. "I am so ashamed. Max has always been good to my mom and never complained about her coming to live with us."

"You went to the dark side to think that of Max," Rachel said with a moan. "I was really worried about you. You definitely were a steroid mess."

"The dose was high and contributed to my psychosis, but it didn't help that I kept stopping and starting my medication. And then when Dr. Barnes told me to take the prescription that would calm my psychosis down, I was too scared to take it."

"I just thank the Lord all that is behind you," Rachel said, wrinkling her nose.

"Me too. I'm also so thankful for the teachers' and staff's kindness during all this." She would be forever grateful for the kind way her fellow teachers and administrative staff at the school had treated her after her fall and diagnosis. Between them, they had prepared homemade meals for her family for two straight weeks after she fell. Even Sara surprised her by bringing a lasagna. Then, when she was finally well enough to return to school, they had given her a warm welcome with open arms. Oh, how she loved them. Lainey smiled to herself. It was so great being back with her class and enjoying the support of their parents too. "It was a crazy time."

"How did your mom deal with all your craziness?"

"She made a lot of weird faces; particularly, the *please don't touch me* face, when it was time to give her an insulin shot. Once my steroids were lowered, I became calmer, so I tackled that again." Lainey laughed. "I didn't blame her. I was scared to death that I would give her too much, but my mind was clear. Now my mom is more worried about getting rid of her health aide than what's happening with me." Lainey thought for a moment. "I'm glad she didn't understand her daughter and granddaughter were in the hands of a murderer."

Rachel nodded. "That's something to be thankful for."

"One thing I want to do after this horrific experience is volunteer at the Lorianne Falls Women's Center. With Carla dead, they'll need someone to take her place. If it wasn't for Carla, and her affection for Bobby, we'd have both been left tied to our chairs and died in that awful trailer explosion." She sighed, reflecting on their fortunate turn of events.

"Your Bobby strategy worked," Rachel said in agreement.

"Thankfully, but Carla's not the only reason I want to volunteer. I witnessed so much abuse of women by

Walter, and then there was Adler, who treated his wife and girlfriend so poorly. I want to help those women create a new life for themselves."

"I'll never remember that Isaac's name is really Walter," Rachel said before sipping her lemonade and placing the cup back on the table. "I'm going to volunteer to work at the center with you." She closed her eyes as if in prayer before opening them again. "I got to know Carla at school. She was a different woman than what we saw at the trailer. It's so sad." Rachel slumped back in her chair. "I guess it's what happens when you get in bed with the devil."

Lainey gasped. "I hope she didn't sleep with him. That image makes my skin crawl." She flinched with the memory of that horrid kiss, then said, "He is an evil monster." She exhaled. With murder and kidnapping, and the federal charges Max hinted at, she expected Walter to spend the rest of his life behind bars.

Rachel nodded and the women were quiet for a moment. Eventually, Rachel grinned. "But we got through it together."

"We did. I'm just so happy to be sitting here with you."

"We can get back to the normal conversations we used to have before the murders and your psychosis."

"I'm all for that." Lainey lifted the puppy off her lap before she stood. "How about another brownie?"

Rachel smiled. "Count me in."

Lainey came back with two brownies and handed one to Rachel on a napkin before she sat down. Holmes jumped back up onto Lainey's lap and settled in.

"Remember when all we talked about were your mom and sister? This last year sure put them on the back burner," Rachel said.

"It was kind of a relief not to feel the hurt every day. I didn't know that when I lost my dad, I would lose my older sister too." The words reared themselves in Lainey's memory once again: *I've done my role. Don't ever expect to see me again.* Her sister's words.

"It's just family dysfunction after a death. You'll get through this and so will your sister."

"I hope so." She closed her eyes. Rachael made it sound so temporary, but, as it had already been so long, it didn't feel temporary. It felt like forever.

Rachel smiled. "I do have one request since we're back to your problems. Could we do a retake of the year of Rachel? This year was mainly about you."

"I agree, yes. The year of Rachel will be extended!"

"Pinky swear?"

Lainey gently pushed Holmes off her lap, moved closer to Rachel, and extended her smallest finger. "Pinky swear." She smiled at Rachel. "Can I get you more lemonade?"

"No thanks, I'm fine."

Thunderous knocking on the door caught Lainey's attention and Holmes suddenly began barking. "Who in the world is banging like that?" Lainey asked, getting up and heading for the front door. When she peered through the peephole, her body tensed and her mind began to race. Her eyes widened and her hand trembled as she held tightly to the doorknob. She turned around and sought Rachel's eyes. "It's my sister."

CHAPTER 92

THE HAND

A dim light from the small prison cell window spread over the open journal. The hand wrote what the mind thought, so the hand wrote:

> *Mischief Maker*
> *Mischief Maker*
> *They think I'm done*
>
> *Mischief Maker*
> *Mischief Maker*
> *So lurks the one*
>
> *Mischief Maker*
> *Mischief Maker*
> *Bide the time*

Mischief Maker
Mischief Maker
Till the crime

The hand twitched and the fingers held tight. *So much fun still to be had.* A bloodcurdling shriek erupted across the cell block. *Hee-hee.* The hand stopped.

ACKNOWLEDGMENTS

If you are reading this acknowledgment, it probably means you have just read my first novel. I hope you enjoyed being a part of the lives of the people in Lorianne Falls, Maryland. It was an exciting journey for me to write this book and I have many people who helped me along the way to thank.

I am grateful for Crystal Heidel, Founder of Byzantium Sky Press, for her encouragement, her guidance, and expertise that has brought this book through to publication. I am thankful for the wonderful cover she designed for me, the interior design, and her work to get my novel ready for publication. I am especially grateful for her kindness, understanding, and grace as it became evident that I knew nothing about the process of getting a book published. I would like to thank Jennifer Westervelt, the proofreader recommended by Crystal Heidel, for her thorough dedication to proofreading my work and her extended notes to improve my writing. Another example of the high professional expertise I found at Byzantium Sky Press.

Many thanks to Maribeth Fischer, Executive Director of the Rehoboth Beach Writers Guild for her encouragement and expert instruction in the craft of writing. I want to thank Cindy Hall and the rest of the RBWG Writers Chat for their encouragement and for the enjoyment I received in sharing our writing journeys every Wednesday. I want to thank Nancy Walker, a member of the Writers Chat for being an excellent Beta Reader and encouraging me to get my mystery out into the world. I am grateful for the Millville Free Write group for sharing their creative stories with me and listening to mine. My time with them inspired and encouraged me along my writing journey.

I'm grateful for the support and encouragement from my three sons and their spouses, and from my seven grandchildren. Their love and belief in me inspired me to keep working at my writing dream until I reached the wonderful satisfaction of completing my novel.

Finally, I want to thank my mom for showing me that it's never too late to make a dream come true.